Incoming
the piteous recognition of slaughter

by
Richard Baker

ISBN - 97809705148-8-2

Library on Congress Control Nimber: 2012921779

publisher - Stephen Banks
final edit - Stu Winnie / Gerry Lester

Ink & Lens, Ltd.

To Gerry Lester for his continued friendship

From Henry the Fifth

Let us on heaps go offer up our lives.
Let life be short; else shame
Will be too long.
...with blood he seal'd
A testament of noble-ending love.
Then call we this the field of Agincourt,
Fought on the day of Crispin Crispianus.

In 1415 Henry V, king of England, attacked France. After achieving several victories, his army, down to about 6,000, decimated by casualties and disease, he attempted to withdraw to a port for safety and recuperation. The French stopped him at Agincourt. Henry attempted to avoid battle with the 35,000 French and asked for free passage. The French, full of fight, attacked on Friday, 25th of October. They far outnumbered the English, were completely fresh, and felt themselves far superior to the English common army.

It had been raining for several days making the field a quagmire. Henry lined his bowmen along each side

of the field and his other 900 soldiers across the field. The French attacked and were decimated. French

knights, falling from their horses, drowned in the mud. In disbelief, they launched two more attacks with

the same results.

Estimates place the English dead between 100 and 400. The French lost 10,000 - the result of mixing power with arrogance.

Writers on the works of Richard Baker

"Each story created real people for me and set them
down in impeccable realized times and places. ...a
wonderful writer."
Evan Hunter *Blackboard Jungle*

"An extremely well written story which I found both
compelling and moving."
William Manchester *The Glory and the Dream*

"I like his writing a lot - it's strong, deft and full of the right
feeling."
William Stryon *Confessions of Nat Turner*

"His poetry brings the war closer to the gut than any
novel."
Tacoma News Tribune

"Baker has presented some fascinating ideas and created wonderfully memorable characters. His style
is a rather unique combination of Hemingway and
Faulkner.
Mooring Mast

"The book is excellent and is most assuredly one of
recommended reading."
Pacific Veterans

BOOKS BY RICHARD BAKER

Janus Rising
Shellburst Pond
The Flag
Smoke Tales
Feast of Epiphany
Looking for Jimmy Wilde
The Last Round
Gecko
Shattered Visage
Stone Island
The Hands of Esau
First a Torch

Chapter 1

This story has nothing to do with men at war or about Vietnam but about war itself, any war at any time, although you shrinks, or should I say head doctors, might have difficulty understanding that concept. You will want to look into the mind of Pete and see what made him do what he did, how he thought, his emotional state; but you will never understand him unless you come to believe that he was War. There are enough stories about men at war to choke a general. They fill books, poetry, and movies - easy stories to tell because the drama is built in and it doesn't have to be made up or embellished. In the end you'll think I'm full of crap, that this is a story about men at war. You'll be mystified by what you mistakenly think is a tale of a troubled man and you'll think you understand him because you're all shrinks and believe you are smart and I'm just an orderly, a stupid grunt with one leg blown clean from Anh Khe to Qui Nhon, and tapping around on my plastic foot like a wind–up toy soldier. I never forget that shrinks came up with the lobotomy as a viable treatment for brain disorders. And why not? No brain, no disorder. The amputation here is one of mind, not body – a separation of a man within a man, the mirror image within all of us where glass reflects flesh with such revealing light that our true self becomes a distortion. So kick back with your note pads, nod in agreement in all the right places and occasionally throw in some of them "how do you feel about–its."

The rest of you, trying to cover your butts so you don't screw up your government pensions, report the story any way you like. It's just another death and the government won't hold you responsible. Just remember one thing. Do not think for a minute that because there are men at war floating around this language, they all actually exist. The war here resided between Pete and Clifton, one good, one evil and, as you already know, so close together they could have been the same person. In fact they were the same person, two people, two complete people, two aspects of war and humanity residing in one mind.

I met Pete for the first time in Building 7, the one with the bars across the windows and the solid iron door that clangs through the ward when the outside bolt is slammed. That's the building with the doors locked including the bathroom, the place where a single white bed in a special room waits for new patients, and a nurse watches them all night as they sweat out pints of Thorazine doctors have pumped into their system to keep them quiet. He was leaning against the wall between chips of curled green paint, a knee bent up for support, a smoke in one hand, a book in the other, a look on his face as if he had been frightened by something so horrible he was unable to scream.

I had just scooped up a pail full of turds that had rolled out of Jackson's side. He's the black kid who keeps tossing his colostomy bag into the coffee pot, the one who thinks you're trying to kill him because you dress like the K.K.K., all in white and wearing masks. Pete looked harmless enough, just frightened, and I asked him who he was reading. I spent three years studying literature at the University before dropping out to scoop turds and was rather pleased to find someone holding a hardback. This place doesn't cater to a literary crowd and those that do read seldom get past the printing on a cigarette pack. He gave me a shy wrinkled look, the kind a kid gets when he wants to be friends but is afraid to say anything. He lifted the book, rotated the cover toward me like an offering. I bent down for a better look. It was a book of World War One poetry: Blunden, Sassoon, Owen, Graves - that sort of verse.

"I killed him," he said, as if he had been holding a

massive secret for years and I was the one destined to be to be told.

"What else is new?" I said. After all, Building 7 is for the first class loons so I didn't expect him to ask for a cup of tea. Almost everyone here has killed someone, friend or foe, and are here because they feel either remorse or joy from the act, and it doesn't matter which. He handed me the book and, as I thumbed through the pages, he grinned.

Doctors make everything complicated and would have analyzed him for years for reading. He continued to grin and again he looked a little afraid. "His name was Clifton," he said, "and he liked pinching his thick hands around the throats of the Vietnamese, squeezing until their eyes bled out. Do you think that's strange?"

I continued to thumb through the book. Now I had my introduction to Clifton; a fine fellow to the Gook killers in here, not that there are many because the ones that go for killing don't usually have any mental problems, but not so fine to the guys with remorse for killing folks they probably would have liked. Someone had written a long paragraph on the inside cover of the book. The handwriting looked dilapidated: off—centered circles and bent lines like the thoughts had come faster than the words. I later learned that Pete had scribbled the inscription in an—effort to encapsulate his madness. I borrowed the book enough times to memorize everything he had written:

War consolidates the epitomes of every emotion bringing them to a fine point of overwhelming misunderstanding. The idea is simply too much. Neither the mind which, through various tricks of mystic and glorious misconception, tries to house war nor the body which, through exhaustion tries to evict it, can handle this unruly and clangorous tenant. Even if the torn body could cry for peace the mind would not listen. To chew off a piece of war is to experience an enormous indigestion, a suffering of confusion, excitement, guilt, emptiness and alienation. War is nothing less than an emotional-maelstrom of gastric imperfections. Nothing lies beyond this experience, no insight, no meaning, no grand lessons to be learned.

War simply – IS.

At the top of the page he had written "for the Weasel," a shrink who had left a year before you guys arrived, a rather ignorant bastard who accepted everything the patients said, or neverlistened to them at all since sometimes it's hard to tell. I remember the time he asked if I could tell him about any event in Nam I couldn't remember. That's your high-class shrink, for you. But mostly he neverreally listened to anyone, anyway, just went through the motions and collected his paycheck. No one blamed him; how many times can you hear the same old stories and still remain interested?

Pete was trying to invent his life, to understand the forces eating within him. War lived there. But nothing written about war ever comes close to the reality. Some images might land on the page, but not the smell, the absolute stink of it all. Soldiers can only be bitter. We hate everyone except other soldiers. Even those of us with regular jobs, the ones still rising in the world, think people are ridiculous and ignorant. If I spit and piss a little it's not because I'm trying to be nasty, it's because you wanted all the facts of this incident and I'm not a bit like Pete. He refused to hate anyone. That's what drove him crazy. Hate is the primary driving force in us all. He had none. In fact, he had no emotions of any kind and survived as a living, breathing mass of protoplasm.

During the year I knew Pete, he never said an unkind word about anyone. As far as Pete being crazy – being locked up in the VA psycho ward – well, he was as mad as any combat soldier. Once a man has been to war he is good for little else, never able to sleep quietly or sit for any length of time or even to love again. The animal instinct, the smell of blood, the indiscriminate killing done as easily as tossing a beer can, is his only world. Going to war is not a problem - living through it is. Everyone liked Pete, probably because he was so quiet and inffensive, personable and incapable of lying. Truth is not something on a page, truth is something in your chest and his goodness lived in everyone's chest.

In the short time I knew him you might say that Pete and I were friends. He seemed afraid of most people and spent much of his time in the library. I often brought him books from downtown or the University, mostly religion or philosophy, his favorite subjects. Something about evil lounged in those subjects and he was determined to dig it out. He wanted someone to listen to his theories. I wanted someone to seriously discuss poetry with, someone who thought a little deeper than "There was a young maid from Madrass..."

We both had a love for the old soldier poets, Owen, Blunden, Sassoon, like I mentioned, and Randall Jarrell, and my special favorite... well, what dfference does it make? Pete decided that if all things are within us, then war abides there also. At first he was looking for some single thing, a thing he could not describe, something intangible yet as real as any apple or chair. He was unable to get war into words. War is not a thing but an illusive contradiction, a reality untouched by words. Words only scratch and nip at the edges, never eat their way through. James Jones couldn't get at it, nor Hemmingway, or Remarque, or a dozen others. Just a mention of war is a lie tricking and scheming against interested listeners, something to suck them in, something they will never understand or feel until it is too late and they have been tossed into a war at where the reality out-paces language and resides in the world of emotion. And whatis emotion? Nothing. Emotions have no weight, occupy no space, cannot be described. Yet, they are everything.

Nothing importnt fits into words. Mention the horrors of war to any young man and watch his eyes light with romantic wonder. He imagines himself shot and broken in some forgotten jungle, injured, but always alive, always going to pull through. What he wants is the excitement, the challenge, the ancient ritual, the trail that leads to the passage to manhood. To a kid glory is the nature of war, the thing that defines it. Every boy knows he will survive. Every government uses that old lie to suck them in. Look at the ads, bright uniforms, fancy weapons, artillery fire belching smoke, strings of crisp marching soldiers. Be all you can be, says the army. But the image is never accompanied by a row of flag draped-coffins. In the military, that's as far as you can go. They never say Dead is All you can be. Nothing exists beyond that.

Pete understood: war is in men, a curled venomous lizard that's crawled through every generation since the first, a lizard waiting to be prodded awake. Maybe that's why I gave him the wire he wanted, the cord strong enough to hold several hundred pounds. War and peace can not occupy the same space. Pete had flowers and sunny open fields. Clifton had rocky crags and shadows. Light and dark tried to occupy the same space. Maybe I finally understood what he was saying, the thing about war and about men. In any case, I won't lose any sleep over what I did. I saved a man from himself.

Pete lived with Clifton, not as another part of

himself but as his best friend. Although only one man stood on the deck of the U.S.S. John Pope, about to sail for Vietnam, two men carried on a conversation. Evil comes with an ingratiating smile, slick talk, the feel of excitement and adventure. Evil is the candy of downfall, the inviting light that eventually turns to darkness. Clifton was no apparition, no curvy smoky image rising from the ship's deck. He appeared full blown in Pete's mind, alive and real and vibrant.

At the time of sailing, Pete understood nothing about war, a young innocent, fresh from one semester at a private Lutheran college wher he seemed out of place parking his used Triumph Tiger Cub motorcycle among the new Chryslers, Buicks, and MG's in the parking lot. People, clothes flapping in bright array from the Puget Sound breeze, crowded on a dock seeping creosote. Worn train tracks gleamed in the sun behind them as a Green Burlington Northern engine pulled flat—cars of slick new up-ended Chevrole Vegas. Lumber mills snorted great white clouds of smoke drifting over warehouses, decaying railroad ties, and pyramids of logs. Waterside bars and junk yards diminished toward the Tide Flats Road. The 11th street bridge appeared toy—like in the distance and St. Joseph's Hospital, on the heights of Tacoma, scemed little more than an aid station, a silhouette backlighted by the coat of awestering sun.

Standing on the dock, the 26th Army Band played

the ship into Puget Sound. Pete gripped the rail and hummed along. He was also a musician, a trumpet player who had enlisted in the wrong Army band, an infantry band. The music drifted out as the ship stopped then rocked and groaned forward in a froth of snorting white water. Their destination was listed as Southeast Asia.

Southeast Asia equaled Vietnam. No one on board said the word, as if the letters contained some kind of hex, a disease easily caught. He knew nothing about Vietnam except he was not interested. Let people run their own countries, fight their own battles, he thought. Everyone knew where they were going. Even without the word, they had caught the disease the moment they stepped on board. As a musician, Pete felt confused. What did the army want with him, or with anyone else in the 4th Infantry Division band?

Pete released the rail and looked around for Clifton. He had been there a minute ago. Clifton understood how the world worked. All Pete understood was how to keep a constant rhythm, know when to vamp and how many refrains to blow. Clifton seemed to know everything, not in a blustery way but with an air of confidence.

Pete looked back over the side of the ship, watched the waves roll upon themselves. "Vietnam." He tried the word on like a smallpox blanket. "Vietnam," he said again stretching the word into his mouth. Nothing happened. He had not fallen overboard or been struck down with a massive stroke.

The other men hung on the rails, pale fears hushed with smiles and laughter. Pete scooted to the cold deck, his legs going numb over the side. Soldiers started to bunch together on the bow and stern. "Vietnam." Pete mumbled the word into his folded arms.

The first advantage was his.

Chapter 2

Soldiers crowded the deck, bunched beside hatches, hung from ladders and perched on railings like green pigeons in contrast to the gray ship. The air, usually smelling of evergreen trees, now carried hints of salt water, fish, musty wet moss. The city of Tacoma faded as the ship chugged past two Foss tugs and a rusted white Alaska steamer heavy with faded, bent, red containers. Pete walked once around the deck pushing between soldiers, gear, cigarette smoke, littered cans of pop, several unstowed du☐el bags, as he looked for Clifton. Clifton never strayed far except to smoke in a dark passageway or to read a book after finding a little light. The two had discussed joining the Army. Clifton wanted to enlist, the Rangers maybe or even the Marines. He wanted war, excitement, and killing.

Not Pete. He thought if he joined the band he would not have to travel to Vietnam thus, fulfilling his military obligation without going to war, or to jail, (a perfect solution said the recruiter) so joining the Army band was a compromise for Clifton if he wanted to be with Pete. So far things had not gone as planned.

Under five hundred feet long, the ship had a feeling of haste to it, incomplete and unsettling. The ship had been built in the forties, an old Liberty ship used to haul troops to and from Europe and the South Pacific. Now it was in business again, more wars, and more soldiers. Pete examined various joints and connections on deck. The paint was layered in gray. The shadows, the corners and bends, the swinging lifeboats, even the rims around the portholes, were all uniform in color. At the stern of the ship, Pete wedged between two soldiers and notched a small V cut into the railing. Layers of paint resembled age rings on a felled tree and the metal looked thin and rusted.

Crowded water bubbled from the stern. Pete's chest emptied. This was his first time away from home. He breathed through his mouth to hold back any tears attempting to leak out. He kept his head well over the side so no one could see him. Heavy shadows darkened the deck.

In the distance hills slowly ticked off one slope after

another. He tapped a finger against the rail, let a Chet Baker ride drift through his head. Music made sense of the world, kept everything in order. For years he had worked bringing emotions to life, to place each feeling momentarily into the world. The frustration of such brief creation, of striving to make an idea solid, was disappointing or, impossible. Creative desire made Pete an optimistic, idealistic manic depressive. Sometimes he felt the music was making him crazy, the incessant rattle of notes, the constant twitching of body parts.

Pete was eighteen and knew everything people of eighteen know. Since musicians were not really soldiers, he felt safe from the war. With an M.O.S. of 02B20 — trumpet/coronet player - he would never fight.

Clifton was the fighter. He liked the Army. Knocking people around in basic always put a grin on his face. He liked being beaten just as much. As a kid he razored off Henry Bilow's lower-lip, jumped him from behind drawing the straight razor from one corner of his mouth to the other. Since they had been best friends, Henry never suspected Clifton had cut him. Clifton kept the lip, wadded up the little sausage in a Blackhawk's comic book, and later fed it to the neighbor's cat. Pete was confused about going to Vietnam. Nothing confused Clifton.

High banked cliffs, small islands and a gentle wind left the Sound flat. Water flowed smoothly to the stern as the screw beat and whipped it into a foam before gathering itself again leaving a triangle of waves drifting out. The water was a long way to jump, maybe thirty feet or more. Pete felt tempted. His foot rested on the lower rail and on the top rail, one hand topping the other. He watched the water as he bent over the side and could almost feel its cold hands pulling him down. He thought of making a break, leaving the ship and Clifton. He knew nothing about fighting or about Vietnam. A life preserver hung from the railing, a clear invitation to escape, drop into the icy water, swim for the nearest cabin on shore. Let the U.S. have its war. Except for his friend Clifton, he just wanted to be left alone.

Clifton could find other fun than war, although war and violence always seemed to be his choice. He killed birds as easily as a turkey processor and often pinned their bodies, wings outstretched, against the sides of abandoned buildings. He called them THE WALLS OF CHRIST, a sanctuary of crucifixion, the birds resembling angels, pretty and innocent. Clifton understood the need for worship, the need to prey upon virgins. Besides, no one was innocent in this world, even angels. One thing ate another, not according to size, but through skill and cunning. Deer ate grass, man ate deer, bears ate man, and the tiny maggots ate the most ferocious creatures of the world. Man constantly ate other men, devouring towns, cities, nations - governments feasting on their populations, religions on their flocks. No two people lived who did not attempt to devour one another to achieve dominance, wealth, success.

Pete reached for the preserver, then brushed it against his arm to check for any movement. When the ring lifted over his shoulder, almost without his control, he stepped away. Confronted with a solution to avoid war, he realized he was more afraid of jumping than staying. He might drown, get chopped and minced by the single out–of–balance screw cutting through the water. Or hypothermia might leave him adrift on the outgoing tide, a floating lunch for dogfish. Yet, he was tempted as he turned away and looked down the length of the ship.

Pete walked forward past the bulkheads, the ladders, the hatches, past the groaning vent pipes, the puddles of mumbling soldiers. He walked up where the wind blew cold and fresh, up where the yellowing sun nodded toward the water. He spotted a new Gerber hunting knife latched to a pack of unstowed gear. He stopped. The knife was a real beauty, slick and long. He started to turn, felt a grip on his arm, smelled Clifton's cold breath. "Shit," Clifton said. "Go for it, man." Scar tissue framed one eye. Although clean shaven, signs of a heavy beard gave him the appearance of a dirty face. He stood under six feet with broad shoulders and hands knuckled–up and rough. Because of his kind and friendly eyes, people liked him almost instantly. His throat coaxed out words, little lines and phrases that pushed into the air.

Clifton seldom told the truth unless it was to his advantage, and viewed the world as his own fiction. His favorite saying was, "Who needs truth if it's dull?" He met the world head–on and arranged it to his liking unlike Pete who gathered his experience through old re–runs of "Ozzie and Harriet". Clifton fought club fights in Chicago, spent the small prize money on friends. The money gone, only the scar over his eye remained. He had split the world open like a fresh orange and let the juice run down his throat.

Unlike Pete, who had only slept with one woman, Clifton had screwed many including Murphy Malone's retarded sister, Joline. She had been sterilized and Clifton photographed her naked, sold the prints to friends. He and Murphy took turns jumping her and he split the money from the pictures on Murphy and his pals. When Joline said she loved Clifton, he bought her a giant panda, kissed her on the forehead and never returned.

Pete saw Clifton in his mind, as real as any other person – Clifton the man of the world, of decisions, the man whose black hair glowed under the yellowing sun, a man to be admired, a man of the world not afraid to attempt anything and accept the results without whimpering. Clifton tapped his heel against the deck and grinned.

"Not the knife?" said Pete.

"You say something?" A skinny soldier looked up, cracker crumbs framing his mouth. Wrinkles covered his fatigues. He glanced at the knife then back at Pete.

Pete waved his hand, shook his head and stepped back. The wind felt good against his face and if he licked his lips he could taste the salt from the ocean air. He watched the water turn away from the hull of the ship.

"Going to be some trip," said Clifton. He seemed to ooze charm and confidence. Pete glanced again at the pile of unstowed gear. The handle of the Gerber knife showed clearly. Clifton spoke loud enough to pull in several soldiers with his conversation. They pushed closer to Pete who only heard Clifton's voice. "Hell, I been to Nam before," he said, scratching his head. "Anybody else been there?" The soldiers remained silent. "My cousin went there," a scraggly redhead said, his eyes bulging knowing his comment made him more than he was. Clifton said, "The place is filled with babes and the army will give us all the ammunition and rubbers we need."

"What's it like?" someone else.

"The usual kind of place filled with strange people. All we got to do is kill them." He relaxed, his arms resting behind him on the ship's rail. "Lots of action." Pete held in a laugh knowing that Clifton could not go into any detail since he had never left the States. Vague generalities usually sufficed in these situations as people conjured up their own images. Whatever he said, people always believed him.

More soldiers, eyes wide, ambled over to listen. They were green, real green. Anything Clifton said would be believed. Yet, Clifton played politician and dodged all specific questions about the war. He shrugged here, nodded there, said things like "well, you know what I mean," or "hey, I don't have to tell you guys," as if they had already had some experience at being men. The soldiers pushed in even more tightly until his tale corralled them. He wanted that knife, could almost feel the cold blade along his thumb. Distract the troops, that was the way.

"You want to know about Nam? See what you can see on that speck of land dangling under the horizon." Clifton jabbed a slender finger over the bow and directly toward the setting sun. All eyes squinted. Clifton slipped between the shoulders of two corporals, dipped as he passed the knife and slid it into his fatigue shirt. Without turning around, he ducked between another four soldiers, parting them cleaner than the Red Sea, scatted across the deck – first one side, than the other – climbed between vent pipes and over a bulkhead until he worked himself to the stern of the ship where Pete waited. "Jingle bells, jingle bells," he sang. "Christmas is here.

"You're a regular Santa," said Pete. He was not totally disgusted. Anxiety and excitement over the knife buzzed in his chest although he knew it was wrong.

"Gifts are for soldiers. If you want to be a damn musician, you don't get gifts," said Clifton. He smiled the same contagious smile he always did when he was in trouble. "We're part of the same Company, Headquarters Company and Band. Only soldiers get knives. What you get is rhythm."

"I could never take anything." Pete fumbled with a button.

"A lot of suckers on this trip need to be taken. Think of it as a learning experience. How else are we going to grow as men, I mean, every one of us."

"Leave me out of it," said Pete. "I have a girl and I don't need any trouble."

"The world's full of ass," said Clifton. "The way I got it figured we can go hog wild in this war. We'll never get another chance to know how nasty we can be and still be legal. This place is going to b wild, wide open. This is where we find out what we are. What do you say?"

Pete would have been better off saying yes. A man who refuses to admit that good and evil are two sides of the same flesh, a man unwilling to confront himself, is a man in chaos, his veins already cut. Pete shrugged his shoulders.

"I was going to get married before I got orders." He thought of Sharon standing on the dock against a dirty piling, one gloved hand threaded through the handle of her purse, the other hand waving just below her wet eyes. Above the oiled planks, her white dress looked misplaced, too clean and too bright.

"There's no percentage in marriage," said Clifton. He scratched his chin. "One roll in the hay after another, that's how I like it. You've never even been in the sack with her." In the distance, the land become a shadowy lump. Sharon would have never approved of Clifton. Clifton removed the knife and drew the blade down his sleeve. "This baby can remove a head like that..." He sliced the air, watched an invisible head tumble overboard, and handed the knife to Pete.

The blade was double–edged with a long taper to the tip. It balanced perfectly in his hand and felt sharp in a way that was not quick to dull. Energy seemed to run through the metal and up Pete's arm and he suppressed a desire to clench his teeth and jab the thing into his own arm.

"Here's the best way to use it," said Clifton. He flipped the knife in his hand and pointed it at Pete, his arm straight out. He danced a little, lunged forward, sliced the air. His rough knuckles slid past Pete's ear.

"Knock it off," said Pete, stepping aside.

"Don't have the blade stick from the bottom of your hand like they show in the movies," Clifton said. He held the handle in a fist and the blade protruded from the bottom toward the deck. "Too easy to knock out and you can only stab down." He flipped the knife over again. "This is best." The blade pointed toward the sky and he tipped his hand toward Pete and jabbed again. "Only Smith and Wesson make a better one."

"Not guns?"

"Sure, guns. But they make knives, too. One of them has a kid in Special Forces and he makes knives for the whole bunch of them. The blade is thicker and you can rip ribs clean in half." Clifton whacked the railing with the palm of his hand. "There's a wire inside for garroting. One slice empties a man of words, thoughts and breath." He held his hands up before Pete, the knife still tightly gripped in one hand, and jerked his arms wide as if he had opened a stage curtain revealing his raisin–like eyes and anxious grin.

"Try it again," he said. "Feel the power, the energy the metal gives you. You'll grow an inch every time you use it. It turns guts into muscle, apathy into conviction."

The knife's power rushed into Pete like molten metal and he felt strong and important. The world sizzled into a flaming dream and winds lifted his feet through clouds. Here was domination, authority, vigor. If a man was anything, he was steel: 440 stainless, unyielding and cold. Pete struck the fire at angles until his arm stopped instantly and his body shook. Through the clouds he saw a large black fist clench his wrist. He felt the pain as the man jerked him to the deck.

"So you the muther–fucker what got my knife." The man smelled musty like old peat moss. "You, whitey. I axed you a question." The hand, with pink nails and creases folded over the knuckles, looked enormous. Long and chipped, the thumb nail hung stiffy in the air like a weapon. "I oughta shove this up your ass," the man said as he twisted Pete's arm.

His wrist burned and the bones inside crowded together and he wanted to cry out. Where was Clifton? From Pete's position, the man looked like his head was taller than the ship's spars. His thick chest pressed at the buttons of his uniform and his sneer resembled dried welding slag.

Please, Pete wanted to say. Please don't hurt me. You can have the knife: I found it, I really did. His arm burned like fire and he was willing to do anything to let it cool. As he opened his mouth to speak, he heard Clifton say: "Piss off, man." Maybe it was just his eyes filling with water, but what Pete saw was Clifton stepping away from the railing, Clifton's voice, Clifton's actions. Several soldiers gathered around.

"Dis ain't no fiddy–cent blade, " the man said. "This muther fucker stole my knife and now he gonna sit on it." He looked to the other soldiers as a warning. He twisted the wrist again bending Pete's body to the side. Sweat dribbled from Pete's forehead and his face wrenched up as if he had been slapped. Please, he wanted to say: please, please.

"This ship's full of knives," said Clifton . He spoke without urgency. "Shit gets lost. People find it. Back off."

Pete attempted to see everything, without success. By now, his eyes had filled with tears. Silhouettes, shadows, soldiers rippled behind thick glass. Someone yelled "Get the bastard!" Pete's ears swelled shut and only the rumpled tick of his heart thumped against the drums. Please let me go, he wanted to say. The wrist felt as it would break.

"I run this boy all around the boat. Now, the white boy's gonna pay." He leaned in close. The smell of tobacco rolled off his breath and filled the air.

"Some officer's going to give us shit," said Clifton,, stepping closer. "Don't break the arm and we'll talk this out."

The soldier twisted even more. Pete tore at his trapped hand like a fox in a trap might do – but he then restrained himself. He could not breathe. He knew that this moment would define him to the men, mark his boundaries like beating up a bully the first day of school so you'll be left alone the rest of the year. An act of defiance left a wake of peace. All the ocean seemed to pour in, blending Clifton with the other soldiers.

"You gonna eat shit, white boy," said the soldier as he gave one final twist.

Pete watched the grin widen. Pain shot into his own head. Please, he wanted to say. As he opened his mouth to beg, his hand jerked free. He lunged forward and heard the soldier groan. Then he was running, limping, running into his own dream, everything a blur, a mist of confusion The soldier doubled over, grabbed between his legs. He staggered forward then back as Clifton held him by the shoulder. Again, Clifton's knee shot up from the deck catching the soldier on his bunched–together hands. The man bent into a hard bow, fell to the deck and sucked air like a grounded fish. Other soldiers crouched around as Pete tried to shake his head clear. Clifton snatched the knife and, like a buzzard, beak down, talons clinging into the flesh, perched on the soldier's chest. Saliva dribbled from between the man's lips. Clifton drew the knife to his throat.

"You've been fucking with the wrong boy. The knife is mine."

Clifton struck, the knife pressing deeply into the man's throat as layers of black skin folded over the blade. "Now, if you want my knife, I'll give it to you – right now." Pete liked watching the man hurt, grinning like he had spit. "What do you say, boy?" Clifton moved the blade enough to draw a fine line of blood.

"It ain't my knife," said the man. His voice squeaked like a drawn string. The palms of his hands lay flat against the deck. "A mistake, man: a mistake. Theys all looks alike."

"Real sweet of you," said Clifton. He sat back drawing his knees up under him. He held the point of the knife against the soldier's chest and rested his hands on the pommel. "You keep on your part of the ship – that's anyplace away from me." Clifton jumped up against the rail and almost knocked Pete over. The soldier rolled to his side and someone bent to help drag him away. "Remember, you see me, you hide."

"You sure had him fooled, buddy," a soldier said, slapping Pete on the back. "Some real scary shit," said someone else. "Best bit of possum I ever saw."

"Let me look at that arm," said Clifton, as the crowd mumbled itself away.

Pete flopped to the deck and leaned his head against the rail. Salt on his lips had formed from the thick ocean air. He let Clifton cradle the arm, swing the hand from side to side. The wrist was red and swollen.

"He had me," said Pete.

"No one gets had who doesn't want to get had," said Clifton. "The iron a man has is in himself, not in his nuts."

Pete watched the mast sway into the last of the twilight, the sky about to tumble into dark.

Chapter 3

All vibrations from the wind, the sea, the engines, rumbled up through the tall smoke stack tossing black ash across the ship and onto a frothy trail of wake. Waves riveted against the ship in gentle strokes then rolled against the hull soundly, solidly sending kicks through the hull. Metal deadened the sound of the water causing whispers to vibrate the railings and down the stairs snaking in rattled Z's deep below decks, deep into the hull where the pressures of air and water equalized. In the stern diesel engines slapped a steady methodical buzz. Pistons strained to strangle diesel fuel and air until it burst into flame. Pete lived in this pit. He felt the vibrations, the quivering, the heavy thump of drudgery straining the metal. Everything solid tingled. An object so large, so solid, yet unstable, caused Pete's hand to shake. His world was too close. Here, every life appeared to be a part of his. If the ship sank, everyone died, not a select few, not just the poor huddled masses or the rich; everyone. Any attempt toward the stairway would only bind them more tightly together in that space where poverty and wealth purchased an equal fate. Pete started to sweat. He rolled toward the bulkhead, placed his hand against the cold iron. Paint flaked down where rust had pushed through. Time ate everything solid, ashes to ashes, dust to dust. He slid from the bunk, parted the heavy cloud of cigarette smoke, and clamored up through the decks as night broke free of light. No stars, no moon greeted him. The air smelt of diesel fuel. No lights shown on deck.

"You trying to strangle that railing?" Clifton rubbed Pete's shoulder.

"I'm starting to choke."

"You'll get used to the dark. Don't think about it. Breathe in and out and no one will know you are afraid. You must travel down, down as deep as you can before you'll understand. Face your fears and you will find they are not fears at all, just a tricky mind."

"You'll be there?"

Before Clifton answered, Sonny Provo walked past, stopped long enough to tip his shoulders and smile before easing down the steps. His butt rolled from side to side.

"Don't bother. He's too much woman for you," Clifton said.

"What if I get into trouble?"

"You mean, like with Sonny?" Clifton drove his tongue between his fingers and wiggled the end like a snake's angry head.

"Everyone likes him. That doesn't mean he's a fag," said Pete. "And what if he is? He does his job."

"I'll be there if you need me, believe me, I'll be there," said Clifton. "No one cares if Sonny's gay or not. What difference does it make what a person is, what a person does?"

Clifton pushed Pete toward the hatch. Pete felt better with Clifton behind him. Pete held to the railing as he descended, the metal tingling with monotonous consistency. The air thickened like a wool blanket, hot moist and scratchy, heavy with smoke as if the world were upside down and smoke fell instead of rose. Caged light bulbs hung like insect nests and cast strange wire shadows. Water continued to scratch against the hull.

The Company had already settled in. Puffy duffle bags rolled into corners radiated the odor of canvas. Men piled up footlockers to make chairs and tables since the musical instruments had been packed into a huge wire cage making their cases unavailable as seats. Shaving bags, a fatigue shirt, one boot, a bayonet and a Mickey Spillane paperback, staked out bunks. Five young soldiers wedged between a row of bunks surrounded by fog from smoking

Muriels, Camels and Viceroys. On a stenciled foot-locker, they flipped cards, anted into the game with a tie clasp, two Dough Boy condoms (antiques from another war) and a handful of coins. They each chewed seriously on the tobacco and, like generals do with men, fanned the cards, pinching them up and down, swapping them in cupped hands into different ranks and order.

"My bunk's here," Pete said, pointing to a bed of tight canvas wedged under a canopy of wrapped pipes.

"Good place for you." Clifton helped lift Pete into the bunk. "I'm across the way, a bottom bunk you can't see from here. I can roll to the side and pull my pecker in complete privacy. Of course, if we all get horny at the same time, we can go up to that string of shitters they have on the next deck and pull at the same time. Team work counts in the army." Pete felt his face redden. Clifton, like most young soldiers, constantly talked about sex.

"What did you mean about Sonny?" Pete scratched the canvas on his bunk.

"Like I said, he's a fag." Clifton sat on a footlocker and flipped the retaining latch with his finger. "It's nothing to me." He leaned back and rested his arm on a bunk. "He'll get such a work out on this ship we'll never be able to erase his smile."

Sonny was the first man to welcome Pete into the outfit. He looked Spanish, at least he had brownish skin, and pretty hands like a priest's, and long fingers that he used to finger the hair off his forehead. No one called him a "lifer" although he had reenlisted at least once. Standing too close to people seemed to be his only fault. Yet, he looked natural with being close to people. Other soldiers - those less liberal than musicians who often lived a counter-culture life of back alleys, transvestites, lesbians, and homosexuals - might avoid him, but he could not be disliked.

"When the pot fattens, I'm going to get into that poker game." Clifton nodded toward the card players. He unfolded a wad of bills from his pocket. "Have enough here for a pretty good stake. Got it down on Pacific Avenue outside the Anchor Tavern."

Clifton shot a hole in the floor with a large hairy finger. He scratched through the hair on his forearm. He had been in several club fights, yet his upper arms were small for a fighter. His shoulders were thick, however, and pressed against the seams of his fatigue shirt. Pete had seen him often enough without his shirt: he had a thick line of hair that rolled from one armpit to the other and fell from his neck to his navel giving the impression of a dark fuzzy cross. That's how Pete imagined him, anyway: an ape—like creature with small ears, a thick neck and a face that remained blue after a shave. Thin scars had been knocked into his eyebrows and the end of his nose was larger on one side than the other. This is not to say he looked in any way hideous. No. He had a smile chiseled into his face and eyes as large and black as river stones. His laugh rolled with the tide and just as easily. But a sense of unpredictability surrounded him, something animal-like that might lick your hand before suddenly ripping your throat apart.

Pete might have tried to make him totally grotesque, but tha would have made Pete grotesque because only someone twisted could love a rusted wire. Pete only innocently found him grotesque the way Sherwood Anderson found people grotesque: not freaks of nature, but freaks against nature. If anything, Pete refused to gawk at three legged midgets not because it made them uncomfortable but because it made him uncomfortable. What Pete had before him was Clifton: a tough, rambunctious Clifton; the same unacceptable Clifton that is within everyone. Pete's acceptance of Clifton was his own denial, a refusal to deal with his own dark recesses, to accept, then repress or control them. Had he just confronted the Clifton side of himself maybe things would have turned out differently, especially for Sergeant Biggilo, a man they both hated.

"Integrity wears a person down," Clifton said. "You think you have it, that's why you're decent. I met a man in jail once, who suffered from integrity. He was an albino black named Willie Jenkins." Clifton held his hands up in front of his eyes. "He had hands as white as yours and they kept getting him in trouble because the did white things. He sold his integrity on Saturdays and tried to buy it back through the church collection plate on Sundays."

The only time Pete had been in jail was when he had doused his headlights to run a stop sign so he could get home and watch the Clay/Liston fight. He had stayed too long at his girl's house. In the car, a '53 Hudson Hornet – seats smelling of leather, yellow glow of the radio flickering against the windshield – Pete had been fighting with the emotions of love: surprise and confusion. Baby birds pecked at his stomach. When he thought of kissing Brenda, the birds grew carnivorous and he shot through the intersection. Pete leaned over the bunk and told the story to Clifton. Clifton wound his arms in wide arcs and laughed. Pete felt cheated. Clifton had not taken the story seriously and Pete had done nothing to fulfill the requirements of a musician scoundrel. Musicians needed jail, and booze, and smack, and women: all wondrous and evil things. A complete physical breakdown fell in there someplace, usually around middle age. Death from pneumonia, or VD, followed. So far, nothing had worked out. Although people said that Pete was a hell of a horn man, his attempts at evil had been dismal. Even the slightest lie left him tossing at night.

"Integrity," Clifton said. "Integrity once sold can never be repurchased." He feigned a cough. "Never thought you would hear a line that sophisticated from me, did you?" He continued, "That's what Willie Jenkins didn't understand. He thought he could let those white hands run over an unwilling woman, then sing in the church on Sunday with a clear conscience."

Pete's mind drifted. On several occasions Pete had traveled downtown to buy a woman. Drunks and cowboys lined the streets or piled against the curbs of Pacific Avenue like stacks of greasy discarded engine parts. Streetlights laid a dim yellow gash over the people and flashing neon cut straight across wet pavements. Lights hung to the bottoms of low clouds making them glow warmly.

Pete had slept in a three dollar room over Ezmarilda's Tavern. Paint peeled from mildew and wine and the air smelled stained from sweat, dirty sheets, and unflushed toilets. The bent quarter notes of country music scratched through the floor and limped from wall to wall. A dancing neon sign – a woman hung on rusted wires from an overhead pole – flashed through the cracked window where Pete stood alternating the room from blue to red. On the sidewalk, aided by parking meters, a wino crutched his way along.

Cowboys, came in only two shapes: thin like a chalk line, or bell shaped with cascading rolls of fat straining buttons on plaid shirts. Trails of spit tobacco guided them into the tavern. Pete didn't like good old boys, or their music. He preferred music from the adjacent black clubs on Broadway. But there he had to content himself with standing under a light post and listening to the music of two bands fighting from between the doors. He was afraid to get too close, to choose one club over another. The music from the twin clubs confronted each other like good natured bums: one note refuted another, notes repelled notes, sometimes notes almost blended in an uproarious clatter of powerful sound.

Earlier, Pete had been there. But when he tired of refereeing the musical onslaughts, he had returned to the room over Ezmarilda's where the atmosphere was antagonistic. Ascending the stairs, reading the prophecies tattooed on the colorless walls, he had been confronted by an aged prostitute. She smelled of Woolworth's perfume and under the yellow light of the bare bulb her pale face looked emotionless as if it had been melted onto her skull and plopped onto a thin pile of Goodwill throw-aways. Only her painted lips danced in the dark.

"How about a tumble?" she said, brushing at the small scabs around her hairline. "Ten bucks honey, for the ride of your life."

Pete felt the handrail pushing against his back.

"I don't have any money."

"Your mama give you some." She forced a smile. "You don't look like no kid what goes around broke. Ten bucks won't kill you. Five for a blowjob and I promise not to bite." She stepped closer and speared him through the shoulder with a dirty fingernail. Pete looked past her, down the hallway. A door oppened and someone spit. Music rolled up the steps, something by Hank Williams. "Five bucks, ass–hole; five bucks for the time of your life." She rapped her knuckles against the wall and speared him again. "I'll treat your little prick like it was my own. Ask anyone in town. Five bucks, five stinking bucks."

Her breath smelt of tarpaper and her eyes, sucked dry from the street, tried to pull him in. Her nails cut deeper into his arm. She was filthy, yet he wanted her, wanted any woman, wanted the feel of sex and not just the idea. Mostly he wanted to rip off her clothes and beat her with his fists before he had her. How did a naked woman look? How did their secret parts smell? Pete jerked past her, confused, afraid and ran into his room.

He leaned against the window and watched the drunks on the street. He needed someone like Clifton to strip him down, guide him between her legs, make the grunting noises, push at the right times, slap her in the face and laugh when it was over. Later that-night, as he rolled on the stained mattress, she came to him: a refugee image, an imaginary succubus who left him wet with semen, tired and alone. What was the wasteland called Woman? What did he want with them? Attempts at reason left him addled and perplexed. He was willing to pay just to see the parts that made up a woman. That only added to his confusion. They had no parts. Their complete nothingness fascinated him. He sat on the bed and felt ashamed and guilty, the semen going cold and sticking to his underwear.

Now it was too late for her. He was on a ship sailing to Vietnam and she was gone. All the women were gone, except Sonny Provo. Did he count? Only Clifton knew. Pete could wait. Already a day had passed. Pete walked to the starboard hull of the ship and lay his head against the cold metal, closed his eyes, let the straining ship cradle his head as it ratcheted his eyes closed. A cloud of images filled his mind and he drifted off as that night, a week after the first prostitute, flowed into his mind..

She stood spotlighted under the streetlight... the rosy cone of luminosity flowing over her body painted on the sidewalk... her hair ebony dazzling straightened rolled at the ends... eccentric face sculpted with a tiny nose and rounded cheeks dark... a shadowy neck slender where light dripped from her shoulders leaving more shadows at her waist... legs embracing nylons printed with webs under a miniskirt down to her feet... red shoes spiked heels deadly against the concrete... bright straps veining up her ankles toes turned toward Pete stunned like a kicked cat crouching on a fire hydrant and him feeling her eyes cupping his shoulders pulling him in like a fly on a toad's tongue... hands around his head... a finger crooked over his ear down and swirling around his lip before parting them as they drifted from the spotlight... the glow falling as if it were tired of holding her up... to the flop house hotel brass door handle dull green the clerk reading a nudie magazine bulging with him not looking up from behind the greasy fingers... the cigar cold for hours wet chewed to twice its size as if picked from a toilet bowl brown stagnant water... the woman piloting Pete up... the center bare carpet through the ice floors coaxing his reluctance... glossy red nails scratching the chipped wall dipped sunken pock-marked a puking light swirling her skin to chocolate... reaching into his pocket for the room key sliding into the loose shaky doorknob... the inside knob clanging on the linoleum floor and rolling to the trash can a dream of faded New England winter snow clinging to the tin and dented side like a billboard of a never existing time alive only in the minds of advertisers... Pete on the bed held by fear and embarrassment her clothes unwrapping puddling on the floor the lips warm parting compassion against his... him feeling the tongue slipping in and out between kisses over eyebrows his shirt stripping away in fear... shoes socks pants a snake shedding skin... her arms painting down his sides head and tongue a creek meandering down to blank out in darkness... the sudden lipped shock between his legs hands earmuffng her head holding it in time before laying back her rolling over... knees up like railing him mounting then falling through the slippery slit involuntarily instinctively pumping her ankles caressing his shoulders cigarette burn marks dimpling the table black plastic ashtray made in America chipped in two places... her legs falling to the sides him leaning forward confused by her strength her ability to lift him over and over again with the thrust of her tiny hips... the lingering odor of puke and urine rising from the mattress... air warm air blowing past his ears dragging moans of ecstasy so great he could not stand it... the emotion unleashed squirting pumping out his soul... her tiny scream as if surprised the gift of astonishment faked forced wonderful... him enjoying the lie of it as he leaned back struck by the sudden radiance as a raging accusing moon screamed through the window and him falling in a bundle of pant.

Pete rolled out of the dream, sweat soaking his body, as Sonny rounded a corner and, before dropping down a passageway, tipped his head and grinned. Clifton rose from Pet's bunk, shoved his hands into his pockets and followed.

Chapter 4

Pete awoke seasick, his stomach awash with bile, as he rolled from side to side, tried to clear his head. Where was he? Everything seemed a blur, his eyes unfocused as he reached up to touch the pipes. Dust floated down from the wrappings and scratched his eyes. The canvas bunk caused his hips to ache and left him stiff as he lifted up to one arm. Dim light filtered through the smoke of the room. His stomach felt close to bubbling over and he lay back down, tried to sleep, to wake, to sleep, always on the verge of drifting in or out of his life. When he tried to wake, grasp his surroundings, his senses deserted him, wandered across a sea of fog. There was no stopping the swaying of his world, the equivocation of mind over mind, emotion over emotion. Who was he?

A sound filtered from a corner of the hold, a quiet sound, and fine, like sand rolling across steel. The sound drifted up, mixed with the throb of the engine, the rolling water pressing against the hull. Pete felt nauseated and twisted toward the noise while trying to get his bearings. The wrapped pipe caught his shoulder causing his stomach to turn and jolt and he ducked under the pipe as his stomach pinched together. The puke burst over the bunk and landed into a large garbage can. His world swirled again, and again the vomit rose up: small chunks of cheese and crackers that clogged his nose.

"Good shot," James said, jumping back slightly. He was the prettiest man in the outfit, the silver band of his watch contrasting with his roasted chestnut skin, dark eyes sparkling in the light, a smile like grateful hands curled at the sides below his high cheek bones revealing Cherokee blood mixed with African. He crossed his arms across his thin and delicate chest. Pete had never seen him without a smile. "I placed the can here to puke in; didn't think you were going to make it."

Pete lifted his head, slobber dripping in strings from between his lips. He saw Clifton sitting on a footlocker sharpening his knife. His arm rotated in steady rhythmical motions over the whetstone. The puking o□ered Pete only temporary relief. The world straightened, then spun away clouding his chance, maybe his last chance, to recognize his situation. Clifton rolled out of view behind James, replaced by canvas bunks and gouged footlockers. Pete's throat and chest ached for surrender. Clifton returned to view long enough to say, "Stop when you get to something round and hairy – that'll be your ass–hole." Listening to those imaginary words, Pete focused on Clifton, a home-rolled cigarette dipping loosely from his mouth. Unlit, half chewed, the tobacco showed visibly through the licked seam.

"God, I've never been so sick," Pete said. His body was a circus. He wanted to go home where his mother might bring him soup and crackers, some 7–up, plug the TV into the socket above his dresser, ease the heating pad under his lower back.

"I scrounged this 7–up," James said. "It won't help much except to sweeten the chunks as it runs through your nose. It's warm and flat the way my Dad always give it to me on the farm."

Pete rolled to his arm and licked at the can. The air in the ship smelt like it came from an old bottle that had lain for too long in the sun. "Last night was dif-ferent," Pete said. The pipe seemed to catch his voice and hold it there.

"My Dad was in the navy during the big war, the Big War, that's what he called it," James said. "He sometimes said, "I seen sea's roll like a hundred dollar whore at a plumber's convention." James tossed Pete a bottle of Dramamine.

"Pills?"

"Must be a thousand people in sickbay. I got these right off knowing folks might get sick."

"Sure," said Clifton. There are only two kinds of people in this world: those at the front of the line and those at the back." Clifton scratched exclamation marks on the air with his knife.

"And you're at the front, I suppose?" Pete said.

"Lines don't exist for me," Clifton said. "I'm an apparition, an idea, a mist of what everyone wants in this world."

"I happened to get lucky," James said. "If you need something just yell. I'll be across the way with Fibo."

Pete listened to Clifton chuckle as he continued scraping the knife blade across the whetstone with monotonous redundancy, stroke after stroke after stroke. With the remaining drink, Pete washed down two pills. He was sick enough to have welcomed death, if he could have welcomed anything. But even death seemed a laborious imposition and he let the Dramamine and the swirling blade mix him down into a maelstrom of dreams.

Cushioned by the dreams, Pete became many things: a snake snapping an unsuspecting rabbit, the rabbit quivering against the bite, on its side, legs kicking the air, head back and red eyes turning in on themselves as foam ran from its mouth; a boy, naked in a classroom trying to hide behind his desk afraid everyone will see him, confused that no one is paying attention to him; a young girl frightened and proud at the blood on her sheets as if this wounding had made her a woman; an old man being fed through a straw, his hand dancing against the arm of a wheelchair. Pete drifted in a half sleep watching the imagined sun flicker pink through closed eyelids. Deeper and deeper he drifted, his temperature rising until finally the delusion of water thickened into a muggy molasses of tender and distorted sleep.

When Pete awoke, he felt trapped, caged in a timeless hold of metal: no days, no nights, no seasons, this day or night the same as the last. Drab honeylight from the pulsating light bulbs stuck to everything and the ship, at least below decks, appeared to be seen through old Scotch tape. The pipe stopped Pete, catching his shoulder, when he tried to roll. A canteen, hanging from a steam line, swung above his head. Taped to its side were two Dramamine. The pills stuck in his throat as he attempted to wash them down and water spilled over the sides of his mouth and into his ears.

He had to pee and crap and, easing over the side of the bunk, he slipped and fell to the floor. Standing with James, Harvey Pitkala, the stage band drummer, helped him up. Pitkala's thin frame was deceptive. For three to six hours a day, his arms worked, beat skins and cymbals and his legs ran hundreds of miles on the peddles of the double basses. He scratched at his freckles and his red hair.

"I'm sick," Pete said. He leaned against a beam and

felt his legs shake.

"You been out for two days," Pitkala, the drummer, said. His head shook from side to side. "Sergeant Biggilo wanted us to pour a bucket of water over you. He's a prick. James gave you the water and pills."

Pete tried to forget about Biggilo. Clifton hated the sergeant and just the sound of Biggilo's name sent him frothing.

"I'm sick. I have to piss."

"You'll regret it and end up sicker than you are if you go up there." Pitkala tipped his head toward the stairs.

"I can manage," Pete said.

"You're an odd one, all right," James said. "We'll at least take you to the stairs." They grabbed his arms and placed his hands on the railings.

Pete started to heave as he staggered toward the stairway, the metal clanging under his feet. He crawled more than walked up the rattling stairs, the chain handrail loose in his grip, the mumbling sounds of men void of activity behind him. As he stumbled to the next deck, the terrible sharp smell of wet rotten shit and piss ripped into his lungs and he gagged again. He heard water sloshing. He edged along the bulkhead and looked into the head. The toilets had backed up and four or five inches of raw sewage rocked with the gentle roll of the ship. Slop splashed up one side of the bulkhead, then the other, leaving behind a smear of dripping paper and globs of shit.

Pete held his nose and heaved again. He tasted the

bile and spit it to the floor. A brown wave splashed by, held in by a ten inch hatch stop. The bathroom was the full width of the ship. Double rows of toilets, over half way through, faced each other. Six showers filled the remaining space. Having no choice, Pete jumped behind a rolling wave and trailed it to a center toilet. As he sat, Pete held his stomach. Like an oil pump, he rocked back and forth raising his legs each time the sewage passed. But his timing was bad and twice slop splashed over his feet. He rubbed his toes against his slippery thongs. James, and Pitkala standing behind him, reached through the hatchway and placed a bar of soap and a towel on a beam.

"Imagine how deep this will be in another twenty days?" James adjusted the towel, "Do you remember the stories of Buddy Bolden, the trumpet player?" he said. Pete held his head and remained silent. "You remind me of those stories. They say he went crazy and ran down the streets of New Orleans naked. You're about as changable as him, all mixed up. But man, could he play." He scratched at his nose. "Anyway, you're going to need these for a shower."

Pete made no connection between James and the pills. If the note on the pills had been from Clifton, then the note was from Clifton. If Clifton was scraping a knife beside Pete's bunk, then Clifton was scraping a knife. Any visual facts were facts because of his mind and his mind saw what his mind saw.

Pete crawled into a shower stall, removed his clothes, then moved into the next stall. The shower had only one handle and cold saltwater dribbled from the faucet – spit, coughed, then belched against Pete and the galvanized stall. He had imagined hot water massaging his ragged body. Now he sucked up his breath unable to breathe under the chill. The soap refused to lather and Pete scraped the bar across his chest leaving his skin red and sore.

The bunk felt good and homey and Pete nestled against the canvas and decided not to take another bath. Even the wool army blanket with bristly hairs and smelling of mothballs felt good. He found such joy in a common thing as a blanket comforting. Everything about the ship started to feel like family: the cozy smell of oil and sweaty bodies; the friends forever gaming at the footlockers; the solitude of the ship plowing out the cold sea. The world was a pleasant place and, for the moment, warming under the wrapped pipe with Pete breathing in dust from another war. Pete did not need Clifton.

Soon the burden of questions arose and bore into his head. He attempted to chip and sort out the answers like a sculpture whittling rock into gods. "What am I doing here?" Pete thought.

"I'm a musician." And then the big question. "Why am I? What am I?" And for a minute he thought he heard himself mumble: "the bastards, the dirty bastards."

As he started to doze, he listened to Pitkala tapping out a rhythm in three–four time. Tic tic tic – Tic tic tic - Tic tic tic... Pete caught he beat. What will they Do with us? What will they Do with us? What will they Do with us?

Chapter 5

The man fell hard against the deck, face down, his arm broken in two places. Just below the elbow his forearm protruded at a ninety degree angle and the elbow itself twisted back toward the shoulder.

He had tried to catch himself on the railing before hitting and flipping off, twisting and hitting the deck. His luck had not been good. The man fell from someplace above, maybe on the off limits deck where a gray cork raft hugged the smokestack. He flipped through the air and, if his toe had not hit the railing and deflected his body, he would have tumbled into the sea. His arm drove into the deck first to cushion the fall, yet his head smashed against the metal, twisting his neck quickly to one side but not hard enough to kill him.

Two soldiers, who had ducked to avoid the falling shadow, hesitated, blinked toward one another, then moved to kneel beside the man. He lay half curled, his wrist, also broken, hanging at a right angle toward his body, opposite the direction from the elbow. The wrist bone, sharply slivered, stabbed through the skin of his arm, the tendons firmly attached like bridge wires, the looped artery throbbing blue. The wrist did not bleed badly and the white bone, like wet porcelain, looked almost pretty against his black skin. The deck twisted his neck folding his head to the side. His chin, at the one end, and his forehead, at the other, were on a horizontal plane with his shoulders

Pitkala pushed the other soldiers aside and knelt beside him. The injured man's breathing was thick and heavy and his chest quivered with each breath. A thin layer of greasy blood and saliva dribbled from his mouth and puddled on the deck. Pitkala handled him gently. James joined him and together they rolled him to his back.

"Get a medic!" Pitkala said. The man's head jerked when Pitkala attempted to straighten it.

"What happened?" said James. Theories echoed from the gathering crowd.

"I think he slipped on the deck."

"Naw. He tripped coming out the hatch."

"I saw him bounce off the rail. Maybe he was going to jump."

"He just come out the sky, out of nowhere."

"It was from way up there. I swear it was. He just came plunging out the sky."

"Wait," a small man in a tee-shirt said. He leaned in close. "That's Bo Samuels over from transportation. He's the one who lost his knife. It's upset him ever since but I don't think he would try and kill himself over it."

"Pete. Is that you?" James said. Pete watched him from between the crowd. "Call someone, call a medic." Pete stood panting in the rear as if he had run from a distance. Maybe he was attempting to get some fresh air when he heard the commotion. He could not remember. He only knew that he was breathless and, when he landed on the scene, he thought he witnessed a shadow on the deck above, a flash against the sky, something dark crawling away from the light. Pete trotted to a hatch and passed the word to a soldier just emerging. The soldier dropped his hands, tried to look over Pete's shoulder, then turned to run back inside, his footsteps tiny little clicks against the metal. Pete returned to a larger crowd, as if the entire Fourth Infantry Division had mustered for inspection, and had to ease his way through. The mad excitement of destruction, a twisted body, an injury, drew him to look in fascination. James had torn his fatigue shirt and tied the cloth around the man's bleeding wrist in a tourniquet. Medics shoved their way through.

"What happened?" a young medic said. With slender fingers he brushed his blond hair over his ears.

"He fell out of the sky," someone said. "I swear."

Pete recognized the injured soldier and did not want to implicate Clifton. He thought the shadow he had seen looked familiar. He tried to draw away from any questions.

"What do you mean, the sky?" the medic said. He shoved Pitkala and James away, worked the injured man's head and mumbled toward the deck.

"The sky," said Pitkala, annoyed at being pushed aside. "Home of that big fiery thing. I was standing here." He pointed to the rail.

"He came from the sky and almost crushed me. He must have been dicking around up there."

"Up there?"

"Yeah, that space above your head."

The medic looked at the crowd.

"Don't be a smart–ass," the other medic said. He unlaced the man's boots.

"What did you do?" the first medic said.

"Ducked, what do you think?"

"You didn't try to catch him?"

"I forgot my baseball glove."

The second medic unsnapped the stretcher when it arrived. The first medic looked up.

"That's off limits," he said. "You sure he came from there?"

"No, I think he came from Mississippi. Maybe he was trying out for the Olympic Deck Dive Competition."

Pitkala rubbed his knees and shook his head in disbelief. Pete moved in and helped with the stretcher. The soldier lay almost dead except for his jerking chest and raspy breathing.

"His neck's broken, roll him easy."

Pitkala and James helped roll him to his side. Pete and the medics eased the stretcher under him.

"Be careful with him," the blond medic said. "The son—of—a—bitch is in enough trouble for being on that deck."

"Maybe command will break his other arm," Pitkala said.

Pete let someone else take his end of the stretcher. The crowd gathered together again when they passed, mumbled for a few minutes, then paired off and disbanded.

"Bad news," said Pitkaka. "Haven't we seen him someplace before?" He rubbed his hands together and smelled them.

"That guy said he was the one that lost his knife," said James "In fact, you know him real good, don't you Pete? Isn't he that fellow you beat the crap out of?"

"He'll be all right," Pete said. Still out of breath, he leaned against a fire hose on the bulkhead. Pitkala rested his foot on the bottom rail.

"You never know." Pitkala turned to spit. "He shouldn't of been screwing around up there." He jabbed his chin toward Pete. "That's him, all right. I wasn't sure at first. He's the one who accused you of stealing his knife. Some guys have no sense; they screw with the wrong people and ask for trouble." Other soldiers moved to the rail and Pete started to fidget with a button on his tunic.

"I just came up for air," he said. "The stairs took my breath, nothing else."

"Sure," said James, tapping him on the forearm.

"I've been sick and never hurt anyone before. I don't like it, I don't like any of it."

"You're a card, all right. A regular Buddy Bolden."

Waves rolled like twisted prairie. The sun hid behind a flat sky. The air, fat with salt, blanketed the deck dribbling over bulkheads and railings. Pete crawled deep within the ship, there to fall into a half sleep, into his childhood, into a morass of troubled thoughts, sick again and sweating. He tumbled from one side of the canvas bunk to the other trapped by an idea. On a card table before him sat the idea of war: heavy cards, thick cards, all suited in red. Beside them stood the hand of childhood: good cards and bad ones, mostly innocent ones. No that's wrong. Children are seldom innocent. There was also the hand of dreams: meaningless loose cards which rarely helped a good hand.

Pete held the hand of war, felt its power. How should that hand be played? What cards might work against him? As a kid, he often played war. The hand consisted mostly of bodies. What was it about the game he could not grasp? Death, the concept of death, of many deaths, of a universal spectral image, was overwhelming. He placed the bodies into stacks separating them into suits until he held the image of a single death, a single person, one crumpled joker.

He still could not grasp the idea of death. The dead man looked warm and his chest twitched. Television had ruined Pete. He could not get a true picture of death.

Pete tossed down the cards and picked up the hand of dreams. Reds, greens and blues tumbled about like a kaleidoscope, a pale purple triangle here, a bright orange one there: faces, trees, thoughts, ideas. He wheeled about in a muddy galaxy of constant temperatures and engine noises and drew into his hand a childhood card. On the card was an empty lion's den of stone and clay. The nasty odor of the den frightened him and he sprouted an erection. Strong sunlight pried through the overhead bars. Shade pooled to one side of the den. Sand burned his feet. He was Jewish. He had never been Jewish before and he did not know how to act. A flea chewed at his brown toes. The erection fascinated him and the sun felt good against the taught skin. When he grinned and grabbed his prick, the dream was replaced.

Cold air blew across his shoulders. He stank. He was naked in a cement shower at Dachau. Children hung like boils from the legs of their clutching naked mothers. A low, disjointed gurgling ruptured his ears. The people looked burnt, gray, twisted. Pete tried to look away, close his already closed eyes. The naked images crowded around him and the ragged fingernails of the concentration camp women started to claw, claw at the concrete walls. They were hideous creatures yet he wanted to touch their tits, reach into their bushes. He screamed at his own shame and flipped away the cards. But the game had changed. He no longer needed cards and he awoke in the dream under the covers of his own bed at home.

Under the covers he smelled his own breath, and held a flashlight on a picture book of W.W.II. The sheet rubbed against his ears. On the page, row after row, naked women stood in line to be gassed. He felt sick and ashamed at his erection. Even when he tried to look away, the pages held him. He grabbed himself, jerked his hand up and down, released himself and rolled to the mattress ashamed. Don't touch it, don't touch it, he thought.

He grabbed himself again and started to pump. He touched the magazine, placed his fingers on one woman who did not look confused or even concerned. Her breasts were large and between her legs was that beautiful black V for which he longed. What was the feeling to have nothing between your legs, nothing to scratch, nothing to ache? All the women looked wretched and exciting.

Pete closed his eyes and jerked faster and faster until his arms were removed, tied to a cross, hands nailed, feet nailed, head split. Shit dripped down his legs and his belly had swollen black. Flies ate at his eyes. All the bodies, all the dead Jews, stood at his cross. They stoned him quietly, slowly, the pitter–patter of rocks bouncing off his flesh. Pete smiled. For a moment everything made sense. Yet, he was unable to put that sense into words.

Pete finally awoke into another dream, the dream of a musician deep in the innards of the troop ship USS John Pope. He had been sweating and he felt the gooey soup of a wet dream clinging to his shorts. He tried to punch the air awake with his clenched fists. Toward the wire that held the musical instruments, two soldiers passed around a cigarette. The card game was still in progress, a continuation of the original one. He looked for Clifton.

"Get your butts on deck for P.T.," Sergeant Biggilo grumbled.

His voice was not unlike the sound made by a wolf protecting a fresh kill. He was the First Sergeant of the band, the company, of anything in which he came in contact. Pete saw him as a large, grizzly man, inadequate and uneven. Clifton viewed him as a repugnant little weasel who had worked his way up in ranks through the thighs of the wives of commanding officers. Still, there was no denying the fact that even in the shadow, he was a handsome man: half Mexican, half Black, a uniform that cracked in the wind, when the wind could bend it at all.

"He's sick, Sarge," said Clifton.

Biggilo stepped across the deck and soldiers snapped to their feet.

"Some kind of problem here, soldier?" Biggilo rocked back on

his heels.

"Ain't we got it bad enough," said Clifton.

"I'm talking to you, soldier."

Pete tried to look up. He fumbled in his pocket.

"Fresh air is what you need. Get your ass on deck like everyone else."

Biggilo shook the bunk. When Pete did not respond, Biggilo grabbed him by the arm. None of the other soldiers had left. They bottlenecked at the foot of the stairs.

"You don't know what bad is, soldier." He stepped back. "Five minutes. On deck. Everyone. Ev–ery– one." He glanced over his shoulder.

"He's got a note from the doc," said Clifton. "And you can't tell about his folks. You make him any sicker and they might write their congressman. Besides, he could even get sick right now." Clifton grinned and pointed at the sergeant's shoes. "He might puke all over that shine. I sure would hate to see that."

Pete worked the note from his pocket, hung it over the bunk. When Biggilo reached for the paper, Pete started to gag. Biggilo jumped back, looked at his shoes, stomped toward the stairs. Everyone there rattled up through the hatch while everyone else folded toward the shadows.

"I brought you these oranges," said Clifton. One landed on Pete's chest. "That shithead's orders aren't for us. If you want air, we'll go up later."

"Thanks." Pete fumbled with the orange.

"We're in for trouble with that bastard. Let's just say that something happened to him. They would come after you. So we'll have to cool it for now. Besides, the sarge can't figure you, and that's to our advantage. His time will come and I'll fix it so you're in the clear."

Clifton dug at his fingernails with the knife point.

"I don't want to get mixed up in anything."

Clifton tossed the rest of the oranges beside Pete.

"You need food."

Pete felt a hand against his arm, a soft but firm hand like the

one his mother used when he was sick. Sweat was wiped from his

forehead.

"Do you like the oranges?" said Sunny Provo, standing on the lower bunks, smiled down at him. His arm rested on Pete's bunk and when Sunny spoke, he spoke very close. "You shouldn't bad mouth the sergeant. He never forgets."

"I'm sick." Pete's eyes felt like two stones.

"I can talk to him." Sunny's voice sounded secure and light. "We have an understanding." His fingers pressed and circled Pete's temples, the sides of his neck. "Sergeants have needs, like everyone else. I'm available, that's all I'm saying. You have a dark side. I like that in a man." His fingers knuckled up and worked the side of Pete's head. Pete avoided looking into his eyes. "I'm not forward," said Sunny, "just available."

Later, on deck, under a sky colored like solder, Pete gathered in his own fresh air. The wind tasted of salt. The masts hung wet and cold on the sky. A soldier, his stomach folding over his belt, squeezed a zit on his chin. A friend leaned close and watched the operation. Farther forward, past the outer bulk-heads where the ship leveled out leaving nothing except space between the port and starboard railings, soldiers draped across wires and equipment like laundry. Several men pooled together around a wench. "I got her to do it after the senior prom." A short man flashed a photo from his wallet. The others tipped in for a closer look. "I've seen plenty of girls doing that," someone said. The first man pulled the picture away. "Then you don't need to see. The second man reached for the wallet. "Well, they didn't do it exactly like that."

For two weeks, cutting a small bubbling wake into the gray Pacific, the ship sailed toward some blank destination. The exercise program of Sergeant Biggilo lasted only a few days before he retired, his uniform crisping in the air. Other routines settled in: the chow line which, for three times a day, cir-cled the ship with slouching and shivering soldiers; reading books below decks; smoking cigarettes topside, ashes flipping toward the stern; jerking off under the covers and in dark passages; the endless poker games, canteen liners filled with stale coffee piling high on footlockers crowded with mashed cigarettes, rin-............................ed cards. Days die... evening, blown b.....................................

On the day the band was to qualify with a Colt .45, the standard side–arm of the army, a firing range was erected on the stern of the ship. Pete had been helped to the deck and stood on shaky knees in one of the two lines separated by a weapons sergeant. He paced and grunted instructions. Sunny stood shoulder to shoulder with Pete. Each day, he and Pitkala had brought Pete food. Pete tried to listen to the sergeant and not puke.

"All right ya god–damned pecker heads, nothing can be simpler than qualifying wid this weapon." The sergeant chewed on a dirty toothpick. "I ain't got time to fuck wid you guys so all yer gots to do is come out here in single file, one at a time." He lifted the pistol in the air. "Dis is yer standard sidearm, a .45 caliber Colt automatic, one each. Da safety is on da side." With his free hand, he pointed toward the weapon. "Because yous ain't got sense enough to load it, I already done it. All yous gots to do is come out here, point dis weapon that–a–way, release da safety and pull da trigger. If yous hits the Pacific, yous qualify." He stepped to the middle of a line and grabbed a soldier. "You, bozo. Come out here and show da boys how to tie your shoes and how to fire dis weapon."

Qualifying went smoothly. The sergeant placed the weapon into each soldier's hand. He aimed and ripped the Pacific. Even Sunny, smiling wildly, fired three rounds, shell casings clanging to the deck, before the sergeant jerked the weapon from his hand. Although he could hardly stand, Pete managed to hold the pistol with both hands and get away his shot. Sunny winked and clapped his hands quietly together. Pitkala was not so lucky.

"I hate guns," he said. "I'm just a drummer." He teetered from one foot to the other. "No one in my family ever owned a gun."

"You made it through basic," said Pete. Another shot tore the air.

"One day at the range. Big deal. And no one paid any attention to me. This is different."

When it was his turn, Pitkala stepped beside the sergeant and looked skyward. He grabbed the pistol and turned his head slightly. Pete took a step back and motioned Sunny to do the same. The weight of the pistol seemed to pull Pitkala's freckled hand downward and he pinched his eyes together and jerked the trigger. The bullet ripped from the barrel, sparked the ship's lower rail, bounced back to the deck and up through a porthole where it skittered down the stairs and below decks.

"You dumb simple bastard," the sergeant said, trying to regain his composure. "Get the fuck out of here. Every one of yous are dumb shits - leave." He snapped the weapon from Pitkala and stomped away.

After everyone had left, Pitkala still stood in the same spot from which he had fired. Pete held him by one arm, Sunny by the other. They tried to steer him inside.

"Nice shooting," said Pete. He helped lift him over some rusted cable. "You may be the only man in history to shoot at the Pacific Ocean, and miss."

Back in the hold, Clifton sat on a footlocker and worked his Gerber knife across the whetstone.

"Will we get any more training?" said Pete. He crawled back into his bunk.

"Some VD films. You'll be able to shoot the ocean and also know what the scabs are on your pecker — a full rounded soldier." Pitkala played his drumsticks against a beam and laughed at his joke.

"Don't think about the training, don't think about the army," said Clifton. He ran the blade across his fingernail. "Staying alive is all that counts. Thinking about survival is a full time job."

Clifton flipped the knife in the air and caught the handle. He sat quietly as if waiting for Pete to speak. The din of the engines vibrated through the metal.

"You all right?" said Pitkala.

"A bad stomach."

"My ass." He leaned against the bunk. "The other night you were sweating and mumbling, going on about all kinds of shit. You looked right at me but didn't see shit." He started drumming on the beam again. "You looked lost, real lost. If you brought a few hits with you, maybe you could pass some around. I'm no prude, no junkie either."

"Forget it," said Clifton. "Worry about saving your ass." He pointed the knife at Pitkala. "Some little yellow fucker is right now thinking about cutting your throat."

"Don't get pissy." said Pitkala. "You looked lost, was all."

"Everything's so complicated," said Pete. "I don't know how to be."

"Be what?"

"Be something; I don't know."

"Just don't get pissy with me." Pitkala hung his head and missed a beat. Pete wobbled topside and spit into the ocean. Everything was quiet except for the hum of water slapping the hull. He dug his toe into the deck and checked his watch. He walked aft toward a small hatchway marked "off limits." The steps rattled and he moved back behind a life preserver. Sergeant Biggilo emerged, winded like he had climbed a small hill. He straightened himself, tucked in his shirt, patted the crease in his pants together and brushed back his hair.

When he was out of sight, Pete jumped down the hatchway and climbed deep into the ship where the air smelled hot and oily. He eased himself down a narrow hallway, through another hatch and into a small room cluttered with working equipment. One bulb badly lit the area and light soaked into the wrapped pipes. Pete felt lost, exhausted and he crawled into a corner to rest.

"Hey, sweet lips," he heard Clifton say. "You here, baby?"

Clifton stood by the hatch, eyeing the dim area. The heat was thick, like a sauna, and he had already started to sweat. He slowly walked around a large padded tub that reached from floor to ceiling. A pipe dripped moisture leaving a yellow/orange stain around its edge.

"You here, sweet thing," Clifton called again.

Pete was ready to call back, to tell Clifton he was lost and he needed help. He started to speak when he heard:

"I'm here, over here."

Clifton followed the sound back to where the light trailed off the bulkhead.

"Where?" he called.

"Here, over here."

Clifton peered into the dark. Sweat soaked through the back of his shirt. He waited for his eyes to adjust. Someone touched him on the arm.

"I'm here, right here."

Clifton pulled Sunny into the light. Sunny stood naked and looked almost embarrassed. His dark hair, his deep eyes, his bare chest and shoulders, his prick slowly starting to firm, all appeared in contrast to the woman–like shape of his trunk. Sunny moved closer, his head down. He slid his arms around Clifton's waist, his thumbs working over Clifton's belt.

"Back off," said Clifton.

"I hoped you would come, I wanted you to come and to do what I asked you to do." Sunny tugged at Clifton's shirt.

"No shit." Clifton drew his hands over Sunny's body, up, down then around his shoulders. "You're going to treat me just right?" Clifton continued. "I'm no fag; don't forget that. I also don't care if you're one. That's your business. I'm just here for anyone who wants some fun, for anyone who can't resist me, for anyone who wants a favor."

"I'm for you, I'm for all soldiers." Sunny looked impatient. "I'll do whatever you want."

Clifton webbed his fingers around Sunny's head and tipped it back. He dipped his head close to Sunny as if to kiss him. Sunny closed his eyes and his face softened waiting for the kiss, the warmth of sunshine below decks. Clifton tightened his grip on Sunny's hair. He drove his knee between Sonny's legs, twisted his head to the side and rammed him against the bulkhead. Sunny slumped into the dark and his body jerked violently.

"You got it all wrong. You want something, not me." Clifton's balled up fists resembled stones.

"No," Sunny whimpered.

"I just saw Biggilo leave." Clifton mashed Sunny's cheeks together but not until he had opened his fists so as to leave only burning skin. "You've still got juice running from between your lips." Sunny curled into a tighter ball and tried to catch his breath. He reached a hand toward Clifton. "I want to kill the bastard. Now you want something from me." Clifton kicked Sunny hard on the thigh leaving scratches from his boot laces. Sunny hugged the leg as if he wanted to pull himself into himself. Dirt had already powdered his body, the dust collecting on his forehead and starting to drip in thin black streaks. "You're a filthy little faggot," said Clifton. "You say you want me, and then take him. You're a filthy whore."

Sunny attempted to stand, brush himself off, lift up his head to regain some dignity. When he tried to talk, all he could do was to squeak out, "He made me. I didn't want to. He made me. You're the one I want. The one who treats me right." Sunny reached for his pants, only to be kicked in the stomach. He retched, gagging against the blow, fell to one knee and rolled toward his pants.

"Biggilo threw me down and tried to strangle me with his tool. I could do nothing." He spoke quickly now, trying to shove the words out between sobs. "He left me lying here."

"Right," said Clifton. "Left you lying here with a smile on your face."

"He was bigger than me."

Sunny crouched on his hands and knees. He shoved Sonny to the deck, rolled the buckle into his hand and snapped the belt hard against Sunny's ass. He flicked the belt out again and again cracking the air like a snake's tongue. Sunny shook with each blow until he finally fell to his stomach, whimpering. He rolled to his back, hushed his sobbing.

Clifton wiped his forehead and tried to catch his breath. He reached into his pocket and lit a smoke. The light from the match flared against Sunny's wild eyes. "I'm not hitting you too hard am I? I think you're O.K. and I don't want to hurt you but this is what you wanted. It's not really my thing."

"It's just right," said Sunny. "It truly is. Pain is my greatest joy." He touched Clifton around the ankle. "Whip me again, just a little, and I'll tell you a little secret about our next stop. It's not where you think it is." He hunched up and waited for the blow.

Chapter 6

The ship continued to sail leaving in its wake a trail of rust, oil and garbage before land was finally sighted. Hills rose from the sea like a steady dark swell and slowly became the ragged shape of color, greens and browns. Pete managed to climb on deck and hang over the railing.

"You said we'd stop," said James. He rubbed his simple face, a face with a constant smile, and two black eyes like islands surrounded with moats of white. James played trombone in the stage band. Of course, like everyone else, he also performed in the concert and marching band.

"Land is land," said Pete, his head swirling in time with his stomach.

"You said we'd stop and here we are." James twisted a finger through his rough hair. He ate around the bruise of a large apple and juice dribbled down his chin. He sopped up the juice with his shirt-sleeve and bit in again.

It seemed forever for the ship to move into the horseshoe harbor and the water surrounding the hull turned from black to navy, light blue then to light green. Sailors tossed lines overboard, thick strands of wheat-colored rope. The water started to film with oil reflecting a spectrum of glistening blues. Barebacked roach-bodied men secured lines to the wooden dock, their muscles as thick and wiry as the ship rope. The dock jutted from below a high cliff. A dirt road cut from between the cli☐ and slanted down toward the dock. Except for the natives work-ing around the ship, there were no signs of life. Soon, clouds of dust rose in the distance over the cliff.

"Ain't you ever going to get over that seasickness?" James sounded more annoyed than concerned. "Rumor is, rides will be coming, enough for all of us. Maybe that's them." He perked up even more than usual. "If I don't get some hard practice on my axe in soon I'll forget how to play. When we get back maybe we can get a jam together."

The cloud of dust in the distance steamed higher and moved closer to the ship. Pete heard the faint and fine buzz of revving engines, angry hornets fighting toward the ship. The noise and dust grewuntil hundreds of rattling three–wheeled Cushmans topped the hill and raced down the road. Snarling Orientals twisted machines for space, pushing to be first in line, as they smashed into one another, bumper car style. As the vehicles banged off one another, drivers shook angry fists, screamed and spit. The lead machines spun to a halt at the dock's edge. More fists flew and blood flowed as men continued to knock each other about over position. One Cushman was shoved to its side, then quickly righted by the driver who rocked it several times back over the dented roof until it bounced on the wheels as puffs of dust emerged from under the tires, the driver flipping his finger to the rest of the drivers in defiance, his mouth snarling around jagged orange teeth like a rabid baboon.

"We need to get below," said Pete "A whole dock full of cars and people fighting for no reason.   It doesn't make sense."

"Like hell." James spit over the side. "As much as you like to fight, this should be your kind of place. Let's see what the Captain has to say."

Down below, the Captain was careful not to scuff his boots and he scratched thoughtfully at his pressed pants. He was the Captain of all Headquarters, Headquarters Company and Band. One finger traveled down the stem of his glasses to a small ear. He scratched the lobe. Stiff bars on his shoulders reflected cabin light and his hair was cropped so closely that its color was indeterminate. He shoved his hands into his pockets and, when he passed, he winked at several of the men with his left eye. He paced the compartment, not from nerves or from any kind of equivocation (as Captain, he always knew where he was) but more from boredom. As he paced, he spoke in a manner the men appeared to appreciate: never looking at a single person, never making any personal contact, yet each man thought the Captain spoke to him alone. Between sentences, he looked up and gave his left eye wink at no one, and everyone at once.

"Men," he said. "We'll be tied up in half an hour. You all have passes and are welcome to go ashore providing you wear your class A's. Again, you may all go ashore." He interlocked his fingers behind his back. "Leave terminates at eighteen hundred hours. Enjoy yourselves. Remember the VD lecture. Don't be late."

His voice contained a touch of mothering that he endeavored unsuccessfully to conceal. Without looking up, or breaking stride, he turned to one side and walked up and out of the hatch as if it had been just another piece of horizontal deck.

By the time Pete had worked his way to the deck, the dock had grown to a swirl of tan soldiers all moving in mass. Workers grunted over boxes, hooked to webbed pallets of freight, fork–lifted rows of black barrels. Steel cable hoisted conex containers high above decks and tractors off–loaded trucks. From the ship, a wave of disembarking soldiers surged forward and back like a weak rubber band. Dust twirled through the air as troops filed into Cushmans, swelling them beyond capacity, causing them to tilt dangerously. When filled, the machines lumbered away in a dusty vision of arms and legs flapping in the breeze like giant blow fish.

Pete flowed down the gang plank with James and Pitkala. To avoid the crowd, they skirted the edge of the dock and climbed down to the water over large chunks of slippery rocks and finally worked their way back to the small road away from the crowd.

Pete, still too weak to walk far, was assisted most of the way. He sat on the dusty sand as Pitkala hailed a ride. The Cushman driver rounded the pack and slid to a halt. Red, orange and green paint peeled in several places on the machine and rust poked through. Two seats, facing one another and covered with ripped canvas, formed the accommodations in back. Bent poles, welded in several places, supported a flapping top made from a parachute silk. The wheels wobbled when the machine moved and the whole machine much resembled a giant crushed and rusted beer can on wheels.

"Ride, one dollar each," the driver said. His lipless grin framed his orange teeth. "You get drunk, get woman, all good price." He knocked his legs together.

The Cushman kicked up dust as the driver threaded the machine through a pack of other machines. Pete held on tightly and James howled like a siren. Few people appeared along the way, some farmers, an occasional ox pulling a cart. The driver dropped them down an alley of wet stones, naked children and long rows of buildings so close together they appeared to be connected. Some buildings were built of rough black wood, some of stone. They were laced together so tightly, the street so narrow, that daylight could not venture through. Pete felt like he was standing in a damp tunnel. Torn curtains hung limply from misshapen window frames. Small yellow and brown faces looked from behind the frames, always from a lower corner. There were no doors, as Pete knew doors, mostly strings of beads or cloth or bamboo strips. The buildings stood on log pilings under which dogs with scruffy spikes of fur and vacuous looks, lounged. Several children sat in pools of stagnant water, their feet deep in mud. Pete had never heard such stony silence. Clifton motioned them forward. His shoe moving against stone sounded like years of hollow echoes.

Farther down the street, on a porch, stood a soldier from a transportation company. He spoke with a middle–aged woman holding two small children. She placed one of them on the porch and dipped out her right breast. The soldier weighed the breast with his right hand, nodded and handed her his watch. She called into the house and a rumpled old lady, bent at the back, emerged and held the children. The first woman led the soldier through the curtain.

"Some stuff," said Pitkala.

The event seemed to Pete like one more unsorted dream. Even the bar, where they finally stopped, carried the air of illusion. The girls, staring from the windows, appeared to be a part of the glass, like brown discolorations, or faded Christmas decorations hung for too long. A girl, more an apparition of pastels, of fog, of disjointed light which had stumbled onto the street by mistake, motioned them in.

They moved into the room, a small rectangle with walls of bare and rough wood. The room smelled of mud, beer, whisky and sugary perfume. A man, his yellow shirt stained brown under his armpits, rested his hands across his stomach which, in turn, rested on the bar. A curtain door nailed to a frame opened to another room. Something like a wind–chime tinkled from behind the curtain. A large fly buzzed between the whisky bottles and another fly tapped and prayed his way across the red and green neon of the juke box.

Outside, a dog barked in the street, yelped as if it had been kicked, then went silent. Clifton flopped into a chair in the middle of the room. Pete followed him and motioned to the others. He breathed deeply, smelled the perfume and something else, something like sawdust and puke.

Pete drew into himself when the girls arrived

as if he had accidentally seen something forbidden or secret. One of them stationed herself at his back. She scraped her nails across his temples and around his neck. Her bold actions frightened him, although he tried not to let on, forced a grin. The other girls hovered around the table like kids to new unopened toys. Pete felt dizzy. Something in him liked being a toy, something liked the soft warm fingers on his neck. He liked being touched. The girls were welcome to his watch. Yet, he was afraid to offer it. A man needed a relationship with a woman to truly enjoy sex. This was nothing but masturbation, an orifice to drop sperm into rather than have it spurt onto the floor or into a wadded clump of toilet paper. Clifton bought him a beer. Flat foam covered the glass rim. Clifton urged him to fondle the girl.

Each girl took her turn rubbing Pitkala's red hair. They pulled at his freckled white skin, bought him drinks, refused his money. He represented good luck, a red-haired oddity among the dark parts of the world. One girl pushed her breast against his cheek. When he blushed, his freckles blended into his face.

"Looks like the drummer is king," he said.

Within a very short time, James became drunk. His head bobbed from shoulder to shoulder and his eyes rolled about his little black head.

"Don't we get any women?" he mumbled.

"If you want a bitch, you grab a bitch," said Clifton.

He clutched a girl to his side and twisted her wrist. She looked surprised but quickly caught herself and forced a grin. She brushed back strands of hair that had fallen over her face, a face featureless and plain like most oriental faces, indistinguishable to American eyes. Under her left eye she touched an old scar that had been carefully painted. She had plucked her eyebrows almost out, replaced with thin lines of black pencil. When she smiled, one front tooth tilted slightly ajar. She would have been prettier later at night. Clifton did not care.

"These are just bitches," said Clifton. "You bend them over a chair and fill them with happy stick. Toss them a few bucks and everyone is delighted. They want the money. We want the sex. No harm done and everyone gets his wish."

He pinched her cheeks between the knuckles of his clenched fingers. She drew back and her eyes looked dangerous and afraid.

"Don't get into one of your nasty moods, Pete" said Pitkala. "There's enough women here for everyone, although they're a bit stuck on me." He motioned them away. "Give me some breathing space. James, you take this one. I can tell she's an expensive one. And you..." he pointed to Pete, "...you need one a little more willing, so I'll trade you for this short one here."

Pete tried to pretend he was drunk, although he had drunk only one beer.

"Let's have them all," said James. "My Pap would

be proud." He tried to dip his hands around the girl's breasts but they landed on her hips.

At first, Pete did not understand. He had never witnessed anyone change so quickly. James was the quiet one never speaking of women, never looking any way except pleasant. He pulled at her dress trying to jerk it down, then lift it up. She motioned toward the back room but when he wobbled to his feet, he tumbled back to his chair.

"It's like this," he stammered. "I used to talk to my Pap and he never answered back. He wasn't no indifferent   kind of nigger, he just didn't need no language." He sat the girl on his knee and pointed his finger at her to make her understand. "I used to sit on the porch with my trombone while my Pap plowed the fields behind a mule named cow."

"What do you mean, cow?" said Pitkala.

"Cow. That's right. Pap and cow went around that field and around that field and every time they got to the far corner, old cow stopped. Pap took a bottle of Kentucky Gentleman bourbon down from the nectar tree. He tipped his WWI campaign hat and downed a swig of that juice. Then he would walk up to old cow and scratch him between the ears." James burped and drank more of his beer. "He never would give me none of that juice or ever let me help with the plowing. He always said 'you just practice that bone of yours and you ain't never going to have to walk behind no mule. You be playing in a big band for all the folks.' He always told me that music would get a man all the liquor and women a man could handle, and that's the truth."

"Let's make the old man proud," said Clifton. "Booze and women for everyone." He raised his glass in a toast. "All we need is some music."

He dragged his girl to the juke box, her free arm flapping behind her, her tiny feet skidding across the floor. She stumbled and knocked over a chair before falling. Clifton threaded his hand through her hair and lifted her to her feet. The bartender never moved, never showed the slightest emotion or reaction except to examine the dried spots on a beer glass.

Clifton bent the girl over the juke box and kissed her hard. Pete knew it was wrong, yet he could not say anything, was not man enough to deal with Clifton, did not have the guts to do anything except feel the evil, sexual rush pour into his chest. Clifton continued to hold her by the hair. With his other hand he clutched her wrist, shoved the arm around her back and lifted it up toward her shoulder. She tried to pull her lips away and scream. He locked his mouth around hers and continued to lift. She danced on the very ends of her toes. Pete could almost hear her arm break. Clifton drove his tongue deep into her mouth. If she could have, she would have stood on air. Tears shot down her face.

When the arm had reached its limit, twisted in the socket, stretched every tendon, Clifton released it and smiled, in the place where her scream now stood, as if nothing had happened. She dropped back against the wall and held her quivering arm with the small fingers of her other hand. Clifton fed the juke box a coin and handed the girl a dollar. She quickly slid the bill into her dress. Clifton punched in a few numbers. He motioned to the girl. She stood back until he showed her a ten dollar bill. She moved to his side and hugged him around the waist. He held her gently like a piece of thin silk ready to blow away.

"Fish on the line," he said. "Life is simple. All people want is what they want."

Pete had watched everything, everyone's reactions. He always saw Clifton as if viewing his own self in some kind of out– of–body experience. He never directly felt Clifton, the emotions of Clifton. The feelings were always his. Clifton was a specimen to be studied. To have his emotions would be to admit that some part of him was the same part of Pete.

The girl moved next to Pete and he felt her warm hand on his neck. She stood over his left shoulder and stroked his neck. He liked her touch. What difference did it make if she were a whore. She was a woman. His body wanted a woman yet his mind fought with itself and he was afraid. Maybe under the pressure he could not function as a man. Maybe she would hurt him. Maybe he would end up with VD or clap or one of the many incurable diseases rumored to be carried by oriental women. All he knew for sure was that he wanted her. He turned slowly to face her. Her feet were small and her ankles tight. Her legs, where they emerged from her dress, were nicely shaped. Every curve of her body dipped and protruded in the right places. Her waist was like a sculpted glass inviting to be held. Her black hair framed her face and deep eyes. Pete wanted to touch her, to rest his head against her tiny perfect breasts. All he had to do was to lean forward, take a chance, tip slightly toward manhood, toward a soldier's world. Here was life, straight ahead and full bore. But he was not ready to decide his own decisions. He turned toward the table and shoved another beer toward James.

Good old James, a man born to nature. Screwing came to him as natural as it did to any animal. Sex was something creatures did and, like any aroused bull, he did not care who watched. He raised his glass and dropped his pants.

"I was born for soldiering," he said, and he charged one of the girls. His feet fumbled in eight–inch steps within his pants. "Love's got a hold on me," he said, and he stumbled around the table.

Pete grabbed him from behind and tried to force his pants up. One of the girls motioned James toward the back room. He dropped his pants again. Pete handed him another beer. When James started to drink, Pete yanked up his pants. James dropped the beer, and his pants. Pete surrendered and flopped back into his chair. James reached across the table, his limp prick falling into a beer glass.

"That's the girl I want," he said.

"Pull up your pants and you can have the girl," Clifton said. He slid the beer away from James. James' face broke into a grin. He fastened his pants, wet from the beer he had dropped and glistening with small slivers of glass. "Take enough money to pay the bitch but leave your wallet here or she'll snatch it all."

"Good thinking," said Pitkala.

"Here, finish your beer," said Clifton. "Don't worry if it's a little salty."

Pitkala muffed a laugh. The girl squeezed James between the legs and directed him to the other room.

As he sat at the table, Clifton's mood turned surly. He rapped the table with his knuckles. His girl sat close beside him. She played with the hair on his arm and worked her way down to his watch. The cream face and gold hands were ringed with worn gold plate. She picked at the grease, from sweat, that had collected on the watch band. Clifton looked away. She squeezed his thigh and smiled. Clifton removed the watch and tracked it around his fingers.

"You'd like this," he said, "wouldn't you? You'd like to show this watch off, to show what a cool bitch you are."

He slapped her in the face with the watch. The band left streaks of red across her cheeks. She drew back and held her face. Clifton dangled the watch in front of her. She leaned in, touching his thigh.

"Touch it, touch the watch," he said.

Her fingers were colored like agate. She cradled the

watch and flashed her dark eyes at Clifton. She lifted the watch to her mouth and licked the face. She knew her job well, the way the tongue, just the tip extended, rolled around the face of the watch.

"Stinking little slut," Clifton said. He jerked the watch away and turned back to his drink.

When James returned, he almost fell into his seat. Apparently, his mission had been more, or less, accomplished and he sat, stupidly picking his nose.

"Nice job," Pitkala said.

"I can handle them."

"A good one, huh?"

"I can handle them."

"Give us the details, the whole works." Pitkala leaned across the table.

"I can handle them."

Another girl sat beside James and she started to rub his chest.

"Well, how about the details?"

"I can handle them."

Without taking a breath, James drank a whole glass of beer. He grinned. "I can handle them," he said. He reached into the girl's dress for her breasts, stiffened his back, grinned again and passed out flat on the table. Pete rolled him over. He had been looking for an excuse to leave. "I'll take him back to the ship before he gets hurt." Pitkala helped lift James to Pete's shoulder. Pete weaved out the door.

Outside, away from the action, the world looked different: better, cleaner. He realized that, for the first time, the seasickness had gone. The driver of a Cushman, a boy of about twelve, helped Pete roll James to the floor. Pete gave instructions about the ship, which the boy already knew, and left him a few dollars.

"You come too?" the boy said. "To the boat?"

"No," said Pete. He turned toward the bar and rocked back on his heels. "It's early yet."

Chapter 7

Pete sat on the deck of the ship looking down into the water where he had just puked. Soldiers were straggling back in, long lines of them tumbling from Cushmans, long lines of quiet bewildered men dragging trinkets and shirts behind them, many to be followed by cases of venereal disease. Pete had puked in the Cushman and driver had charged him an extra dollar. The driver told him there had been fighting on the island during the last war: 200,000 people killed. This place looked too pretty for killing. Europe: mud, rats, rain, there was a place for death. Or Korea where soldiers watched their toes freeze off. But not this place of luscious greens and minty air.

"James has been a bad boy," Sunny said. Sunny had walked up quietly, suddenly. "A good thing you sent him home early. I had to wash his little pecker two or three times before putting him to bed. You don't look so good yourself."

"Guess I got drunk." Pete did not want to talk.

Sunny leaned down to rub his shoulders. Pete brushed his hand
away.

"Pew," Sunny said. "That breath is nasty." He unwrapped a stick of gum and folded a stick into a little quare. Pete worked the gum over all his teeth. "Where'd you get all these scratches?"

"Maybe I fell. I don't remember. What di□erence does it make?"

"Just asking. Can I get you something – a glass of water, a personality?"

"Knock it off."

"You're a little too testy for me." Sunny backed off. "Still, I could give you a nice sponge bath."

Pete continued to sit, to hang over the lower rail, to atch the oily water lap against the pilings, until lifton appeared. Deep scratches ran down his neck and, where his watch had been, only a white strip remained. Pitkala was with him.

"She was good, damn good," Clifton said. "Having her was like driving around an old truck. I kept shifting gears until I got her up to speed, then there was no stopping her." He made sounds like a motor and bounced up and down. His eyes were

90

like dry ice. "Well?" He bumped Pete on the shoulder. When Pete did not respond, he rolled to his side, laughed and walked away.

"You're a real bastard," Pitkala said. He unscrewed the lid from a Coke. He still looked tipsy, red hair standing on end, eyes heavy and glassed over. "Is that the way you think people – women – should be treated?" He took a long drink. "What started out fine, ended like crap. You should have gone to the ship with James."

"I've been sick," Pete said. The final ropes were being loosened from the dock.

"The whole thing turned to shit." Pitkala lowered his head and started tapping his feet. "Dancing with the girl, playing music on the juke box, all that was fine. But the slapping. Why? Why the slapping and the rough stuff?"

"I've been puking over the side. Look, we're pulling out of this place."

"She did nothing to be slapped for. And there was nothing cute about shoving her head between your legs, not with her resisting like she did." He stepped closer and leaned his elbow on the top rail. The floating oil below was like a thin mirror. Pitkala did not look directly at Pete but spoke as if he were writing lyrics to a song, trying to remember the words.

"What difference does it make?" Pete said. "What we see isn't always there. You've mistaken a tub of beer for an incident." His stomach started to float and he felt the seasickness returning. "I'm too sick to talk."

"Even the worst whore deserves some respect. You can pay for the flesh part, maybe even the pain, but there's no price for the dignity part. She begged to be behind the curtain, to be taken back to some privacy. I should have done something." His voice still sounded distant. He grabbed Pete by the arm. "I should have done something – I should have. I never even tried. The problem belonged to everyone else: the bartender, who never did a damn thing; to James, before he left, too drunk to even stand; to the other girls, who looked more distant than me. Why would anyone do that? Why wouldn't anyone take a stand?"

"There was too much drinking." Pete jerked away from his grip. "People are always trying to show other people they're something they're not. Pretty soon, it's too late." He touched Pitkala's hand and held the hand in his. "Listen, sometimes the world gets crazy. Everybody had a hand in it like we all had mixed up some crazy recipe. No one meant to hurt anyone. It's life and we're mixed up in it."

"I did nothing." Now, Pitkala tried to pull away, to stand, to turn away as if it were him that could not face anyone. "She tried to get away. You slapped her hard in the face and she fell against the wall."

Pete gripped his shoulder. Pitkala spun away. "You got me confused with someone else," Pete said, his voice curious and pleading. "After the slap, we left her alone, right?"

"One of the girls finally tried to help. Shit, you

know damn well that nothing would help. Things had gone too far. You rolled up ten bucks and rammed the bills up her nose, as if a tube of money was all anyone needed. Blood ran from those bills."

Pitkala flopped to the deck and leaned against the bulkhead. He circled his belt buckle with his finger.

"I was afraid," he said. "But I ain't afraid now."

"She's a business woman," Pete said. He slid his hands into his pockets as he paced the deck as if trying to unravel a mystery. "Bartenders help out if things don't look right. You said he just stood there. Besides, she took the money, didn't she? You didn't hear any complaints about that?" He waited for a response. "Anyway, it's over."

"She had eyes that were afraid," Pitkala continued. "She covered her face and tried to rise. Blood dribbled from her lip. What could I do? The bartender. Big help. He came from behind the counter and shoved the girl trying to help her into a chair so you could get at her as he laughed. The whole thing was none of my business, like this whole Vietnam thing is no ones business. Even the air was mad." He tapped his feet again. "I wanted to help; I even stood making some kind of pretense at bravery. Then came the part with the watch, dangling it before her eyes like this..." He waved his clenched fingers in the air. "She started to follow the watch to the back room as if she had been hypnotized."

"Nothing to worry about," Pete said. "She wouldn't have followed if she was hurt, if she didn't want it.

A beating was part of the deal for her."

Pitkala tapped his feet faster and faster.

"The girl weighed the blood against the watch and followed you into the room," he said. He moved to his knees and motioned Pete to kneel. "It was then the screaming started." He placed his hands on Pete's shoulders. "I just wanted you to know that I heard the screaming."

"Stop talking crazy," Pete said. "You drank too much. Maybe she was paid to make a little extra noise. You can get a lot of sound for a few extra quarters."

"I don't know what happened," Pitkala said. He held his head like nothing made any sense to him. "She went through hell, I know that much."

"It isn't so," Pete said. "Sometimes the world catches us wrong. We think we see and hear things that aren't there, especially when we're drunk. Piss on it."

"Piss don't start fires. Something's burning here in you that can't be doused."

"Just think about it," Pete said. "That's all I ask. Things don't make sense because things don't make sense. We need to do something else, get back to playing music. Music straightens out everything."

The ship had been cut loose from the dock and was already under steam. The setting sun draped the sea and horizon with red silk. Warm air blew across the deck. The ship left a smooth gash in the water as Okinawa dipped into the sea like an exhausted lantern. Pete stayed on deck for several hours until the

moon rose and flashed each wave of the sea in silhouette, splitting them down the middle, puddling
one side in glimmer, the other in darkness.

As he walked to his bunk, he thought of holding
his horn, feeling his emotions expand and pump
against his ribs. But mostly he thought about the
bar and the girl he almost had.

"Get a little jam going," Clifton said. He appeared remarkably refreshed for looking so terrible
such a short time ago.

"What's the use?"

"All the hard feelings will disappear. Musicians are
like that, all of them crazy." He drew deeply on his
cigarette. The smoke rose only slightly before spreading through the stagnant air.

"What do you mean?" Pete said. He squeezed at his
knees. He had lost almost fifteen pounds.

"Musicians gotta play." He flicked at the ash and
watched it fall to his boot.

James was on his feet again, although his steps were
not solid, and he leaned against a post with
Pitkala. Pete motioned them over. James moved
with one arm out as a beacon directing him toward
Pete's voice.

"I'm trying to make things up to you," Pete said.
"We're all stuffed up in here and we need to play. It
will get our heads straight. You must be tired of
banging on footlockers," he said to Pitkala.

Pitkala looked skeptical. Pete tried to work some
feeling into his legs and he laid his head against the

wrapped pipe.

"Who for?" Pitkala worked at his own legs. "Who we playing for?"

"Us. Just us. It beats exercising and messing off."

"James, you better get some shots first." Clifton was trying to worry him.

" Shots, for what? I don't need no shots."

"When you've been with a woman, you need shots. Haven't you been watching those VD films?"

"I never ride bareback." From his pocket he produced a tight wad of condoms.

"How many you take with you? three? four?"

"I don't remember. Enough, though. I always keep these and a bottle of slide grease."

"No one cares how many you took. How many you brought back is what counts."

"I don't remember. I was pretty drunk."

"It makes no difference to me," Clifton said. "I hate to see you crawl out of bed some morning and find your pecker is still under the covers."

James knocked his knees together. "I got something to do," he said. "It's got nothing to do with getting any shot."

"I know some great tunes," Pitkala said. His depression and anger appeared to be lifting. "We could work something up. Nothing big; a few tunes on real instruments." He started tapping his knees. "I'll get Ron and Johnny Paul. You can blow that horn like you do sowell."

"Not me," Pete said. "I've been too sick. I don't

want to play untilmI'm ready."

"Yeah, right." Pitkala pushed through the footlockers and into the open. "Listen," he said. "Maybe I got it all wrong. Maybe I didn't see things right." He was on the road again.

"Give them what they want," Clifton said. "There's nothingdiffcult about that."

The following night soldiers packed into a small, hot room filled with smoke and situated below the water line where the air had not circulated for months. The talk of a jam had spread through the ship and the jam had now been labeled an open talent show, a brilliant idea whose credit had been taken by some Major in a transportation company. The men sat on the deck and razzed a sergeant, who sang very badly and wobbled from side to side, standing on a poorly lighted stage.

Pitkala, who had talked Ron and Paul into the venture, appeared next. Paul twirled his beanie and picked at his fake nose. The large white nose against his black face already brought on laughter. He cradled his bass and with his heavy calloused fingers he plucked out solid root tones in the key of F.

Pitkala spun his straw hat, thumbed the loud Hawaiian shirt. His enormous sunglasses pulled his ears down like the wings of an airplane. He hopped to the drums and tapped out a steady rhythm. Ron, who had been drafted straight from the Woody Herman band, wore nothing but large boxer shorts patterned with red lips. One band was as good as the next to him and he never minded that he was drafted as long as he could play. He did all the stage band arranging and also played trombone and piano. From the piano he looked at Pitkala. Pitkala had placed a fake arrow under his hat and through his head, old and corny gags that still brought a laugh. Pitkala announced the group:

"Wees like to welcome you all to the Steamboat Hilton." He farted between his lips. "If you don't enjoy yourselves you can transfer to another joint. I understand the supply sergeant will issue you a snorkel and shark repellent." He nodded to the crowd, and to Pete and James just outside the spotlight.

"On bass we have a man known to women everywhere; Paul, Short-Shot, Cromwell." Pitkala quivered a short drum roll. "On piano, skin flute and upright organ, we have the amazing Ron." Another drum roll. "And on drums it's your's truly, Panama Red."

As they played he called out such tunes as *I've Got Tears in My Ears from Lying on my Back Crying Over You*, and *I Chased Her up a Tree and Kissed Her Between The Limbs*.

The ship was starting to become a home and everyone seemed comfortable and content. Pitkala named the band "Joe Banana and his Music With-a-Peel." Pitkala continued to laugh and joke and the soldiers soon became intoxicated with the music. A force took hold of the band and worked its way through the notes and showered the audience. The crowd cheered Pitkala and he danced over the drums playing them one way and then another. More yelling. More cheering. Pete did not know if James cheered loudest but, because of the V.D. shots he had taken, he was having some diffculty sitting. He moved from one cheek to the other and groaned.

Pete actually laughed. He was not a man of great humor, more a serious artist: constantly brooding, withdrawn. Now, he was thrilled. The music cleaned his system. There was life and truth in the army. The seasickness had not returned. He would soon be playing again, his lips warming the brass trumpet as he blew it to life.

Pitkala spun in circles and flopped back to his seat. A silly blank look crossed his face and he cocked his head rigidly to one side and started to slowly slide off his stool.

"What a riot," James said. "That cat never misses a beat. Even Ron thinks he's cool."

Ron, still playing the piano, was saying something to Pitkala. Pete slapped his hands together and laughed until his eyes watered. Family, family, he thought. We are a family.

Pitkala slumped down slowly and with such skill that, as James had said, he never missed a beat. Down he went, his head tipped to one side, his tongue hanging out and his eyes as blank as wood. Down he went beating the snare. Down he went banging the ride cymbal. Down he went until he hit the floor and lay sideways still banging the cymbal with one arm. The troops were hysterical with laughter.

The music stopped as Ron, who had continued to watch and talk to Pitkala over his shoulder, rushed from the piano. He pulled on Pitkala's arms trying to get him up. Everyone continued to laugh.

Pete sensed something wrong. Was this supposed to be funny? Some kind of slapstick? Was he supposed to laugh? James had stopped laughing and was up on his knees. Pitkala, with his blank stare, continued to beat the cymbal, then the air. The lights shone empty in his eyes, stars against the black. His arm would not stop. Ron tried to lay him back and lift his legs. The troops continued to cheer demanding more music. Ron cried into the mike. "Christ! Someone get a medic."

The room fell quiet. Eyes screeched from the dark as Pitkala jerked rapidly and, for the first time anyone could remember, unrhythmically. His arm still spun against the night. Ron could not hold the arm still and Pitkala's wrist, thin and weak, spit from Ron's grasping hands like a serpent.

No one approached them, not Pete, not James, not Paul who let his bass hang over his slumped shoulder. Pete could not make sense of the situation. What he thought to be real, was not. The fun was pain, the joy, sorrow. This was a music of fits, of some kind of stroke. And now, under the spotlight, some kind of play was being acted. Were Ron and Pitkala fighting? Were they dancing, one arm around another, body parts kicking in and out? Were they making love, one on top the other? And the hopeless stare of Ron, the eyes blazing from ecstacy or blank cinders where hope died down?

Medics pulled a stretcher into the light, tipped Ron aside and rolled Pitkala onto the canvas. They hauled him through the crowd, the arrow still bobbing through his head, up and down over the edge of the stretcher. He faded from the noise and the smoke, drifted under the wire cage lights and down the narrow, ever darkening hallway.

After everyone left, a slow procession sucked through the hatches. Pete remained in the room, his back pushed against the bulkhead. He watched the empty stage for several hours. The cold metal throbbed against his head and he hugged his knees.

"Been looking for you." James sat carefully. "I brought you a Coke with some rum." He handed Pete the bottle. "Greatest act I've ever seen. No better way to go than to be beat out by music."

He squeezed Pete's knee.

"Funny world," Pete said.

"They got him doped up." James motioned for Pete to drink. Pete continued to watch the stage. James took the bottle, drank quickly and handed the bottle back. Pete held Pitkala's hat.

"Cerebral hemorrhage," James said. "One side is paralyzed." He tipped the bottle up in Pete's hand. He drank.

"We can't touch anything about us," Pete said. "I don't think anything is real in this world. Someone once told me the Hindus call this veil Maya. Funny name."

"He sure screwed the army," James said. "They have to make a special stop to dump him off. What a laugh." James slapped his knees. "Drink that down and I'll get you another. Pap says a bottle gets you over the humps and through the valleys. Of course, he kinda uses it on the flatlands too."

Pete finished the drink without tasting the liquor. He carried the hat on deck and breathed the thick air. He walked to sickbay and looked through the porthole where Pitkala lay in the dark. Nothing on him moved. A crisp sheet draped him. Only the tops of his shoulders and his bandaged head showed. Pete looked for his hands, to see if they moved, if they still held some kind of rhythm. He was not sure why it seemed important. Nothing but outlines shown in the darkness. He stepped back until the porthole framed Pitkala's head.

The bow of the ship was empty and Pete moved to starboard. Salt from the air rolled clean against his face. Pete twirled the hat in his hand then tossed it over the side. The hat drifted out, turned twice in the moonlight, then angled away on the wake of the ship as if it were the only thing left on the ocean.

Chapter 8

Late at night, off the shore of Vietnam, the ship stopped its rocking stuttering self, ground down its screw and dropped anchor. On a flat sea of heavy heat the water voyage had come to a quiet end. Pitkala had been left in the Philippines, his wrapped body lowered over the side to the launch. It happened quickly, hardly a stop; even the ship's screw turned slowly wrinkling the water, tossing heavy spray to the side. Within minutes, Pitkala was gone.

The idea of Time first entered Pete's head, the idea of something here, then gone: a person maybe or a thought, the idea that there was no clear line between coming and going, living and dying. Time had no constant to the individual. An hour sitting in a classroom seemed to take forever while an accident, instantaneous. Keeping busy moved time quickly; doing nothing made it drag. What were today and tomorrow and yesterday? How did life and death fit within that framework? An animal was alive, then dead. There never was a time, a space, an instant, where it traveled from the state of being to the state of not being.

Heat lay across his arms as he looked toward a land that, in the dark, he could hardly see. No breeze, no otion of any kind, only black filled the air. Any rays of moon or stars deflected before hitting this land. Toward shore lights freckled the night and appeared to move, to drift slowly. He tried to see something, anything, tried to perceive some shadow of land, a mountain, a building, something. Even the water over the ship's side had gone blank. Nothing could be seen yet everything could be felt. He knew the water was there, could sense its presence like he could sense the oppression of the land.

Pete tried to concentrate on the lights. He held up his index finger and marked out two lights, one at a finger tip and the other between his first and second knuckle. A few minutes later, he again held out his finger. The lights now fit between the end of his finger and his first knuckle. He looked to the water twenty or thirty feet below. Still nothing. No moon lit the water, nothing glanced off the ripples as they hit the ship's hull or the shore. For a moment everything, every mountain, every ocean, every building, every thought, every person, everything he crammed into his mind, felt dull and gray and lifeless. Only the black appeared real and in a bizarre tingly way, vibrant. Pete rubbed his face and thought "Fear No Evil." But Pete feared everything and he was afraid.

He looked around the deck for Clifton. The deck was completely empty, no sound, no movement, nothing except the ship's dim lights reaching toward the dark and falling overboard. Evil, he thought again. The balance is in religion. Yet, any comfort he sought from religion only confused him. Evil lived in the dark and Pete was afraid of the dark. Religion felt just as dark. He tried to put God into his heart. A benevolent god of love and passion could find room there, nestle in some small corner. The attempt gave him a headache. He had difficulty separating the god of love from the destroyer god, the flaming hot-tempered god of destruction and death. One kind of god offered kindness and understanding. Stories about that god were few. Pete remembered the god of storms, a god splitting oceans to devour soldiers, cracking apart the earth to swallow people who only wanted a little singing and dancing, a tilted god willing to destroy one people for another, a god set against free thinking, a god that allowed fathers to sleep with daughters, have many wives, many concubines: a god that often picked the worst of the lot to be his chosen leaders, blood-thirsty men achieving rank through killing and the severing of his enemies foreskins.

Pete fought with the two gods until he became a blank slate of empty religious myths. As an adult he no longer wanted myths. Religion was for kids and few adults ever traveled beyond the bed- time stories. He wanted something solid, comforting words, love. Religion was not the answer. He waited for a sign, a thunderbolt of insight.

"Screw that bastard Biggilo." Clifton nudged in be- side Pete. "The prick wants our M-14s cleaned. Kiss my ass." Clifton flipped off the night. "He's going to win the Gerber knife award. Right up his ass. The way you ran out when he gave the order, I thought you were going to bawl."

"Where is everyone?" Pete asked. Clifton ran a finger down the rail then tapped the rail on the way back.

"Big party. The whole ship's gone crazy. Troops are shaking in their boots and hiding the fear in beer jokes and farts." Clifton spit over the side and watched the spit fall out of sight. "You ain't scared?" He looked at Pete with hard eyes. "We're buddies. Nothing can change that." He slapped Pete on the shoulder. "You're a damn fine musician. Now we got to make you into a killer, a killer right out of the old testament. You'll be whacking them up in no time."

"They gave us guns."

"Everyone here has a gun. Come on below. Show them you ain't scared, show them you're just as calm as John Wayne, even though he never went to war."

Stale air below decks mu□ed the laughter of the band. Tonight was a night for being close. The nervous rattle of anticipation buzzed finely against the bulkheads and small groups of men gathered in circles between rows of high standing bunks and piled footlockers. They all were bare-chested or in green shorts or green tee-shirts, except for Sunny who was never out of uniform unless he was really out of uniform. Cigarette butts littered the deck or hung from the lips of men, or found their way into half empty cans of smuggled Pabst, Lucky Lager, and Olympia beer cans. Between some bunks the endless card games continued. A Playboy magazine had worked from hand to hand as Miss August of 1966 took a beating and was tacked to a footlocker. Someone peeled an apple, ate the skin like a snake and shared the slices by shooting them between his fingers.

"Get up a jam," said Clifton. "Your axes will be boxed tomorrow. Give them hell tonight. Go on, get your horn and show them who's boss."

Pete found his horn in the wire cage. Dust covered the case and he wiped off the brass latches. One of the latches caught and he pried it open with a finger nail. Everyone nearby was watching him. No one had gone near the cage since the voyage. It was not off limits. The band had simply accepted the trade of one instrument for another. Pete lifted the lid, folded back the cloth and lifted the horn. He walked slowly to his bunk as if the instrument were a great discovery, one no one would believe. James raised a can of warm Olympia over his head. "I christen this session 'The Night of the Last Jam.'" He smashed the can against the butt of an upturned M-14.

The group rushed to the wire cage and complained as the instruments were passed around. "This ain't my ax, man...get back Jack and let me blow...like dig, daddy, I got the wrong bone...." Pete fingered the trumpet. The instrument had not been blown for twenty three days and the mouthpiece felt foreign. One valve stuck open and the others were stiff. The horn was a brass Bach supplied by the Army and Pete imagined it was his own silver Conn. Pete unscrewed the valves and applied the valve oil. The Schilke 14-A- 4-A mouthpiece sat in his pocket. He inserted the valves and blew air through the horn bringing it up to temperature. He placed the mouthpiece in his mouth, the shank hanging out. He liked blowing the horn wet. He had more control over his lips and the way they slid over the mouthpiece.

Pete blew softly into the horn and listened to the quiet notes sneaking out. He would not be able to play long. The notes crept through a fog, each sound wrapped in the fuzz of a peach, Jack Sheldon style, just the way he liked them. After a long chorus or two his lips would swell due to inactivity and he would be finished. He blew several random triads and went through the circle of 5ths. The horn started to feel natural again, the one place truth resided, a place that needed no words or explanations.

"Damn good idea," James said. "After that spat you had with Biggilo, we thought you might have jumped ship."

Everyone in the group had warmed up as Frank, on bass, plucked out a medium blues in F. He had a steady hand with thick calloused fingers and he moved his body against the instrument like a slow dance against a comfortable woman. James rode first, a two octave run of triplets sliding from high to low and back to center. His years of practice on trombone were apparent and he blended the discipline of sophisticated notes and articulation with the feel of plowed footprints, knifing the earth toward the 'Nectar Tree,' as a solid black man left his mark on the earth. Ron with his bone, rode next. James and Pete blew riffs behind him until, from another bunk, Louie drew a chorus on oboe. The ride was good, emotional and precise, the tone of the instrument adding an eerie unusual quality everyone appreciated. Music and beer rolled around the ship.

"Piss on Biggilo," James yelled, and everyone cheered.

Frank corded a slow blues that seemed to dim the lights. Pete entered with a wail and a moan, his playing emotional rather than sophisticated. He had never been a technician, like Mendez, never wanted to become one. He blew for more than he understood, the notes originating from someplace outside himself. But he blew. He blew for every bit of truth he could find.

The tempo increased. Soon the whole band was playing like a happy disease that rocked about the ribcage of the ship. Joyous sounds bounced from everywhere as if they were returning from a New Orleans funeral.

Frank increased the speed, his fingers forming a flat edge that tripped across the strings, no string louder than another, each note unrecognizable as an individual, only as a piece of sound reverberating within a barrel of rapidly rolling chords.

The band worked themselves into a musical frenzy. As each ride stopped, another took its place. Those who quit riding, lips shot, blew riffs and broke into small groups with one trying to outdo the other. The music tumbled round and round like a giant carousel, each player bobbing and sweating, pumping out sound and muse until the song lasted almost two hours and everyone was split apart, their souls and emotions laid bare, creatively blown out. It was for this moment Pete was a musician, a moment they all were musicians, a moment they could be exported from the ship, from themselves, and placed on that special aura that separates man from all other creatures. The music came from someplace they did not understand and they, just interlocutors between muse and sound, laid about the ship, no longer thinking about tomorrow and that irreversible step into solitude.

And that was the end of that.

The last dying notes of music drifted toward land over the beach at Qui Nhon, across rice paddies, under an abandoned truck at Anh Khe. The notes filtered into the quiet, through the smells of shit, napalm, cordite, diesel, drifted one hundred miles into the Central Highlands until they became nothing more than wind blowing dumb against the barbed wire of some forgettable jungle outpost where a private from Missoula Montana pissed against the side of his bunker and cocked his young head as if he heard music. His startled face knocked back with the punch of lead as one quick AK–47 round burrowed into his forehead. He fell dead and grinning against the side of his bunker as the sweet melody of war passed through.

Chapter 9

Pete awoke early in the hot stillness of the ship and screwed a finger through the wrappings of the overhead pipes. Did they still carry the dust of some Japanese held island? How many troops had lain on this same bunk and thought of home and sweethearts and families? They must have had a reason to fight, a solid enemy, an evil filled with overwhelming corruption. All Pete knew about Vietnam was that it felt muggy. The ship jerked and Pete jumped from the bunk. The hold was empty. He was already clothed and he laced up his boots and held the M-14, a foreign, clunky piece of equipment that he quickly tossed onto the bunk before climbing to the top deck.

Soldiers bunched shoulder to shoulder between stacks of piled bags. The sun rose over the water and already the air was unbearably hot. There was no city, like Pete had imagined, just shacks stretching for a mile to the left and to the right of the ship. The land was so flat, he could not see if the town had any depth. Fishing boats nudged the shore and nets draped posts driven into the sand. Something resembling a dog moved along shore although it was too far away to see clearly.

An armada of supply ships surrounded the U.S.S. John Pope. What Pete thought was a town, a city with electricity, and not just shacks, had been the ships. He chuckled. Nothing real, everything an illusion. A Portuguese sailor adrift at sea for months with only an imagination for company had a better grasp of life. Besides, the U.S. Army brought their own lights. The better to see you with, he thought.

"Check this out," said Clifton . "Ever seen such a mess?" He pushed a hole through the crowd. "That's the killing ground." He pointed toward shore. "As long as the bastards have been here and they can't even build a high-rise. Why call them civilized?" He spit over the side. "We'll whip them into shape soon enough. Put in a few missiles to further encircle the Chinese. We'll teach the bastards progress or die trying." Clifton handed Pete a stick of gum. Sailors unloaded cargo over the side and into barges.

"Maybe they're happy without high-rises," said Pete.

"Until we push them into the twentieth centaury we can't sell them anything. People like this don't know what they need."

"What am I supposed to do?" said Pete. "Maybe beat them down with Western music."

"That's the spirit," said Clifton. "Beat them down with music. I prefer napalm, a little gelled gas to curl up their skin like a wood shaving leaving their bones to hang in the air. The nastier the better."

"Music is the universal language," said Pete. He rolled the gum wrapper into a ball and flicked it against the deck. He wanted to sound more like a soldier, or less like a soldier, he could not decide which.

"Guess again." He felt Clifton close now, his breath odorless and cold. "Even Albert Ayler can't save you now. These bastards know the value of a quarter tone scale." He turned Pete around and walked him toward the ship's mess. "Don't forget the napalm. He who kills the most the fastest is the winner."

The mess line snaked its way down two decks. Clifton tried to counsel Pete, put him at ease. "Can you shoot?" he asked. Pete shrugged his shoulders. "Can you hit the side of a mountain if you're standing in one of its valleys?"

"I do all right." Pete shrugged. What difference did it make? He was in the band.

Clifton shoved him against the bulkhead. "You got to do more than that." He turned cold and serious. "We got to depend on each other. We got to

get honest. I can shoot the nipples off your grandmother at five hundred yards. I need to know about
you."

The line eased them forward. "I got a marksman
badge. Some days I shoot real well, sometimes I'm
not so good."

"Shit." Clifton kicked the bulkhead. "The lowest
fucking badge you can get. If you're dead, then
I'm dead." Then he smiled and grinned and circled
a finger around the rim of his lips like people do
when they want a glass to sing. "We'll work on it. My
ass is out on a limb but I can trust you not to get
crazy on me. Besides, you're just as good as I am. Last
night you were the biggest thing on this ship. No one
had the insight or the guts to grab their axes - no one
but you."

"I don't see the trouble. I'm in the band and you're
H.Q."

"Stop with that band shit." Clifton was pissed
and his fists tightened. "You're a big boy now
and you're in the war. Do you think the army
cares if you can play? It's bodies they want. Besides,
your trumpet was packed up this morning. That
music crap is over. You're in a war." Pete only knew
music. He had had no other training as a soldier except basic. Clifton punched him in the shoulder. "I'm
just trying to save your ass."

Pete returned to the deck, the powdered eggs and
coffee churning in his stomach. What little he had
eaten continued to slosh in his stomach. Landing

craft bobbed at the ship's sides. His boots were hot. His uniform was hot. He wanted a shower, a cool draft of air, something to keep down the sweat. How long could Clifton protect him?

He thought about being home as his mind took him off the ship and placed him in his Hudson Hornet screeching down the Mountain highway with a car full of buddies from Bethel High. The breeze whipped his hair and he smelled the leather seats and the spilled beer. The odor of evergreens penetrated the open window in a cool scented blast. He smelled the sapping fir trees and the fresh wilderness of huckleberries, everything green, everything fresh, a newborn world alive with ideas and possibilities, a future, a real future containing hope, nothing dour or sarcastic or cynical, just anticipation and desire, a world of Opie Taylor, the Beave, and dreaming of screwing Mary Tyler Moore, the great lie that was the United States.

They passed another Weyerhaeuser logging truck. The Hudson fell into overdrive and, at 100 MPH, floated like a battleship. Pete pulled to the side of the road and they rolled from the car, stripped leaving a trail of clothes like bright bread-crumbs, and waded naked over the slippery cold rocks of the Little Mashell River to drink

another illegal beer on shore under the moonlight as their blue feet thawed. He listened to the night sounds of the river cleansing its way downstream, carried piggybacked moonlight through the forest and down an arroyo of flashing echoes.

Then a soldier knocked against him and the image of home was replaced by circling landing craft. Several of them had bobbed to the side of the ship. Boatmen on the craft went bare–shouldered and wore cloth caps and hats of different sizes and shapes. They did not look orderly but rather tired and thin as they good- naturedly taunted the new troops hanging stiffy over the railing. The ship's speakers sounded. "All men report to their companies." Pete walked below and never again imagined drinking beer in the woods in a virgin forest.

Below decks the band looked awkward and uncoordinated, not at all like soldiers, a group of bewildered boys. Nothing militarily fit. They had attached shoulder harnesses in different ways, straps latched up or down, and hung at various angles. Weapons poked people in the ribs and asses and already there had been a black eye or cut forehead from poorly slung rifles, the butts slung overhead and smashing others like a hammer. Sunny Provo tried to attach his bayonet and cut his hand. He wrenched on the bayonet, twisting it from side to side, it came free quickly and hit against the bulkhead bending the tip.

Clifton sat on his bunk smoking a small cigar. Frank, the French horn and guitar player, stood beside him holding an M-14. Frank looked unnatural and awkward and was seldom seen without his horn. He was the only musician in the band who managed to practice the whole trip. His life centered on blending the mellow notes of the instrument into brass ensembles or orchestras. Frank fumbled with the M-14. Rifles blended with nothing, hurt and ripped the ears. He smelled his hands. "Guns stink of oil," he said.

"What?" said Pete. Clifton tried to blow smoke rings and looked natural and at ease in his uniform.

"This gun stinks," said Frank.

"Cosmoline and linseed oil," said Pete. "The Army runs on it." The smoke ring refused to complete and horseshoed up before breaking apart. "That rifle," he said. "Don't you remember holding your prick in basic and saying 'this is my rifle, this is my gun, this is for killing, this is for fun'?"

"I prefer Bach rotary oil." Frank fumbled with the bolt placing his nose half inside. "It smells just as bad in here. Guns have no style, no real shape."

"Cosmoline and linseed oil," Pete repeated.

Frank rattled the weapon. "How come you know so much about it?"

"Ten pounds, loaded with twenty rounds of 7.62 N.A.T.O." Clifton attempted another ring that emerged as a thin mist. "Has a tempo of 700 rounds a minute and sings the same song to everyone." Clifton formed his lips into a kiss and blew out a fat ring that widened as the smoke drifted upward. "Blow enough of these," Clifton said, "and they put rings in your shorts."

"Guess we better go," Frank said. "Looks like we're the last two in line."

Like a slow tide, the company had moved in mass to the hatchway and stopped. The stairs held them almost as a curtain holds back a nervous entertainer. Here was fear shrouded in jokes or silence. What might be revealed on the other side of the curtain, revealed about the audience, revealed about oneself? Clifton pushed through the crowd and mounted the stairs two at a time until he was through the hatch and out of sight. His leaving caused a vacuum pulling another soldier through. The rest shuffed closer. One soldier made the vacuum stronger, and more soldiers squeezed through until the vacuum became so strong that soldiers fought to funnel into the hatchway.

Two landing craft bobbed against the port side of the ship. Behind them the beach was long, white and beautiful, the sea clear like blue glass. Rope mesh hung over the side of the ship and the band crawled over and worked their way down the rope and into the craft. Pete crouched in the corner of the craft against the sides, the metal hot and tall. He hunched in the shade of the bulkhead. Clifton moved beside him. The hull of the ship, wrapped in mesh and clinging soldiers, cut the sky in half.

The full landing craft peeled away from the ship and jumped across the water. Nothing could be seen from inside the craft, nothing but the overhead sky. The craft slowed toward shore. From the bow, someone gave the order to lock and load. Pete felt startled because he had not heard that term since basic. He fumbled for a clip and slipped it into the weapon.

"Try again," said Clifton.

"What?"

"The clip," said Clifton. "It's got no ammo in it."

Pete jerked at the clip, pinching his finger as the clip came free.

"The ass holes never gave us any," said Clifton. "No one's got any but me." He tapped his pouches. They looked full and heavy. He eased out his rifle clip to expose the rounds. "Stay with me and you'll be all right, I gave a supply sergeant ten bucks for them."

Pete wanted his own clip filled with ammo. Every round was its own security, its own power.

The landing craft eased against the beach. The lowered ramp, like an opened window, exposed the new world of stench, white shacks and naked brown kids squatting on the sand. Rubbing his eyes with an arm stump, a kid licked snot from his upper lip. Old women, bent at the knees and back, stood behind the kids. Another old woman had rolled her pajama pants past knees that knotted up like two dried fruits, wrinkled and pitted. A naked boy of three or four years old squatted and smoked a cigarette. Most of the people wore large Coolie hats tied with flags of colored silk. Behind them stood the men, bones pushing against their skin, all ragged, all looking blankly and tiredly at the landing craft. These were a different kind of men than Pete had known. The men seemed sexless, dull creatures evoking compassion and repugnance like liberated concentration camp survivors. The spark that lit a man had long since burnt out leaving leather too tough to even smolder. A black and white dog scurried away kicking up dust.

Pete twisted his ankle in the sand and fell to one knee. A Coke bottle, thrown from the crowd, knocked against his rifle. The bottle fell, unbroken, onto the sand. Clifton dropped to one knee and threw the rifle to his shoulder. When he jerked hard on the trigger, nothing happened. He jerked again. Still nothing. "Fuckers," he said, spitting.

"Gedup," a short sergeant, with red knuckles and a woman's chest tattooed his face looked stern, half his mouth smiled and he winked. "Form up down the beach. Things is new for you here but you'll get used to it."

Clifton spit again. Pete stood and kissed his twisted thumb. He had tangled it in the sling. No one in the crowd moved. Every eye looked through them. Pete pointed his rifle down. Sand ran from the barrel as he brushed himself off. Clifton slung his rifle. Quietly they walked down the beach. Pete wondered who threw the bottle and why he was angry.

"Thought you were going to shoot," said Pete to Clifton.

"So?"

"Thought you might shoot the wrong person."

"Not here," said Clifton. He cracked his knuckles. "They're all the right ones. Remember that if you don't remember anything else."

Pete pulled on his thumb. It still hurt. The Vietnamese stood beside a road that lead through the town. "Everyone went down after they saw you in the sand, everyone from the boat, anyway," he said.

"Old hands didn't, not the ones that met us," said Clifton . "They stood cool." He flew his hands in front of him.

"I'm glad you didn't shoot. I couldn't see anyone hurt."

"You have to keep your head. Didn't have much ammo, not enough to waste on these tramps."

"I'm still glad. I've never seen anyone hurt." Pete shivered for a moment, not from any chill but from a tickle inside like something scratching to get out.

"You got to learn," said Clifton. "There's a time for killing and a time for thinking. Sometimes they go together and sometimes they don't."

Pete looked at the Vietnamese again and turned back in time to see Clifton reach under his arm to the M-14. He found the clip then reached toward the stock and flipped off the weapon's safety. So he had made a mistake. He wanted to shoot but did not have the sense to remove the safety. Pete would not make that mistake in the future.

The company loaded onto deuce-and-a-halves that rumbled through the crowd. M.P.s drove through first splitting people apart. They parted quietly like an old gate swinging from the road. Away from the beach the men had the moisture sucked from their bodies by unbearable heat. Pete fidgeted on the slatted seat and wanted to watch, to get a better look at the people. Looking at these people felt like an invasion, as if he were some kind of peeping Tom or a zoo patron gawking at a strange creature seldom seen in captivity. They stood ready for inspection yet no one could really see them, bodies yes, nothing that counted. Pete glanced briefly at one old man. Fillet him, number his bones, formaldehyde the body parts for display in glass jars, make the scar under his one seeping eye your own, but never know him. Specimens were never specimens at all but something we already know in a different state.

Several soldiers heckled them as their confidence and bravado grew. Others threw gum. It all appeared undignified to Pete. I'll stay above it, he thought. It doesn't concern me, not the war, not these people, not the war.

They rimmed the edge of Qui Nhon. The edge, at least, contained no fancy buildings, nothing in the way of Western progress. People had built crude shacks from cement or wood. Food vendors nudged rough carts filled with steaming pots and strings of dead fish and dried snakes. Other vendors tipped into the street with lean- tos made of bamboo frames. Rainbows of silk, straw baskets, pillows etched with brown choppers and silver jets, black jackets covered with red dragons hung from the bamboo. Several bright and vibrant bar girls slid from doors and looked clean and inviting. Red and white dresses were split almost to their waists. A boy with no legs and bleeding hands dragged himself along the cement as the bar girls waived and blew kisses and the regular girls looked away. Three nuns nodded as they walked arm-in-arm. A young woman squatted over the red dirt and crapped.

The trucks split from the edge of town and rumbled to an airfield surrounded in barbed-wire. Tall wooden towers covered with sand bags gave the field a prison look. Everything around the airfield was flat. The driver dropped the Band on the middle of the field and beside a C-130. The trucks drove away leaving them alone and without orders. Between the morning sun and the sand-covered metal-grated runway, the heat baked them down. Yet there was clarity there, no haze, nothing to blind them from the world.

Pete moved to the shade of the plane wing leaving his duffe bag in the heat. Most of the men sat on their belongings. No one appeared to be in command. He would soon learn that no one was in charge in this country. The air-field remained empty except for a squadron of Huey's flapping in the distance.

Pete held out his hand to catch the heat running o☐ the wing, felt it puddle in his hand, tangible, alive, an unseen entity as real as any he had ever felt. Heat also rose from the deserted runway in jagged shudders. Something in this land was dfferent. Things like heat could be carried in a bucket - a clarity of vision presentin what were usually illusions. Complications appeared to vanish. But it was something else, something entirely removed from home, something Pete first discovered on the ship that now started to sort itself out. It was time. Time had become tempo, rhythm, a metronome clicking away at whatever beat it chose. Recently time had accelerated and moved too quickly for him to comprehend. Every image blurred. They were on the ship, the landing craft, the town, and the airstrip. Pete could not fit all the images together. The bits and pieces of time all clipped and pasted over each other. He attempted to piece together recent events, then something as simple and recent as the features of a single Vietnamese. He could not remember a single one. It was too hot, he was too tired and time here pinched off any thoughts of people.

"I feel like an egg in a frying pan," said Clifton, as he scurried under the wing. The shade was almost as hot as the direct sun. "We won't stay here long. Too hot. Nothing can live on this sand."

"What if we do stay?" Pete held out his hand to catch more sun, mold and shape it in his hand.

Paul was talking to Sunny. Neither of them looked hot or
uncomfortable.

"Can't," said Clifton. "Need air conditioning. Look around you." He pointed in a wide arch. "Everything on the base has air conditioning. All those damn brick barracks, hangers, theater, cafeteria, the whole shitting works. "

Pete opened his hand in the shade and inspected it for traces of sunlight. Heat from the metal runway fried through his boots. The rear of the C-130 opened like a large mouth against the runway. Sergeant Biggilo walked halfway down the ramp, his uniform cracking against the still air. He stood like a statue, a new Colt army .45 strapped to his waist. His hip crooked slightly out of line like a gunfighter's and his head rotated slowly from side to side as if to say "I am your beacon, your lighthouse." Tight new leather gloved his hands and starch sharply creased his pants. His eyes stopped directly on Pete.

"Get your ass up and into formation," he ordered. Clifton smiled and gave a little wave back. Since landing in Vietnam the Sergeant's voice had dropped at least half an octave. He stood motionless as they banged about looking for gear.

In the distance a three-quarter-ton truck emerged as a small green seed and grew as it traveled through the heat waves, stopping in front of the company not far from Sergeant Biggilo. A small thin soldier sat on boxes in back. He wore no shirt and fiddled with a mustache, thin and brown, which could hardly be seen. He kicked down the tailgate. "You cocksuckers load up," he said, shoving a box to the ground. "Ammo."

"What specific amount?" asked Sergeant Biggilo. "Have you brought the paper work to be signed?" Biggilo stood with crossed arms beside the truck.

"Paperwork? Fuck man, this is a war zone. If you got to kill someone you ain't got no time for paperwork. I suppose the amount you want depends on how long you fuck-heads want to stay alive. So no, we ain't got no paper work." He pulled on his chin. "You just steal what you want and the rest we sell to the gooks."

"I happen to be a SERGEANT, soldier." Biggilo's face swelled and he pushed through two men to get closer to the soldier. "What's your name, trooper?" The soldier driving the truck looked out, rolled his eyes, circled the air with a finger, and pulled his head back in.

"Yours, sergeant," replied the soldier. He snapped to attention and flipped out a salute. "Yours is the name. Corporal Yours." His feet spread wide to the side and his knees were bent.

"Yours, what?" Biggilo's fingers were almost strangling his gun belt. The soldier snapped another salute.

"Up Yours, sergeant. Yes sir; I'm corporal Up Yours." His smart stance of attention folded into a puddle of laughter and he kicked another box of ammunition to the runway. Pete wanted to laugh too. Only Clifton had the nerve. Sergeant Biggilo shot him a nasty glance, then looked back at the soldier.

"Expect to find yourself on report in the morning," Sergeant Biggilo said, blowing like a tight balloon.

"Up Yours. Up Fucking Yours, that is if you want my middle name too." The soldier continued to mumble and laughed again at the joke. "What's an ass hole like you going to do, send me to Nam?" This time the laughter almost had him in tears.

"Up Yours. That's good, pencil dick," the soldier yelled from the truck. He balanced himself on the running board. He looked to Biggilo. "How about helping unload this damn shit so we can get back inside where it's cool."

"That's SERGEANT, soldier." Biggilo's neck swelled over his collar.

"Whatever you say, buddy," said the soldier tipping his head back inside."

"That's SERGEANT, soldier, SERGEANT. Expect to be on report too."

The soldier circled the air with his finger again as if to say "big deal."

"Right, sergeant," said the first soldier kicking the last of the supplies to the ground. He slapped the truck's side and it started to pull away. "Right, Sergeant Fuckhead. You in the Nam, boy. You ain't shit over here except another victim." He flipped Biggilo off and again fell over laughing. It was difficult now for Pete to think of Biggilo as sergeant Biggilo." The sergeant huffed into the plane.

The company emptied the ammo boxes and moved onto the plane after him. It was a tight fit. Pete sat on the webbing pushing the red straps aside. The plane smelled empty, like a hot tin cave, and of fuel and aluminum. As it rumbled roughly into flight, he fell asleep.

The landing plane jarred him awake. The back opened on another world and the men filed out and loaded into waiting trucks. He tried to clear his head, get an understanding of the place. The heat felt the same, maybe a little cooler. The scenery had changed. Outside the airfield he saw mountains, heavy, deep green mountains rolling for as far as he could see. Nothing was flat. Short dry fields and heavy jungle covered everything. Clouds hovered around the field as they loaded into the waiting trucks. Everyone was armed. Everyone looked tired.

"Where are we?" asked Pete. Clifton shrugged. Pete bent over the wooden railing of the truck. It had no top. "What is this place?" Pete asked the man riding shotgun.

He turned around and stood up. "Camp Pissing Holloway," he said. He dug a stick of bubble gum from his flack jacket. Sweat ran heavy down his bare chest and freckles covered his face. A rough scar covered one arm and he drank something from a Bugs Bunny mug.

"Know where we're going?"

"To hell as far as I know." The flack jacket looked a half inch thick, heavy with plastic and nylon. It was stained with red dirt and almost black under the arms and neck.

"Sure," said Pete. "This truck I mean. Where is it going?""

"Tittie Mountain," he said. "Hell-hole of the highlands. Another Dien Bien Phu waiting to happen." He read the comic on the gum wrapper. "Naw, it's really Dragon Mountain, the only defense in the mountains right now. Of course if we weren't here, there wouldn't be any need to have a fucking defense. Sits outside Pleiku." He handed Pete a cigarette. "What outfit?" The soldier tried to blow a bubble but the gum was too new. He chewed quickly as if limited by time to get the bubble away.

"Mostly the band. Came to play these guys to death, I guess."

"Too bad." He tried the bubble again jabbing his tongue into it twice before blowing. It broke from around his lips. His chewing became frantic.

"Why's that?" Pete held tightly to the truck as it swayed down the road. Red dust started to blow into the bed.

"Last band didn't make it. Some hot-shot Cavalry band, the Seventh I think. Zips wasted them over Anh Khe. Shot the shit out of the chopper, plow! clean out of the sky." The bubble grew large and thin before bursting on the man's face. "Damn, Bernie," he said to the driver. "You see the size of that one?"

Pete passed the cigarette to James. James lit it, choked, and handed it back. Pete declined. James took two more drags and again handed it back.

"I'm going to like this war," said Clifton. "Take a smoke; you're no kid anymore." He pushed the cigarette toward Pete's mouth. "It's a beginning. Take it."

Pete held it between his two fingers. Clifton sat back

with his hands behind his head. The airfield slowly disappeared as the trucks journeyed down a narrow road kicking red dust into the air, dust that made the twilight sun blood red, close and large.

Sixteen rows of barbed wire held together Dragon Mountain Base Camp, erected on a small plateau and built of brown canvas company tents, scattered in groups, and clustered throughout the area. The camp road system resembled a large wheel. Division Headquarters sat at the hub, the only wooden structure in camp except for the offcer's club. Red clay roads spoked out from this center and attached to the rim, another road circling the inside of the wire. Companies were quartered between the spokes of the wheel. Only one road, the road from Pleiku, a mountain town, entered the camp. Working from the right of this road, and going around the rim, were the band, transportation, several infantry companies, the stockade, choppers, armor, more infantry, and artillery. Sliding down the spokes and closer to the hub were the supply, and medical companies.

On the outside of the rim, beyond the wire, rose Dragon Mountain; two mountains (hills really) called "Tittie" Mountain by the troops. A circular road traveled to the tops of the mountains where different companies pulled guard duty day and night. The mountains were not high and easily climbed in twenty minutes.

A large ravine covered with jungle was sweeped

each morning by soldiers looking for signs of tunneling. It dipped to the south of camp and leveled out. The sweep was dangerous work and six men had been killed and several considerably shortened when hidden land mines and booby traps harvested their legs. A smaller ravine, void of vegetation, was used for sighting weapons.

Further around the rim lay a flat plateau and beyond that, a hill containing a lake from which the Division pulled its water. Soldiers guarded the lake continuously and dead water buffalo, dead Vietnamese and dead soldiers were occasionally scooped from its surface. Completing the circle was more plateau on which rested a Montagnard village often strafed by nervous troops crouching in guard bunkers. Every month they buried the unfortunate tribal members with a celebration, a feast, and flaming campfires. They never moved the village.

The band stumbled into this new green world of hills, jungle and confusion, not yet soldiers, not even men. Many of them still jiggled with baby fat and red irritated zits pushed painfully through faces. Ambush patrols, perimeter guards and convoys to Qui Nhon slowly transformed them into men, then soldiers. Pete, knocked forward by time, soon became a soldier and, as he witnessed more and more of it, slowly formed a philosophy about death.

Chapter 10

Time. War time. Not the constant rotation of earth against the sun, around and around and around. War time is a disjointed mosaic of jagged edges parting out space, a large chunk here, a sliver there. Bewildered, chaotic, unable to assert an even pace, war time stutters, stumbles for some men, remains dateless for others. War is a time of relativity, not between things, but between ideas and emotions: a time of broken clocks and clouded sundials. War is littered with bent, leaking hour-glasses. Age advances at the speed of a shell. Events occur in fragments, unconnected, a quick scene here, a ponderous one there. Soldiers march and stumble through chapters of corrupted time unable to grasp any meaning. Nothing, except the insatiable appetite of war, remains constant.

Zip! Time cut and dropped to the floor. First patrol. Men left in disarray. Muddled through the jungle. At a clearing the saxophone playing sergeant stopped. Can anyone read a map? He rubbed his wet belly where the flesh rolled over his belt. A confrontation. Why didn't he tell the captain he could not read a map? No explanation. Better to walk men to their deaths than face a moment of embarrassment before an officer. Pete, taught to read a map by his uncle, became the point man as the men learned to take care of themselves and become a unit. The sergeants were left to tag along like so much baggage crashing through the jungle, little impact, no contribution, dead weight and ignorant of soldiering.

Time swirled. Another patrol. Pete ordered down a ravine. Frank asked to go along, willing to possibly sacrifice his life as easily as sharing a can of pop. Late at night. The sergeant could not afford to lose two men. With those words in his head, Pete crawled down the ravine through the grass and vegetation, bugs swirling everywhere before slipping over a ledge, sliding to his death, his rifle caught in bamboo to save him. His feet dangled. He felt his legs being held, being pulled down, the Viets jerking him toward destruction,laughing, their knives driving into his calfs. No. Nothing there but the night and a chattering creek below. He lay back and panted, his heart racing, chest heaving like a bellows, thousands of gnats drowning in his sweat. Just his mind, nothing more. Just his imagination gouging him with fear. Just becoming a man, a soldier. Later, he shit till his ass bled and he realized there was nothing real called fear. Be not afraid. He rembered those words. Fear did not exist in the world as anything tangible. People created their own fear, made their own cage, their own prison where they crouched trembling in shadows. Fear only resided in the mind. Maybe everything he thought was real resided there.

Another chip of time, another patrol. A medic noticed that the musicians had placed all the Claymore mines backwards, all of them facing the men. Upon their return to camp, the band broke into the supply depot and stole training manuals to learn to become soldiers, to save themselves.

Time. Time. A listening post erected beyond the wire. A battle ensued. Phones to the post were out. For two hours the battle raged. Grenades tossed and tracers shot. A pretty sight, the grenade blasts flashing the night and freezing the action like a strobe, the tracers writing thin, horizontal bars of orange and red twilight that lingered on the air. The battle was fought between two listening posts, between them and them, the band and the transportation company. Two hours and no injuries. No injuries. Big laugh. Becoming a soldier.

Another patrol. Jagged time sharp and cutting. Frank got hit, his leg blown away. Clifton and James trying to hold him down and tie the arteries. Frank fighting them off insisting the leg was not gone although he cradled it in his arms like a dead baby as his life ran through the grass into the soil until the life eventually dribbled away, the leg clutched in his hands and lying across his chest.

M-14s collected. M-16s issued, new jungle fatigues and jungle boots, yellow stripes and insignias removed for black, white T- shirts and shorts burned and replaced with green, dog tags taped for silence, slings taped, ammo magazines taped end-to-end, a new language of sarcasm, denial, greater profanity learned as men became soldiers, men, stepping o☐ the edge of the world yet unable to fall. And the daily mantra becoming *it don't mean nothing, nothing is nothing, something is nothing, all things are nothing and who really gives a fat fuck then, or now?*

In this disjointed rush of time the world jerked past faster than thought, faster than writing. There was no time to understand the people, the weather, the emotions, the history, the new world. Letters home stopped as feelings bunkered down often never to rise again. It don't mean nothing. No hope. No bright future. A happy childhood ex-changed for war. A month passed before time slowed, seeking a new cog. Even then time often tore loose and skipped a slot. As time slowed, sergeant Biggilo ordered Clifton and Pete on a convoy to chase the cog of time, or be crushed under it. Pete's true madness may have started then, maybe even on the convoy with James as the war started to smother him. But from the fateful convoy on, he could never step back. Clifton was with him, that's all Pete remembered. Clifton never left him. It don't mean nothing.

Chapter 11

For three miles along highway 19, from behind
the burning truck to the drag vehicle past the village,
the convoy rumbled to a halt. A mortar round hit the
lead truck and choppers strafed the hills. Soldiers at
the far end of the line ignored the battle and, as engines idled out, had already kicked their boots
up on helmets and started reading books or
napped. Dust from the highway swirled with the
smoke from village cooking fires. A gray dog ran
between two hootches as a young boy handed elephant grass to a man thatching a roof and other
boys flowed into the ditch that separated the village
from the soldiers. Small hands bummed cigarettes or
offered sisters or mothers for sale to the G.I.'s resting

in the shade of truck tires.

"I can't help it," said James. Dust that kicked up from the road covered his face and formed black streaks around his lips. He handed the lit cigarette to a boy. The boy scratched one foot on top the other leaving marks, from the calluses, across the skin. Because his bare chest was colored burnt umber like the earth, he did not look dirty. He nodded approval and cradled the cigarette between his fingers. When he lifted the cigarette to his lips, smoke folded into the red scar covering an empty eye socket. He grinned like any small boy with a gift.

Pete waived the boy away when he came near. "You'll have the whole damn family here," he said. He fumbled with the lid on a can of crackers. Nothing moved ahead. "How long do you suppose it'll be?" Doors on the trucks flapped open and soldiers sat or lay in the shade on their flak jackets. The cherries constantly drank water. Pete and the band had learned that lesson: the more you drank the more you sweated. They had learned to survive on one quart of water a day, although they often carried more. Rifles hung from the open cabs, slings around mirrors or door handles. Lately, between patrols, he had been driving convoys, easy duty.

The boy had moved back to James and he pinched his fingers together. "Tee Tee," he said. "Number one. Two dollars."

"Bargain day for his sister," said James. He tried to scoot the boy away but when he refused, he gave him another cigarette and opened a can of peaches to share. He ate one peach and offered the rest to the boy who knelt at his feet and nodded approval. The boy scooped out one peach, pried the lid back on, and placed the can at his feet. The boy rubbed James' black arms as if they were good luck.

Pete flung his flak jacket onto the seat over his helmet. He tried to wash down the crackers with iodized water from his canteen. In a short time girls would be under the trucks earning this week's wages. Like the boy, they were all deformed, all sick, wormy little creatures, beaten down by years of war. Survival had replaced any pride they once had. Clifton had told him that soldiers were responsible to keep them alive. Screw them, pay them, simple enough and everyone gets what he wants.

"He's a greasy little pimp," Pete said. "They're all greasy little pimps." Pete wanted to go home. He had become testy lately. Clifton was rubbing off on him. He felt angry and nasty even though Clifton had stayed at camp. "Maybe it's a bad day. I feel sorry for them but I don't know how to help except to go home."

The boy became insistent about his sister. He barely stood above James' bent knees. Pete handed James the canteen. The boy jerked on James' pants and grinned. James tipped back his head and poured the water over his hair. Rivulets of thin mud traversed his slick black cheeks and dirty water dripped off his chin and onto his t-shirt. Two planes screeched toward the sky as a cloud of black napalm smoke rose from the surrounding hills. James handed the boy the canteen and made two fists with his thumbs straight up: the sign for O.K. The boy dropped the canteen, bowed, and ran away.

"I can't help myself," James said. "What's the difference, anyway? They gotta live. One minute you're in there tearing off a piece of ass and the next you're not. Make up your mind, saint or sinner."

"We'll be moving soon." Pete shook his head in disgust, folded his arms and leaned against the fender. "What do you suppose these lines are, anyway?"

Against the edge of the road, where the dirt was soft, and up the small bank to the village, little trails dimpled the ground. They looked like someone had dragged them with a sack and rested the sack every few feet. There was a scrape, and a dot, a scrape, and a dot. The boy had entered on one trail and left on another. James shrugged his shoulders. "Hey, I'm the one taking the chance," he said. "You're more apt to give them the back of your hand than offer them a smoke." He rolled to one arm. "He might not come back with the woman."

During his first week in country, Pete had decided never to give them anything, not because didn't want to, but because he did not have enough to give. War made the country a disgrace and they always came back, the freeloaders, the bums, the pimps, the little girl whores trying to feed their families by having sex with people they hated. He

144

thought he was there to help them, yet his own peo-ple had turned the country into a welfare state. In an effort to help them he refused to participate. He did not lack for compassion; he even paid a betel-nut, black-toothed mama-san a buck a week to wash his clothes, although he was capable of doing them himself. Without good honest work, no country survived. Clifton was often mean to them, not Pete. He just ignored them for their own good.

He finished his crackers and shoved the empty can in a cardboard box behind the seat. "We've made a mess of the whole thing," he said.

"Six months and you'll be home," said James. "You're not the kind of guy who takes a country home with him. You've got to give in eventually. We all do. And you can help them without killing them."

"They've got no whores up North." When Pete touched the hot fender of the truck, he jerked his hand away. He sat on the dirt with his legs crossed next to James. "I heard that Uncle Ho only pays his officials ten dollars a month. If they have too much stuff he knows they're involved in something. Greed corrupts us all."

"The boy's pretty chopped up." James nodded to-ward the village and took another drink from the can-teen. "It's fine to talk about that work crap. How do you sleep at night thinking of a kid whose biggest thrill is a free smoke?"

Pete did not know the answer. His father was a cop

and always talked about making it on your own. He tried not to think like his father or like Clifton.

"I'm not an ass," Pete said. "What will they do when we're gone, that's all?"

"We'll be here forever," James said. "Besides, what difference does it make? The kid wants a smoke today, not ten years from now."

"It's not supposed to be like this," Pete said. "Lately, it seems like we ruin everything."

"A big dog craps where he likes," said James. "Grow up, will you. Bright flags and fields of honor only exist in history books. We don't want much, just everything there is."

Pete unfolded his pocketknife and picked clay from between the cleats in his boots. He etched a peace sign in the dirt. Nothing made sense anymore.

Down one of the trails, the boy returned with a shapeless little girl whose teeth had not yet turned black. Under one arm, he carried a piece of old army blanket. James offered them both a cigarette. They squatted on each side of him and the boy patted him on the knee and tried to wink with his good eye. He pushed his sister forward and crawled under the truck to spread the blanket. The girl did not look up, and James made no attempt to touch her except to point his head toward the blanket when the boy had finished. Pete turned his back to James and the girl and continued to scratch in the dirt. The girl whimpered only a little as James pushed into her.

The boy squatted facing the truck, his arms folded

over his knees, smoke rising across his face. Pete tried not to watch him. Three F-16s rolled in formation against the blue sky. In the village, a woman used a stick to place wet laundry on the limbs of a dead tree. Two dogs, without barking, chased each other toward the road. More black smoke burned the sky then tumbled from the hills.

When he had finished, James returned to his place against the tire and fumbled with his belt. He pulled the girl under his arm and brushed the hair back on her forehead. She was not pretty like the bar girls in town. Her hair was matted and stringy and she tried to shake out the dirt as if now was the time to look attractive.

The boy eased the money into his pocket. He moved back to Pete and tapped him on the knee. Pete watched the hill. The boy continued to tap: steady, even, the pressure constant. "Two dollar," he said. "Number one woman, two dollar." Cigarette smoke rolled up past his eye socket. Pete wanted to rip his hand away, to slap him.

"Buy something from him, anything," said James. "Show him you like him."

Pete stood and brushed his pants. Like the boy, the girl looked too young to smoke, too young to be selling herself. She rested her head on James' shoulder in fictitious affection.

From the village, a man called out. At first he looked as if he were crouched behind the brush, then he moved ahead pulling himself with his knuckles. His body, firmly tied into a leather sack, ended at his crotch. The boy yelled back something in Vietnamese. The man ran a finger through the wrinkles in his face, and turned to drag himself away leaving in his wake another small trail: a scrape, and a dot, a scrape, and a dot. Pete watched him disappear behind the grass. He turned and looked into the boy's one eye.

"Here, take the damn stuff," he said. He yanked two dollars from his pocket and dropped the script to the boy's lap. He fumbled in his tunic pocket, found another dollar, a greenback this time, and tossed it at the boy.

"Number one girl," the boy said. "Number one girl."

He rumpled the script into his fist and scurried under the truck to straighten the blanket.

"It's not such a bad thing," said James. "You might even like it, might even level you out." With two fingers, he touched the girl on the head, then moved to the front of the truck to piss. The boy rolled out from behind the wheels and seized Pete by the hand. Pete jerked his hand away.

"Did you see that guy," said Pete. "How do you live like that?"

"You're either at the table or on it," said James, over his shoulder.

"Take the money," Pete said to the boy. "Just leave me alone."

"This girl number one," said the boy. "Tee, tee;

number one girl."

He helped the girl up and patted her behind. "Number one girl."

"I don't want her." Pete stepped toward the truck. The boy moved in front of him.

"Number one girl," he said. "This number one girl."

Pete reached for the door. The boy looked at his sistr, then at James. James shrugged his shoulders and spun a finger around his ear to indicate that Pete was crazy.

"Number one girl," said the boy. "Number one girl." He stamped his feet in the dirt and tried to make Pete face the girl.

"Dee dee mou," said Pete. "Take the money and go away"

Up ahead, the trucks were starting to move. The boy continued to shout and stamp his feet. He shoved the girl to the side and waved the small wad of money in front of Pete.

The girl stepped forward and for the first time, looked up. Pete had already turned to shove the boy away. He looked down and saw the village reflected in her sad eyes. She slid the money from her brother's hand. Pete wanted to touch her face, to place one finger against her lips, to feel the skin, the breath, just one time.

He reached out. She folded the money into her fist. Before he could touch her, she flung the bills into his face. Pete never flinched as the bills drifted to the ground. When the boy reached for the money, the girl lifted him by an elbow and dragged him down a trail left by the old man, and back into the village.

James never said anything as he climbed into the truck. Pete slipped into his flak jacket, started the engine and gripped the steering wheel so tightly his knuckles went pale. James unwrapped a stick of gum and handed it to Pete. Pete rolled the gum between his fingers and tossed it over the hood.

"You bastards," he said, "You dirty rotten bastards."

"She's not a charity case," said James.

Pete worked a case of C-rations from between the seats and stood on the backboard slats with the carton held high overhead.

"Take it, you bastards," he screamed. "Take every god-damned thing we have."

He heaved the case toward the village. The boxes inside tumbled out and down the trails like fingers in the dirt. The boy turned back once, then continued into the village with his sister. Pete slid back into the the seat. His hands quivered against the steering wheel.

"We're starting to move," said James. "We're starting to move."

He placed one foot against the dash and rested the butt of his M-16 on his thigh. Pete eased the transmission into gear. The truck jerked ahead.

Chapter 12

The breeze wandered gently through the ravine, past the barbed wire, around the bunkers, over the dry dirt road, lifting thin blankets of dust lifted and tossed aside. A column of soldiers, dragging into camp after an ambush patrol, welcomed the breeze as it cooled their sweat then moved on folding back strands of dead grass and swirling discarded coffee pouches and cigarette packs into the air. Outside a tent a bare-chested soldier cussed the breeze when dust folded over his wet laundry and flakes of soap scattered from his torn box of Tide. Equivocal in its actions the breeze freely spirited about the base camp sculpting dirt against buildings and vehicles, dusting ammo boxes, pinching through tank slits and skimming down 105 barrels. It teetered the flag outside HQ, rolled like a wave down the camp roads, and sprinkled dust onto Pete's boots as he sat on a row of sandbags beside his tent.

Under the morning sun, he oiled a small cleaning rag. His M-16 was field stripped, the barrel lying across his lap. He had been gone almost a month, ever since Biggilo had sent Clifton and him on a convoy. They had been hit and he was wounded and spent the last month in the hospital at Qui Nhon. He still felt the healing flesh draw together on his leg. He had returned to camp qu
witnessed death and had lear
wanted out. The doctors said he ....
Only Clifton waited for him.

He tried to get the feel of the M-16, a new weapon, a plastic shoddy weapon, that had replaced the M-14. The rifle felt too light to be useful. He tipped his head back, looked past the sun and reassembled the weapon without looking. The barrel was poorly finished and the plastic butt felt wrong. He did not like carrying it by the handled sight.

The breeze blew across his mouth. He wet his lips to remove the dirt. It's like the breeze at home, he thought. Maybe not Washington. More like Cincinnati, where he spent summers as a young kid. The breeze was like the breeze blowing off the Ohio River. At his Grandmother's house, Pete had sat on the banks of the Ohio River under the seven hills of Cincinnati. "Cincinnati is like Rome," his Grandmother said. "The same seven hills." She straightened the crucifix on the kitchen wall. She had never been to Rome and she touched him on the nose. Pete liked her to bake cookies and read him books. She once said her dress was a tent and she asked Pete to be a good little Indian and crawl inside, between her tent poles, and find the bird trapped in the nest. At night, he said grace before supper. He never said grace in Nam.

The breeze blew across his eyes and he tried the weapon again, the parts, every notch and crack. He dismantled it again, closed his eyes and assembled it, a silly exercise. If he were in a position where he could not see, what was the use of having a weapon? He tried to place himself back in Ohio. Grandmother's always knew best. Maybe she understood something about him that he did not. Grandmother's never tried to hurt you.

When he was older, Pete slipped down the mud into the Ohio River and watched river tugs nudge coal barges against the current. His summer friends splashed water and talked about a whore house across the water in Kentucky where everyone eventually traveled. All the whore houses were in Kentucky, none in Ohio. Ben pointed with his wet hands to a peeling, yellow house behind a row of sad–looking brick buildings. Pete wanted to say something about his grandmother, to tell his friends they did not have to go to Kentucky. Grandmothers never hurt kids.

Pete shoved the bolt into the receiver. It snapped shut. He kept his head bent back and let the sun filter in red flags through his closed eyelids as he attempted a return to Cincinnati, to the evenings where he floated on the river under the reflected, flashing thighs of the neon banana girl sign outside the Caribbean Club. Once, late at night, as he drifted on a tube under a lump of grass on the still water, he heard Cat Anderson, from the club, blow a note bluer than sky.

The bolt snapped shut. No one could escape the war, no refuse in Cincinnati or Washington or California. The M-16 was together. He cleared his eyes. The weapon held him as tightly as his grandmother's legs. Pete, too young, too afraid, never floated to the whore house in Kentucky. The convoy to Qui Nhon changed that, took his youth. His body remained young, but his mind had been twisted and driven to some dark ancient edge, he was not sure where, some black web or tunnel he did not understand. His thoughts had aged, grown beards, hobbled – arthritic and tough.

Today, he had the day off and he wanted to ride into town on the laundry truck and sit in a restaurant and drink coffee and watch people eat or sit in the park. He liked the people who hurried, bent double, scurrying from one side of the road to the other. They represented progress. The shops would be in colored disarray from hanging bolts of silk and bins piled high with confederate tin medals: purple hearts, bronze stars, silver stars, any medal one could want, offered at premium prices. There was no war in town, not when G.I.'s were about, not when money was to be made. But the last convoy remained in his mind.

Biggilo had sent him on the convoy. Biggilo was a grandmother with tight tent poles and a bird's nest that snapped like a bear trap. He offered suffocation disguised as cookies.

Pete pissed into one of the cement piss tubes that resembled fields of tombstones, then returned to his tent. His tent held ten mosquito netted cots, empty ammo boxes formed cupboards beside them. Henry, fresh from a patrol, lay face down on his down filled sleeping bag. Sweat pooled in the small of his back and white foam dribbled from his lips. Pete fished in a box, removed his razor, and walked to the water truck for a shave.

The company compound held several rows of tents, the longest rows belonging to the troops. Facing these were the sergeant's tents followed by the off icer's tents, smaller and holding only two men. The water truck was parked at the end of the rows. A detail filled truck and a small water trailer, each day at the reservoir. In the evening another detail sank large immersion heaters into the truck tank and heated the water for showers. The small water trailer was pulled near the mess tent standing alone behind the others. When Pete shaved only cold water dribbled from the tank and he returned to the tent with his face raw and bleeding. Clifton waited on the sandbags.

"I'm going to town," he said. "James and me. Maybe get stinking drunk. You too?" Pete rubbed his face with a T-shirt leaving streaks of blood. "Yeah." He looked suspiciously at Clifton before stowing his gear. Clifton followed him more and more lately. Something about Clifton had turned sour and evil. Since the convoy, Pete recognized that Clifton was no good yet, he could not escape him. A change had to be made. He did not understand that a separation from Clifton was a separation from himself. Clifton was emptying the stuffng from pillows, bright pillows embrordered with scenes of choppers and country landscapes. He restuffed the pillows with marijuana from his pack.

"You'll get caught," Pete said.

"It's a business deal," Clifton chuckled. "Fibo came up with the idea. I'm just helping him out. Eventually everybody comes must deal with me. We stuff the pillows and send them to his friend. No one checks anything from Nam. His friend sells the dope and mails us our cut of the funds. He gets no more until we get paid. That's the only way to keep him honest."

"It's not right," Pete said. "There is something not moral about it."

"Moral?" Clifton rolled back on the cot and laughed again. "Moral? That's a word invented by the rich cats to keep the poor simpletons like us out of the money loop. You ever see anyone moral get ahead? Everyone climbing the ladder has stepped on the rungs of morality, all the businessmen, all the leaders, all the politicitions. The lack of morality is the key to success whether you are a congressman or a preacher. Arrogance and greed don't exist with morality and that's what gets a person ahead."

They gathered at the laundry truck, a shrapnel-shot deuce-and-a- half Clifton had named Rocinante, the same truck they had driven to Qui Nhon during the incident that changed Pete. Two bullet holes still aerated the door and Pete imagined he smelled burnt flesh.

"Not this truck," he said.

"Work it from your system, for Christ's sake," said Clifton. "You live on dreams like they were vitamins. Swallow this dream, or nightmare in your case, and piss it out in the morning."

Laundry bags filled the bed, the canvas bumping the knees of two black-toothed women sitting on one side and holding hands. Pete nodded to the driver, Moses Washington, who stood by the truck with his right arm pushed into his pants. He held the record for V.D. infections and men called him *Bareback Rider*. Doctors had cautioned him about getting sick again since he was close to becoming incurable because the penicillin was less and less effective. Hearing his nickname passed around in bars, Moses always swelled his chest and said, "das me, da Bareback Rider." A huge lethargic man with dull gentle eyes, Moses carried, more often than a weapon, a blank puzzled look. His stupidity came naturally, something everyone accepted. If not for the military he would have been living on the streets, probably hungry since he would not have remembered to beg. The doctors told him to keep a grip on things. He could not remember why. All he remembered was to keep a firm hold, which he did through his pants.

"Hey Mo," said Clifton, walking to the truck. Moses looked up, focused his eyes slowly and cocked his head.

"Hi ya guys," he said. He kept the hand in his pants and scratched.

"We want to fuck around in town. How about a ride? Maybe even buy you a beer later, or a little nooky, some of that slant-eyed pussy you like."

"Climb up with dem laundry bitches." The word bitches triggered something in Moses and he extracted the hand from his pants, smelled his fingers, and wiped his mouth.

Pete climbed into the truck. One woman started to cackle. She held the twisted hand of the other woman and bumped against her. A leg was torn off the first woman, just below the knee, and replaced with an old French rifle stock. The bottom of the stock faced forward like a clubbed foot. The brown splintered wood of the stock matched the color of her skin.

The bones of the other woman stood almost outside her body. Thin skin draped over them like fabric on a wooden airplane. Flies strutted across her dry lips. She parted the lips revealing slick black betel-nut teeth and crimson gums. Only her eyes looked alive, blue- black and mountain creek clear. The eyes were those of a younger woman trying to push her way through the pupils.

Clifton sat beside the one legged woman. "What's happening, Mama-San?" He wrapped his arm around her and pinched her nose. "I hear you give the best blow jobs in camp." The old woman slapped him on the knee and laughed. Lately, Pete did not like being with him. Each day, Pete felt more like a soldier yet, he still found decent decisions diffcult and Clifton was no help. James sat opposite the women. Pete handed him a cigarette.

"You not going to cause trouble are you?" said James. "I've got to watch over you every minute."

"Have the smoke," said Pete.

Clifton squeezed at his prick and made humping motions toward the laughing woman. Pete lighted a smoke for himself and watched the dead–looking woman.

"You going to make trouble this soon?" said James. "At least wait 'till we get to town."

The truck moved down the dusty road and out the gate. Moses missed a gear and the truck lurched. He looked at his new shotgun sitting beside him, a sol-

dier from Maine. Earlier, the shotgun admitted
he knew nothing about truck driving and he seemed
content to sit on the seat and point his M-16 toward
the surrounding jungle and ravines, make shooting
noises, and play soldier.

Pete held his own weapon skyward. The
M-16 still felt undependable. He comfortably
carried three hundred rounds on patrol with
this new weapon, just nineteen in town. Twenty
rounds in a clip might cause jambs. He liked carrying
extra ammo in the field. One hundred rounds
with an M-14 was a burden. Yet, the M-16 felt too
light to be dependable. He fiddled with the clip. The
surrounding country was a spectrum of greens
like an expressionist painting. Only the road looked
out of place: a bloody red gash across the canvas.

After pinching her tits, Clifton grew tired of the
game with the woman. He removed a pipe, worn
smooth and dark around the bowl, from his
pocket. He spit on the stem and worked the pipe together. He crushed several cigarettes into the bowl.

Pete did not want to think and he fought with his
mind. A mind within a mind swirled ever so slowly.
Shit, he thought. Keep out of the convoy. Drive it
from your mind. Then he wondered: Why have I
changed when everything was going so well? Clifton's
pipe smelled good. Think about the pipe, not the
convoy. Think about anything but the convoy to Qui
Nhon. His mind became a deceitful little laudanum
affected by the rising smoke and the heat of day.

Pete tried to fight off time, to stay in the present. His mind refused to respond. He was there, in the truck with the old woman, and looking at Clifton. Then he was gone. Then he was there again as he forbade himself to have the dream about the convoy again, not again. Yet his mind drifted away rummaging loosely through old memories until it stopped on the convoy.

Pete is on the convoy. It is not a memory but a chip of relocated time hissing in his mind and he is there again, really there. Clifton and Pete are in Rocinante, the truck. Clifton is driving. They are returning from Qui Nhon. The trip from the mountain passes to Qui Nhon is beautiful, winding through Anh Khe and dropping to the coast. He remembers the trip. Everything is beautiful, a swirl of deep colors. And plenty of Tiger beer in Qui Nhon. Sergeant Yama is in the jeep ahead. They met him at the N.C.O. club. He is Korean and, like the beer, just as hard and rusty. He hates Communists. He never sees VC, just Communists, and he kills them all. He is ashamed of what they did to his country in the last war and says it will never happen again. His country will never be unprepared again. Communists will never get another chance to swoop down on him and kill his sister and grandmother. Sergeant Yama has two kids and a wife with crooked teeth. He shows Pete their pictures. He bought the beer and now they are on their way back and he is ahead in the jeep and he turns to smile and wave his calloused yellow-brown hand made thick by banging it against tree trunks then soaking it in salt water. Clifton lies and tells him they hate Communists too and they would like to kill North Koreans. Sergeant Yama likes this and buys more beer. It has been a good trip, a great chance to escape from Sergeant Biggilo. Pete says it is a good trip. Clifton says it is a good war. They are having fun. Even Pete agrees.

That's right isn't it? Clifton did agree that it was a good war and that he would rather die than return home. Pete told the doctors what Clifton said. He thought that helped justify everything.

Clifton says he likes war. It is a good war. They do not function as a band. The duty is not bad. Clifton says their combat pay buys a different woman each night. Women are only two bucks. Combat pay is sixty. Clifton is right again. Women are two bucks and there is no bullshit in war.

They move back toward Anh Khe, back toward the Highlands. Pete feels the sun and watches red dust paint the back of Sergeant Yama. He lies back and enjoys the ride. He whistles. The sun sucks the moisture from him and he lets the sweat puddle on his skin. Sun feels good. Clifton says "fucking-A, Jose."

The dirt road is Highway 19. The road winds from Highway 1 on the coast and twists through Anh Khe and through Pleiku and on to Cambodia. The jeep ahead drives up a fine pink curtain of dust. The mind twists and turns. Pete wants out of the dream. The mind   controls time, controls Clifton, controls him. The jeep. Paint peeling from the jeep and curling within itself leaving two shades of green, too green scabs. Flat land everywhere is sectioned into paddies. They approach small hills beside the flat road before entering Anh Khe Pass. Sergeant Yama is thin and is not driving. Somehow that is important. He rides shotgun. Pete rides shotgun. No   difference. Pete starts to understand something: nothing in the world is different, everything is the same. He thinks about that idea. Everything is the same thing, all one thing, one big idea swirling through space which is also part of the idea. None of it important. Everything real, everything that occupies space and has weight has no meaning except as metaphor for everything that is important, the stuff that has no weight and occupies no space, the stuff of importance that cannot be described: ideas, emotions, thoughts, decisions, and more, the stuff that belies description that can only be hinted at through metaphor. The beauty of the country might be a sign pointing at tranquililty because tranquiloity cannot be described, just felt.

Sergeant Yama rides ahead in the jeep. They are the same, all confined within steel and on canvas seats. Clifton brought beer. He hands one to Pete. The beer feels good going down even though it is warm. He is used to it by now. Clifton taught him to like beer. Clifton likes beer. Yama likes beer. The Koreans make beer with formaldehyde so soldiers will rot when they die.

I shouldn't tell you, Clifton...

Good. Don't tell him anything, even now that it's over. Keep your mouth shut. Let nothing out.

I didn't go to the senior prom. Christ! You're going to piss about that to Clifton.

Clifton frowns. The beer is warm. He understands like Pete knew he would. This business about the prom is serious business. The senior prom is part of a normal adjustment period. The Senior Prom is part of growing up. A chance to feel tits. You are a man when you can balance, like a couple of gold nuggets, a set of real tits. The Prom is now serious business on the road from Qui Nhon to Pleiku.

Sergeant Yama's helmet is cocked. Pete liked him instantly. He soon learns that the world falls away quickly when you are having fun and leaves you holding nothing but your prick and imaginary tits. He says his world ended the night of the Senior Prom. He knew nothing then about ending.

Pete tried to snap his mind back into the laundry truck. Nothing made sense on the convoy. Everything made sense on the convoy. Nothing and everything – the same thing. He watched the one– legged woman, so ugly she looked almost pretty. James talked to the shotgun, the sound of his voice blending with the sounds of road noise, a whirling drive line.   Pete fell back into himself, back into the memories.

The Senior Prom. Shit. The fucking Senior Prom. It is the end of high school. Now it is over. He was young and now youth is finished, finished by a single screech in the air like a fingernail down a blackboard. He hardly notices. Pete is getting drunk on Tiger beer and laughing with Clifton.

What is the noise? He was once too young to understand. He is learning to be a soldier. Instead of a happy childhood he now had Nam. The noise is a common one now. How could he have been so stupid? Now he understands about all noises. Young soldiers must learn the world of sounds, of instincts. Listen. What is it? What is that sound that kept him awake years later, right up to the end. Whistling. The sounds of war. The sound of Anh Khe Pass. First the sound. Then the object.

Move, move you bastard. Crawl into a ditch. The object has the mercy of noise, of warning. Don't say you weren't warned. The sound. Louder. Catching him in time, real time, the time Pete tries to understand and not understand. No time then. Too new. Too untried. Pete does not want the sound to hit. Not before the Senior Prom. Not before he becomes a man. Not now, sitting in Rocinante beside Clifton. Not now sitting in a laundry truck. Not now, looking overhead, holding a Tiger beerin his hand. Not now searching the sky for a whistling bird.

Did he see it, that solid black object, silent, far ahead? They do not move as fast as you might think. You can see a mortar round if you look — a leisurely sort of death that comes whistling down from the sky like explosive bird shit. There are flames. Is that what he sees first? Pete does not know then. What he sees, what he thinks he sees is dust on his eyes as he holds the Tiger beer. He spills the beer on his pants. He does not piss them. Many men do that. He does not piss them. The wet is the beer on his pants and the spot is the dust in his eyes.

The flames seem to hit first and he sees them before he hears the explosion. That's right, isn't it? Yes, that's how he described it. First the flames, colorless and flat. Shit! That is not right. The suction comes first, the suction that hugs you close, then knocks you on your ass. It happens to the man in the jeep, to Sergeant Yama. Sergeant Yama and his driver pull toward the shell as if listening to a secret. Maybe that is wrong. That is how it looks. The shell carries a secret and they want to hear, to greet death, to shake its hand. The shell, the driver, Sergeant Yama wrapped together like three friends. Pete watches them hold together as he stands and lets his weapon fall between the seats. That would never happen now. Not now...

Pete's mind stopped. He sat against the laundry

truck, rivulets of cold sweat dribbling from under his arms. He tried not to listen to himself. He lit another cigarette. The dead woman had fallen asleep. Her head banged against the truck slats. Pete burst into laughter.

Chapter 13

Pleiku, mud hole of the highlands. Pleiku, a tight knot of commerce sprawling out to ragged begging edges. Pimps, whores, bars, restaurants, merchants and religions conjoined in mad enterprise. Confucians, offering quiet reason and rational approaches to life, Cao Dai priests, outlawed by government, skittering through shadows and constructing a standing army that worships the many-headed snake and all seeing eye, Hoa Hoa, religion of the poor, offering no ceremony or ritual, no sacrifice, Taoists, incomprehensible, to say is not to know, to know is not to say, worshiping nothing as everything and everything as nothing, Catholics, strict, sure, stiff black and stern telling enticing stories about a mother and her baby God from an educated God quick of temper and just as quick to forgive, Buddhists replacing Gods with compassion, ritual with compassion, suffering with compassion, anger with compassion. These religions, and dozens more, waited to strike the unsuspecting person.

Pleiku, a town of thick mud roads and ingenious low-slung buildings, each building marking a place in life, a financial and social position. From the center of town and moving outward the buildings began as brick structures surrounded by beautiful flowering gardens. The homes quickly changed to dried mud followed by tin, then wood, then bamboo then stacked ammo boxes. Finally, outside of town and across the creek, homes of flattened beer cans reflecting sun, smashed Buds, Pabst and Olys shingling thin frames. Houses built of C-ration boxes reveal creatures of no status, non-beings sucking up good oxygen and little else, houses built of cardboard tolerating only three or four rains before rebuilding.

Pleiku, a slow city packed with Indian merchants in tight turbans speaking the language of the week's conquerors. Thieving children stamping at the feet of soldiers stealing more than money with their looks. On one corner, a legless beggar quiet except for the tattling ring of his arm: a fractured 105 shell. Hungry dogs eating piles of shit and licking the faces of compassionate troopers. Outside, the military school children, dressed in red and white, snapping to attention. A Popsicle vendor peddling sawdust covered ice on a stick. Everywhere, rats as kings. Bicycles rattling down streets or racing smoking, rusted Lambrettas. People shitting, washing and drinking in the small stream.

A city featuring a two pump Shell gas station and a brick theater painted with pictures of ancient soldiers swinging long swords and dressed in red, black and white gowns. Flames shooting from eyes, blood soaking swords.

Temples surround the city and, in the center of town, where the main road split, a tree-covered park hugging a fenced knoll from which waterfalls sprouted. A bird-stained Virgin Mary stands at the apex, her arms clutching tightly to her chest and she, looking blindly down as if she had relinquished all hope for the city's repentance. No longer able to show compassion, she had just enough stiff resolution to cock her head and stare with stone eyes at two yellow flowers growing to the left of her sandaled feet where tiny black bugs had built a nest.

Moses Washington drove past the statue to a row of brightly painted wooden buildings. Rows of drying uniforms hung between walls, window frames and doorways. The clothes looked clean although the wash water made them stink. Several old women, age hanging on them like wrinkled rouge, squatted outside a building. Naked children, thin, brown and dirty were busy beating a crippled dog to death with crooked sticks. An old man hobbled from a building to shit in the street. The truck stopped, pushing red clay before the tires and leaving a foot of tread marks to the rear. The engine idled as each rush of piston shuddered on exploding diesel fuel and slid reluctantly to the bottom of its stroke. Vibrations rolled around the crank, out the main bearing, through the transmission and down the truck frame and body. A shutter rattled the left door and caused the squatting women to jump and rattle like ghosts in the mirror.

The soldiers tossed the bags off the truck. The two women who had ridden along still slept. Clifton kicked the one woman in the rifle butt. She jerked awake and shook her companion. The dead woman awoke, did more than that, actually sprouted to life. She rose slowly and hissed at the women squatting outside the building. The women bitched back and one of them shook her fist. They stood together weaving from side to side toward the laundry bags. Pete lowered the dead looking woman over the side of the truck. She winked, reached between the slats and squeezed his prick. Her drooping flat tits helped drag the lines from her face. He dropped her onto the bags. She smiled, screwed her fist with a finger and pointed to a building across the street. Pete turned away.

The children came running leaving the dead dog in the street. With sad raisin eyes they revealed their unprofitable hands holding them like brown empty sacks. They stood stiffly in a beggar's salute. Pete tossed them two dollars.

"Those little shits will be on us all day," said Clifton, spitting over the side of the truck. "You can't feed them all, and look at them - - they look better fed than you."

"I had the money. If I don't feed them it's wrong; if I do feed them it's wrong. This place has no correct decisions except the ones we make."

"Save us all some grief." Clifton patted his shoulder.

James sat on the railing cleaning his fingernails with a small pocket knife as the kids scrambled for the change he tossed overboard, then tried to surround the new shotgun. He stood in the truck with his rifle lowered and away from the door. Kids climbed in after him. He fought his way out of the truck and retreated to the side of a building. One young boy broke away and ran into the street. He grabbed the dead dog by the tail and dragged it behind him as he chased the shotgun.

A flash caught Clifton's eye. "Look at that building," he said, pointing to a sad collection of leaning boards. He nodded toward Moses. From the building across the street a window curtain was drawn apart. A small shadow formed on the glass. Moses, who had been supervising the old women with the laundry bags, looked up like a jackal catching a new scent. He dropped the bag in his hand and stood stiffly. The old women giggled as the shadow took shape. Moses stared at the window. Across the street two yellow breasts with cork-brown nipples nudged against the glass flattening them like two great eyes. Small hands helped them form until they were perfectly round.

Moses reached into his pants then backed out again. He pursed his lips, looked skyward and took two small steps. One of the old women asked him something. Moses grunted. He took another step and stopped. Again he reached into his pants and he scratched his chin and looked puzzled.

"Hell," Clifton said. "He can't remember what the doctor said. He knows it has to do with his pants, or something in there."

Moses smelled his fingers again. Almost without moving he floated across the street and into the building. The breasts remained against the window and soon two large black hands cupped the tits carefully, directing them back into the dark.

"Moses," James said, shaking his head.

Clifton fished out his prick and shook it at the old woman. She swatted at the prick with a stick and laughed as Clifton kissed her forehead and fastened his pants.

"That fucking Moses," he said; "He can't spot a V.C. at ten feet, but at fifteen miles he can see tits locked in an iron box."

The old women started to pull and sort laundry. They squatted in a circle, quacking like ducks around a trough of corn. The woman with the rifle butt leg paced back and forth, her wooden foot twisting elongated fans in the clay. The dead woman dropped her pants and released a wide stream of yellow greasy piss on the dirt.

"Let's go to OZ for some green weenie," said Clifton.

They traveled past the Virgin Mary to a long row of merchant's shops, most of them owned by East Indians. The shops were similar to stalls seen at state fairs: about ten feet by fifteen feet with fronts that formed shade canopies during business hours, and folded down at night. Two of them had folding iron gates. A turbaned Hindu watched when they walked into his open shop. James fingered the goods. He fluffed a silk pillow hanging overhead. The pillow was cold blue and embroidered with a yellow Huey hovering over pale elephant grass. The inscription read, Vietnam, 1966. James jerked at the V. It peeled off. The merchant bowed, smiled and handed him a different pillow.

Pete plowed his fingers through a bin of poorly painted tin medals and placed one in each hand as if on a scale. A thought entered his head as he clutched them, some kind of realization of how to deal with Clifton. Pete had been looking for something without knowing what the something was. He decided to buy Clifton off. Now he had seen the way, felt it in his hands, felt it long enough to trigger the look on his face reflected in the tin drum. At the very least, a medal might make Clifton more pleasant. If Clifton was happy he would not be so mean, might even let Pete have more responsibility. Pete decided to help Clifton get a medal.

"Got any .38 ammunition?" Clifton asked the merchant. The Indian shook his head. Clifton thumbed some cheap knives. "Got any ammunition?" he asked again. The Indian grinned shaking his head no. Clifton flashed him a twenty. The merchant bowed and disappeared into the back. "Money'll get us anything."

On the street a tank clattered through town. A Buddhist monk, who had been standing beside the street under an umbrella, gathered his orange robes and ran into the tank's path. A small crowd gathered. Pete replaced the medals. The tank drove to a stop rocking back and forth on its tracks. The Buddhist knelt before slumping to the ground and crossing his legs. Gently his finger tips kissed. He was a young man with a clean shaven head that tipped toward the tank.

"This shit could get good," said Clifton. He pushed closer toward the street for a better look. "He'll eat those tracks before this is over."

"The tank will turn," Pete said. "It won't kill him for sitting."

"Ten bucks says he's pleated within five minutes. Don't want to take your money, old buddy, but you need a lesson on human nature."

"Don't treat me like that," said Pete.

"Then it's a bet?"

"He won't run over him."

James removed a ten. "My ten says he won't."

Clifton stuffed the money into his pocket. "I'm holding all bets. You suckers act like kids. There's a war on here, we have all the toys, and we like to use them."

The tank engine roared then idled back. The Buddhist folded his hands across his knees and looked slightly down as the crowd drew tighter but kept well back. Someone stopped a dog from entering the street.

The merchant returned from the back room and produced a box for Clifton. "Be right back. I got business." The merchant's hands blossomed like a brown flower as he offered Clifton the box of rounds. Clifton inspected the green box, manufactured by Remington, and felt its weight. The box was old and frayed with thin copper corners. Clifton removed the top. The rounds were copper coated.

"CRACK!" A shot sounded from the street.

Clifton pushed back toward the street. "They nail him?" he asked. He still held the ammunition in his hand. The crowd had moved farther back. Some of them had already grown tired of waiting and had dispersed. A man selling dried snakes was doing a rapid business and he twirled one over his head.

"Fired a warning shot," said James.

"Double your bet?" said Clifton. James gritted his teeth.

The Buddhist had not moved. Neither had the

tank. Clifton returned to the merchant.

"These good rounds?" he asked.

The Indian smiled and nodded his head then held out his hand for payment. Clifton laid down the box, fished out a round and, with his Gerber knife, pried at the head. The merchant waved his hands in an attempt to get the knife from Clifton. Clifton shoved him aside.

"Good rounds," he said. "All good rounds."

"Piss off."

"This very dangerous work," protested the Merchant looking toward a curtained door.

Clifton popped off the head and smiled. The merchant stiffened. Sand emptied from the casing. The merchant slapped at his own face.

"I no understand," he said. "I got from very reliable source." He apologized profusely bowing again and again and slapping his hands together. He yelled into the back room and disappeared behind the curtain. The tank engine revved.

"Mash him yet?" said Clifton.

"You're about to lose your money," said James.

"Piss on you. I'm open for a bigger wager."

James pulled another five from his pocket. Clifton snatched the money before James changed his mind.

In the street the tank started to smoke as it moved slowly back, the tracks chewing up the red road. The Buddhist remained perfectly still. Pete unbuttoned the top of his shirt. James chewed a piece of Double Bubble. He tried to blow a bubble. He could get no air. Pete's heart took on speed and his hands itched. The tank rolled back and moved slowly to one side, almost in a turn.

"He's getting away," said James.

The tank stopped, rocking once. Clifton placed an arm around James and squeezed him tightly. The left tank track lined up with the Buddhist. The tank ground ahead slowly casting a deep shadow over the Buddhist. The track scratched ahead and nibbled the monk by the knee. The knee wrenched sideways as the track drew him under crushing the leg. A bone sprang through the skin from his thigh yet the Buddhist never flinched. The tank laid him back, the track sucking him up like a rough conveyor belt and crushing him into the road. The tank stopped with the Buddhist in the middle of the track. It twisted to the left making a complete circle, the one track stopped on the monk, the other grinding ahead. The head of the Buddhist pinched o⬚. An arm followed, raised up from the track and appeared to wave at the crowd.

Pete held his stomach and felt sick and ashamed. Why didn't he drag the monk from the street? James leaned over and gagged. Yet Pete wanted the monk to die, to see something he had never seen before, a tank crushing a man, food for his eyes. The waving arm and crushed head were the funniest thing he had ever seen. God, aside from being sick, how he wanted to laugh, to laugh off the whole war, to purge everything from his system in one huge fucking guffaw.

The tank crawled away. Bits of Orange cloth, and the arm, remained stuck in the tracks and resembled someone following a parade, flags waving, people chasing behind. Everything disappeared down a wide alley as an old woman snatched up the monk's umbrella.

"Mashed the shit out of that dumb fuck," said Clifton.

"You OK?" Pete asked James.

"I'm broke," said James, looking like one of the despondent laundry kids. "Loan me some money. I really need a drink."

"Lots of folks don't know anything about life. You're the first one I've ever met that doesn't even suspect anything."

Clifton handed him fifteen bucks. "I couldn't take your money for that kind of show. Get a real pisser on, maybe some hard liquor, and I'll carry you back to camp."

"Some deal."

Clifton helped him up. He had stopped gagging.

"I got business to finish. Then you can buy the first beer."

Clifton stepped to the counter where the merchant, holding another box of ammunition, waited. He grinned and bowed then yelled again into the back room. Clifton stuffed the box into his shirt pocket. The merchant smiled and held out his hand. Clifton grabbed him by the back of the head and slammed his face hard into the bin of medals. The merchant screamed. James looked toward the street, toward the remains of the Buddhist, a bloody patch blending with the red dirt. Someone had already covered the monk's body with powder so he would not attract flies and smell. The merchant banged against the wall his face covered with blood. The needle of a silver star had lodged in his cheek and the medal swung down the side of his face. Clifton spit across the counter and jerked down a row of silk. In the street, the dog had been turned loose.

They walked to a restaurant across from the Shell gas station. A man, filling his Lambretta, spilled gas onto his legs. He threw down the hose, tried to kick the gas pump, lost his balance and fell across the machine. Gas flew everywhere. An old man, smoking a cigarette, hobbled to his assistance. Pete entered the restaurant half expecting to hear an explosion.

Vietnamese crowded into the small restaurant. Smoke filled the room and the room smelled of rice, fish, nuoc-mam (a rotten fish sauce) and tea. A beaded curtain hung from the back wall and a small man with twisted fingers limped in and out taking orders one way, carrying food the other. His face wrinkled more with each step and, where an ear should have been, a hole sat oozing grease.

The only table rested by the window so they pushed their way to it and sat. The Vietnamese customers appeared to be engaged in intense conversations, chattering wildly and throwing their arms. Aside from the rice, nuoc-mam and tea, dishes of pork, noodle soup, heart, tongue, and intestines covered the tables. Coagulated blood, spices, piles of hot peppers, vegetables, pho soup and fresh fruit added to the smells.

Clifton cocked his M-16 and placed it on a ledge. The man with twisted fingers rushed over. He smelled of dead fish and tobacco. The grease emanating from the hole in the side of his head was light yellow. "What's hot today?" asked Clifton.

"Everything good." The man bobbed his head and bowed.

"Fish with nuoc-man," said Clifton. "Fish, fish," he said again and floated his arm across the table. The waiter bobbed his head and smiled. "Shoot," Clifton said to James.

"Pho soup." James shrugged his shoulders. "What's the international sign for soup?" Clifton slurped into an imaginary spoon. "Pho soup," James repeated.

"Also some macaroni and cheese," said Pete. Clifton thought for a minute then twisted up his fingers. He held his breath and squeezed off a loud fart.

"We fix," the waiter said. "Everything to you is ready."

"That shit stinks," said James.

"What?" said Pete.

"Nuoc-mam. It stinks."

Pete's M-16 was loaded, although there was no round in the chamber.

"So does pussy," Clifton added. Why the hell didn't he just shut up, Pete thought.

"I don't like it. I don't like anything here," said Pete, and tensed up and shot a quick look around the room. "I hate it all. This whole damn place."

"Fucking-A," said James. "Eat the damn Nuoc-mam. Just don't go into one of your fits and shoot up the place. It seems I take most of my time these days looking after you."

Pete jerked his chair sideways. James shrugged his shoulders.

"Fucking-A," said Pete. "What the hell does fucking-A mean? What does it mean? Got to mean something. Everyone uses it." He spoke to the floor and expected an answer. This was not a country; they had fallen down a rabbit hole. Monks became roads and people without ears listened to everything and guns became feet and tits attracted dinner.

"Don't mean nothing," said James. "You know that. It don't mean nothing, nothing don't mean nothing. There is no other way to survive. If shit meant something we would all go crazy."

"That's another one." Pete stamped his feet. "If it don't mean nothing, why the hell do we keep saying it. Why don't we shut the fuck up and go home?"

His outburst quieted everyone nearby until the food brought the chatter back. He did not move except to hold his cup of tea and scrape a finger around the rough porcelain edge. He wanted to get into it with Clifton. Just let him say something, anything. Who the hell did he think he was trying to run his life?

"What shit is this?" said James, his voice low and unsure. "We came to town to party and everything is fucked. You act like something's going to kill us. If it did we wouldn't even know it, or probably wouldn't even care."

"Nothing kills nothing here," said Clifton. He dipped his fish in the sauce. "When you get caught up with thinking, then you're fucked." The voice of reason, Pete thought. Just what I need. "You're a danger to everyone." Clifton prodded Pete in the arm with his fork. "You're a good kid. But you're fucked. You won't kill anyone and it's making you a hazard."

Pete spun around and looked Clifton in the eyes. Clifton took a big bite of fish and sauce. Nuoc-mam dribbled down his chin. "Killing don't bother me," he said, jumping to his feet. Clifton poked him in the belly with his fork.

"Keep that damn fork away from me."

"Would you sit down," said James. "If I don't poke you, you don't pay attention."

"Sit down," said Clifton. "Course killing don't bother you. Sit down." Pete slumped into his seat. "Getting wasted is part of the fun. That's not it, not what the problem really is."

"What then?" His face felt swollen.

"You ain't doing no killing." James looked directly

at Pete. Even he knew Pete's secret. Clifton continued. "James won't say nothing. No one else will either. They got feelings. Sometimes they don't like the killing so they understand. I got no feelings. Just my ass."

"Besides," said James. "It don't mean nothing."

Pete jumped up again. "What the hell do you mean? I'm out there with the rest of you up to my neck in bodies. You didn't see me puke when that damn gook got mashed."

"Can't keep this boy in his seat," said Clifton. "Sit boy, sit." This time Pete refused and he tightly gripped his M-16. "We saw you," Clifton continued. "Whenever we hit the bush. You shoot everything but the Zips. Now the killing's getting botched inside of you and you're making things dangerous for the rest of us."

"Fuck off. Nothing's inside me." He stepped back knocking over the chair but catching his balance.

"Nothing but shit. Sit down, would you." Clifton grabbed his shoulders and pushed him back into the chair. He rubbed Pete's head and stood behind him. "Kill someone. That's the ticket, isn't it? Just kill someone." Pete heard the words and tried to hold back the tears. He could never kill anyone. "Kill someone," said Clifton again. He massaged Pete's shoulders. "You been like this since the convoy. You're the best point man we have. No one minds that you aren't killing anyone." He worked up to Pete's neck. "You're brave and tough. It's your guts that are soft. You got to kill someone, any-one to get straight. Drop the hammer and clean yourself out." Clifton kissed him on the back of the head before sitting.

"Can I have your macaroni?" James asked.

Pete tried not to listen. Thoughts raced through him like an angry fly. He wanted to stay in the restau-rant with James and Clifton, never leave. His head spun. Time grabbed him and he was back on the con-voy, back in Qui Nhon on the convoy, before the re-turn trip, before the noise, before the flash.

Clifton sits outside the tent on the sand. Pete sits beside him. The night is cool and wet and they have not yet started to the base camp. Stars shine brightly overhead. Muffed artillery patters and sings in the distance, a dull hollow tenor sound. Tent lights cast yellow shadow on the sand. Clifton squats, Vietnamese style, on his haunches. Did you see him drive that deuce-and-a-half off the road on the way down? Clifton nods as Pete nods and con-tinues to talk. He ran down that old man with his truck. Knocked him a hundred feet. The old guy did nothing. Was walking down the road with a bas-ket of fruit. I know, says Clifton. It's not our busi-ness. Nam requires a different kind of sanity.

Clifton is drinking a beer. No bugs hover near, no creatures of any kind. Living counts, says Clifton. Re-member living.

Pete feels the sand trickle through his hands. The

sand feels good. Clifton knows. Sanity. Fuck sanity and Tiger beer and waiting to get our asses blown away. Pete still talks back then and that is how he feels.

Later, on the convoy back to Pleiku, back through Anh Khe Pass, there is the flash and the passage to manhood. Not now. Now there is the sand and Pete's voice.

Did Melvin show you his pictures? He photographed the battle, the dead bodies chopped up and piled like thick steaks. Arms and legs like twisted branches. On the same roll of film he had pictures of Grant buried in the sand. We gave him sand tits and a seaweed twat. The pictures were returned with all the dead, but with no shots of Grant. The enclosed note said they could not print the shots of Grant – people representing nudity are considered obscene. Such shots are against the law. Shit. All those bodies, people, piled on photo paper and they won't print a phony girl with sand tits and a seaweed twat.

"It only takes one," said Clifton. Pete tried to clear his head as he was drawn back into the restaurant. He wanted to be on the convoy now, to get the images over so they would not return. Clifton leaned across the table. James was finishing the macaroni and had pulled the plate to him. "You won't be killing, not really killing. You'll be letting yourself live." Clifton pleaded. "Drop the hammer on some

poor bastard. Take my knife. Cut that damn Biggilo's throat. No one needs it more." Pete drifted
back into the dream.

Everything is clear. He is there. He is here and there
as if time had no doors. His mind remembers apart
from himself, thoughts and body in different
places. It is morning. He gets drunk with Clifton
and meets a new friend, Sergeant Yama. They drive
toward Anh Khe Pass. They pass the old dead man
who is still beside the road, swollen and black. He
stinks. People walk past and cover their noses.
Pete remembers how much he stinks. Everything
dead stinks, especially humans, as if they started to
rot even before they died. The convoy drives past.
Flies cover the old man like a crawling hairpiece. Cut
him from my mind, Pete thinks. Rip him out. God
he stinks. Pete says nothing about the old man. It is
over. Clifton hands him a beer. He pees from
the moving truck, the yellow stream splashing up
over the tires. They laugh as piss flies everywhere.
I missed the prom, says Pete. This business
about the prom is serious. I wanted to love her
in a touching way like real people, feel the
softness, the gentleness, cover her like a
fine gauze. Not like now where you just fuck
the piss out of someone and are sorry you didn't split
her in half.
Love, he says. Simple bastard. Then it is
love, in the days of National Geographic

and beating off in the bathroom to naked Africans with flat elongated tits.

I missed the prom, he says. The air holds a screech. I missed the prom, he says. Are you sure it's a screech? A screech. He says it was a fucking screech. He's been to war. Don't you think he knows what the fuck a screech is? From making love to beating off and fucking as a punishment because a woman has brought you into the world and so now you hate them. That's what war is.

The jeep flips. It happens too fast. It hangs in Pete's mind. Clifton stops the truck. They run from the truck. There is gunfire, gunfire everywhere. Pete wants to be in love again. He doesn't want to fuck. He wants to make love, the joining of two souls rather than a wet twat sucking his prick. There is an explosion and the jeep flips and Sergeant Yama is gone. This is serious business about the prom. Could change your whole life. Hold on to the thought like a jewel. It could leave scars. Scars my ass. The jeep is over. Sergeant Yama is thrown to the side. Pete remembers everything. They are in the truck drinking a beer and laughing. The soldiers are in the jeep. He sees the jeep flip and the flying Sergeant. Why did they leave the truck? They leave the truck. Dumb bastards. One soldier, two soldiers. They chase manhood, chase a mad world. Pete runs to Sergeant Yama.

"Don't be pissed," said Clifton, trying to bring

Pete back. Pete smelled the nuoc-mam and the smoke in the restaurant. "I'm not pissed." This time, he tried to forget the convoy which only brought it back to mind. He wanted to hold on here, in the cafe. He listened to Clifton's voice as he drifted back toward the convoy. "Sticka knife in someone's ribs."

The air is filled with noise as the jeep springs over. Pete runs to the Sergeant. I am in the band, he screams. We are in the band. The jeep is over. Pete sees it. Where is the other soldier? The jeep. Look under the fucking jeep. An arm protrudes from under the jeep. Pete goes to the sergeant. The prom. It could have been great. I am in the band, he screams. The jeep is over. Someone stop the fucking noise. Clifton pushes at the jeep. The jeep is over and Clifton pushes at the wheels. The jeep will not move. Clifton pulls the arm. It comes away. A stump bloody of hanging meat and dripping arteries. Pete wanted to get a feel of his girl. The arm comes away. I am in the band, he screams. War is not like the movies. Clifton holds the torn arm in his hands. Pete wants to feel big soft tits. He wants one feel of his girl. What is this business about the Senior Prom, anyway? There's a fucking war on here. Snap out of it. Clifton turns, holding the arm. Raw meat hangs from the end.

Pete holds the sergeant, holds him gently. Turn

off the god-damned noise. War is not like the movies. The sergeant's chest is gone. Pete holds the Sergeant and tells him he is in the band, says it quietly, gently like a prayer. Pete holds the Sergeant gently, yet tightly like a ripped toy. He tries to hold the ripped flesh which wraps a pool of bubbling pink flesh. The ribs reach out like white arthritic fingers unable to touch, to feel.

The Sergeant is alive. His body is alive. Clifton is not angry. He drops the arm. Shit, he says. He brought his weapon. Why the fuck don't you shoot? Simple ass-hole. Pete's weapon is in the truck. He never thought to use the sergeant's. He did not need it. Pete did not need it. Shoot? Shoot what?

Clifton drops the arm and grabs his M-16. The other driver is having a beer in Qui Nhon. What does it matter, says Clifton. What does it matter that he ran over the old man beside the road? Clifton did it. Clifton ran over the old man and laughed about the killing. Killing is fun. The government has said so. How many times in boot camp did they have to repeat - this is for killing - the gun - this is for fun - the prick. In war the words reverse. Isn't that what every soldier is taught? It's the price you pay for getting old, says Clifton. What does death matter? he says. Death matters. Death matters. Death Must matter.

Clifton fires at the moving brush. He is not angry. Killing is business, not like the movies. Killing is a way to waste an afternoon in Nam. Shoot he says to Pete. They're coming. They're coming, damn it. Forget the prom. Some things you get over. You have exchanged a happy childhood for Vietnam. Your prom is here. Your dance is with death.

Pete holds the Sergeant. Are you praying? Never! Never again. Nam is ultimate freedom. People are afraid of freedom. Take your freedom and run. Get the fuck out. You can never be happy again once you've tasted freedom, made your own decisions about life, about death.

They're coming. Shoot. The sergeant's weapon is in the dirt. Pete holds the Sergeant. Pete tries to hold in something that is man, that is the Sergeant. He feels the thing there in the sergeant's chest. Pete fails. Without even trying, his wince twisting to smile and tranquility, the sergeant opens himsself up for death.

Pete does not move. He feels the "thing" slip through his arms, a thing not like the movies. Clifton shoots. Clifton also understands something. This is his time, his prom. He stands, grins and fires. Clifton loves this part of war. He is his own God giving and taking life. He laughs. Fuck 'em all, he says. It don't mean nothing.

Pete holds the Sergeant. Blood dribbles down his arms, the Sergeant's blood, the blood growing cold. Pete does not accept the loss, is not graceful, is not willing to try again. He shoots his fucking ass off that day. You should have seen him.

He bleeds through the arms, the sergeant's blood, now his blood. He feels a hard kick in his leg. He bleeds through the leg, this blood warm, this blood his. He does not care. He only feels the cold blood gelling on his arms. Some cold dead blood running onto his leg and mixing with his hot blood. Blood is a living thing. His blood also fails. War is not like the movies. He has lost. He is not afraid. He stands, lights a cigarette and shoves his hands into his pockets. Clifton shoots everywhere. The movies are dead. The prom is dead. Pete blows a strong wind of smoke. Wounded, with his hands in his pockets he walks slowly toward Pleiku.

Clifton shook Pete awake in the restaurant. Pete liked waking to the closeness of the people and their language, unintelligible, coming together in a fine buzz of varying tones. There is something good here, he thought, as they started to leave. The waiter short-changed them but Pete did not care. Life was good.

"I can use a beer," Clifton said. Sun dabbled through a tree webbing the street with shadows. Pete looked back through the window and watched the waiter jabber to an old man. "We'll find a bar by the laundry truck so Moses won't leave us. Get some ass for James."

"I don't need any ass, not in this place."

"Bullshit. You've poked every hole from here to Saigon. The best looking ones too." Clifton slung his weapon. "Makes no difference to me. Sophia Loren or Sunny Provo. You have even less taste but better looking women."

As they walked, Pete tried to change his sour attitude. He wanted to feel good again, to regain his youth and laugh with his friends, the intrigue of attempting to feel a girl's flesh rather than drop two bucks on a dirt floor as she rips her clothes off and you think she's fucking your brains out until you realize she's only reaching for the money that's been placed slightly out of reach. Sex must be more than about that. The convoy dream was gone replaced by sun and good friends. It's a good day, he thought, not believing it. The food was good. A day off was good. Friendships are good. They embraced as they walked toward the laundry truck. Beer, laundry, women and war make a man human, he thought. He was not sure why. It was true, there was something good here that did not exist any place else.

From the bar, a small shack with a yellow front, they watched the laundry truck. Pete scouted the entire building before ordering a drink. The unframed doorway held rows of colored beads, like most places, that kicked with every breeze. Several small tables crowded the dirt floor and a bamboo bar tipped against the wall. Beside another wall stood a juke box. There was a small room in back on which a cement slab was used for pissing and shitting. A ladder sloped to an underground mud cubicle, probably the fuck hole. Pete looked in.

Two thick boards covered with a thin bamboo mat, filled the cubicle. Girls sold themselves between the walls. One bare bulb and a pan of stagnant water rested on a board driven into the mud.

They sat upstairs with their backs against the wall and faced the doorway, gunslinger style. The seats were low to the ground and uncomfortable for an American. They were probably the same seats used for the French. Clifton spun the cylinder on his .38.

"Bring us boys a round of suds," he said in a cowboy accent.

"Make it snappy." He slapped the table. "Been on the trail for ages and we plan to do our riding indoors from now on."

The bar girl looked small and hard, older than most and was probably used by the French. She brought them beer and constantly rubbed her rough powdered face. A soldier at the bar sprouted a filthy look. Clifton slapped the bar girl on the ass.

"You're a good looking mare with a plump ass and a big mouth. We'll call if anyone here wants to break you." He threw an arm around James.

"You buy me tea," the girl said.

Clifton threw his hands to the table and grabbed the thirty-eight. "You want your tits shot off?" He drove her away with the gun.

"Someday they're not going to know you're kidding," said James.

" They got any food here?"

"You're a regular trash can."

"Oh yeah..."

"Good," said Clifton. "Real snappy."

The beer was cold and better than Pete remembered, better than the warm Korean Tiger beer in rusted cans he drank from conex containers at the base. They ordered another round and another. Each time the bar girl brought the beer, Clifton slapped her on the ass. She laughed and asked them to buy her tea again. Clifton chased her off with his gun. She did not weigh ninety pounds, most of that syphilis, and she had difficulty stomping the ground as she left. Pete played the juke box, some Bob Dylan, Joan Baez, The Rolling Stones and Sonny and Cher. He started to loosen up. He liked it here. He liked Clifton playing like a cowboy and he liked the way they sat together singing and drinking.

The soldier at the bar kept turning and staring at them, his eyes floating with beer and so thin his uniform looked empty. Over and over he rubbed his blond hair. Eventually he stood, weaving like a weak girder. He wore a red and yellow Lightning patch of the 25th Division. He was not interested in a good time as he staggered to the table.

"Fucking Fourth Infantry," he said, spilling beer from the bottle. James looked up at him. So did Clifton. Pete listened to the music.

"Problem?" said Clifton. Pete knew he held the .38 under the table. The bar girl stayed against the wall behind the bar. The soldier continued to weave.

"Fucking Forth Infantry," he repeated.

Bob Dylan sang. ...he not busy being born is busy dying...

"Sit." Clifton motioned to an empty chair. "I'll buy you a beer." He cocked the .38.

"I don't drink with chicken shits." Pete felt the heavy bass of the

song.

"...not much is really sacred..."

"We came here first," said the soldier, staking out his territory. "Not you bastards. We cleaned up. You fuckers are getting the credit." He leaned over the table. "We whipped them all."

James slid to one side.

"Appears you missed a few." Clifton grinned, his lips pushed up to one side. "Someone has to clean up your shit, to wipe your ass." Clifton kicked the empty chair from under the table. "Sit."

"...it's all right ma, I can make it..." Dylan sounded rougher than usual.

"Fucking Fourth Infantry. We can kick your ass any day. We did it all, cleaned up everything. What do you say to that?"

"Well," Clifton thought for a moment. "Thanks, I guess." Clifton calmly fingered the weapon, his thumb scraping against the hammer.

"...that's life and life only..."

"Last chance to sit and have a beer." Pete drank from his bottle. The beer tasted bitter.

"We're the toughest outfit in Nam." His knee collapsed and he hit his head on the edge of the table. When he staggered back up he pointed his finger at Clifton. "The toughest outfit in Nam." He worked his way back to the bar.

"Thought you might kill him," said James. "Every time we go someplace you leave a trail of bodies."

"The world's changing," said Pete. "Maybe I am too."

The girl brought another beer. Clifton uncocked his weapon and placed it on the table. The tall soldier whispered something to the girl and she frowned. She grabbed a bottle of beer and smacked the soldier across the nose. He staggered back bleeding profusely. The girl jumped onto his chest, wrapped her legs around his waist, and landed blow after blow with the bottle. The soldier danced and tried to swat her off as if she were an angry wasp. He tumbled to the floor taking the girl with him. The girl slammed him again and again in the face as he rolled from side to side.

"...It's all right Ma, I'm only bleeding."

Walking into the sunlight, Pete stepped over them. Outside, nothing had changed, just the shade grown longer from the trees. Their shadows dappled the hot buildings in gray rivulets. The air was warm and damp like a sauna. People rolled in and out of the shadows.

Pete walked to the small park in the middle of the

street. Clifton and James returned to the truck. Pete stood by the park as the shadows, like the fingers of a blind man, touched his face. His face felt new and young and as easily molded as wet clay. But like the rest of Pete, his face had grown hard and fragile, like porcelain that rejected the imprint of any touch.

Pete reached over to pick a flower at the feet of the Virgin. They looked out of place, cold and slick, like they had fallen from her eyes in shame and now cowered at her feet. Pete tried to derive some kind of symbolism from her, some metaphor, and fancied her trying to find her own symbolism, perhaps in the flowers which had been planted for her pleasure but which had betrayed her. Desperately he grasped for some meaning from her, some greater good. He looked back to the flowers then at her pitted face. Pete wanted to ask her something, to make one final grasp at religion, to return the ultimate freedom he had been given. He looked deeply into her eyes and watched a tear spring from one of them. Pete bent forward for a closer look. The tear became a drooping of fresh bird shit ready to mix with her coat of white shit.

He returned to the truck and squatted in the dirt. James and a woman were in a big discussion. Pete thought of what Clifton said. Kill someone, anyone. It sounded simple. He had a right to be happy. At home, his friends had girlfriends and dances and happiness. He just had Nam.

He pushed out the thoughts. He had his own plan. He had worked out the plan in the hospital at Qui Nhon where he recovered from the leg wound from the convoy. It was a simple plan. He wouldnot kill anyone. They could remove him from the band, they could shove him in a war, they could toss him into combat, they could drop him in North Vietnam. He would not kill anyone. Though he was in the middle of the war, he refused get involved. He would go about his business, would point the patrols, would drive convoys, would do whatever they asked. If the enemy came, he would fire in their direction. If they started through the perimeter wire, he would shoot the warning beer and pop cans that were filled with rocks and hung from the wire. Only if they crossed the last wire, the very last wire, would he aim toward them. Crossing the last wire changed the game. That opened a new perspective and he would be forced to kill. With luck the enemy would never get to the last wire.

"Let's go," said Clifton. He pulled Pete up. "Think about what I said."

They climbed into the truck and nestled between the fresh laundry. Moses drove slowly through town. It had been a busy day and Pete thought about the statue and about getting Clifton a medal. Pete moved to the seat with the M-16 against his arm. The sun sat low on the horizon, fat and orange, large accusing. Although Pete had never killed anyone, he knew he could never kill anyone in the future. Never.

Chapter 14

What started as a perfectly peaceful flight to Anh Khe ended in disaster for Pete. A chopper crew had called the band looking for a door gunner to replace a man on the sick list. Biggilo sent Pete. He did not mind. He knew how to use an M-60 machine gun and, if he took his travel sickness pills, should be O.K. A milk run seemed to be a better deal than another patrol. With just two weeks before R&R he would have rather hung around with James in the small apartment on Shaow Street with James' girlfriend Minou, her French nickname for pussycat. Ling Low was a pretty enough name but la-Minou seemed to fit - his little pussycat – a tiny little minx not rising even to his shoulders, a waist his hands fit around, feet like two cuddly mice, and a face the color of the moon. That's how James described her. James seldom got into town but when he did he always told Pete about her. Pete had never seen her so he had no idea how she looked. Minou always knew when James would awake and she always brought him a bowl of steaming pho noodle soup, careful not to bring chopsticks but rather a fork and a spoon. He had never mastered the sticks, even using one in each hand, and he was just as likely to jab himself in the eye or flip noodles up his nose as to capture any food.

Pete wondered if she would take another lover when James returned home. He imagined the conversation, running the play through his head.

"I will stay with you," she said, dropping her head onto his lap.

"You cannot go home with me," he said. "Not now. Maybe not ever."

"Then I will take another lover."

James stood and placed the bowl on the table then paced from wall to wall. "I will send you money. In my country we don't take lovers when a person leaves"

"I think they hide it," said Minou. "To survive I must take a lover. I cannot feed myself and my family unless you take me home."

"Something can be worked out," said James. "I will check with the general. We've killed enough Vietnamese we ought to be able take some of them home as an endangered species or a war souvenir, if not a lover."

She placed his jungle boots at his feet. He had nice feet and delicate features for an American, who were generally fat, ghostly looking, with poor complexions. Even more than the French, they stank of milk, and opulence and whisky. James was thin with fine black features and short black hair. He looked like everything she had read about concerning royal Africans even though he was not an officer, just a corporal. He laced up his boots and lighted a Cuban Cohiba cigar knowing he would not have time to smoke it unless he dragged it like a torch through the sweltering streets of Pleiku. Smoking was painful during the humidity of the day and best left to the evening when the air covered a man like a wet sheet and the smoke drove away the mosquitoes before they retired for the night.

"You will return tonight?" said Minou.

"We don't fly until tomorrow. Maybe not even then."

"Stay with me."

He walked out the door leaving her standing there dressed in spotless white, a yellow flower in her hair. That's the way Pete imagined it. His imagination had outgrown imagined images. Now that he understood that everything that existed did not exist except as illusion, everything he imagined was just as real.

"Crap," Pete thought. "He's not flying, I am." But

he thought of how nice it would be to have a woman, something warm under him, someone to come home to and to love.

Nothing changed from day to day. The streets still smelled of shit and diesel, fried vegetables, smoking Lambreattas and three-wheeled Cushman scooters with boxes on the back to hold people and guillotined bu☐ alo heads. Food venders hawked fried snakes, octopus, and country fish that no American would eat after learning they came from ponds in which villagers crapped to supply food for the fish who, in turn, supplied food for the people – the perfect eco system. Storefronts showed samples of brightly colored silk pillows stitched with pictures of helicopters, tanks, jeeps, and unit insignias of all kinds. Service medals, pounded from c-ration cans and hand-painted, rested in bowls on tables. Babies played in the dirt on the sidewalks where old men sat on haunches and sucked cigarettes through swollen lips often oozing yellow pus. Old women cackled, swung their arms about as if they had been scalded, and revealed black beetle-nut teeth punched through red gums at odd angles. Children surrounded Pete and begged for gum or money or offered up their sisters for one or two dollars and pinched their fingers together as proof of their vaginal tightness. The American soldier's generosity had ruined them, had ruined most of the people, the young girls spreading their legs for easy money, the street boys stealing and begging. The old people understood that the Americans had brought a great evil to their country and wished they would leave. No Americans, no war. There was nothing complicated about it. Pete had become an old soldier, an in country soldier, and offered the boys nothing, not even a smile that might encourage them. Only cherry soldiers offered gifts until, eventually broke and overwhelmed, started resenting all the people and would just as soon shoot them as anything else. Pete caught a hitch on a three-quarter ton truck that dropped him off at the field.

Sergeant Kelley tinkered with the cowling of the Huey's engine and did not notice Pete standing on a skid. Kelley ripped a fart and laughed at his own joke. He was fond of talking to himself and was the best crew chief in the outfit.

"Don't crap on yourself," said Pete.

"You going out with the crew?" He worked his way down the ladder.

"How many tours you done?" said Pete.

"Big number five." Kelley wiped his hands with a cloth. "How'd you know I been here before? They're sending me home after this one. They think I'm crazy to want another tour. You doing another?"

"I learn fast," said Pete. "Soon as I can I'm on the Freedom Bird to the world. Mind if I look things over?" He climbed aboard and checked the M-60, pulled the bolt, opened the loading latch, checked the boxes of ammo, sighted across the field at a jeep driving by.

"You won't like it," said Kelley. "Everything's changed."

"The protesters, you mean? I've heard of them."

"Not really. It's the indifference that hurts."

"You know, in all my time here I've never shot this thing except at some rice paddies just to watch the water splash. Never shot from a Huey either. I get sick flying."

"You're a lucky man. Few soldiers escape war with a clear conscience."

Heat waves shimmered from the tarmac in slinky little translucent dances that crawled through his blousing garters and up his trousers only to explode in puddles of sweat under his arms and around his chest and back. The wet shirt helped cool him as he entered the Won Hung Low bar, a non-com joint near the tarmac operated by the transportation company. He recognized Gypsy Lee, the other door gunner, slumped over the bar. His kaki Panama hat tilted to one side. They had talked several times before when Pete had wandered down to the choppers or stopped for a beer.

"I hate the waiting," said Pete. "I'll have a Tiger beer. Doesn't waiting bother you?"

"How do you drink that crap when you can have a Schlitz?" Gypsy Lee had bright dark eyes and an odd smile that curled at one side of his lips and regardless of how often he shaved coffee grounds stuck on his face. Honesty was not a word he understood but not a bad person if you ignored any of his deals.

"The formaldehyde appeals to me. If I get wasted my body will last longer." He gripped the rusted can.

"You act like a short-timer," said Gypsy Lee. "I've got another six months. Sometimes things happen to cherries and short timers. In between is fine."

"I hope to get out with no lasting injuries and a clear conscience. Nothing gets better than that. I'm looking forward to going back to work, if only to deliver papers."

"Funny we should be from the same city," said Gypsy Lee. Have you heard of the R.V. car lot on Meridian? My brother owns it."

"I spend all my free time at Esmeralda's, on Pacific Avenue, throwing empty beer bottles at the country bands." The bar had just gotten air conditioning that started to dry Pete's face. "Schoenfield's was built to be the biggest whore-house in the country. Not many people know that."

Pete glanced at the two bar girls chattering at a table. They were not supposed to be there, not inside the camp, but no one enforced the rule. Both wore flowered dresses cut low in front and the back and they entertained for a price, also against the rules. They knew Pete and Gypsy Lee and did not bother to rise and ask them for tea. Prying a dime from Gypsy Lee's hand took a crowbar and Pete never bought a woman. They waited for easier prey or for the rare occasion Gypsy Lee got drunk.

"Rose is the pilot," said Gypsy Lee. "He likes the officer crap, you know. Call him Mr. Rose. He's a warrant offcer; a dead rank that hardly counts. He's a damn good chopper pilot."

"He comes here every time?"

"Always" said Gypsy Lee. "He'll be here to get a snoot-full like he always does before going up. He's probably found a dice game in an alley. I've never met anyone so lucky on the ground or in the air."

When Rose finally waddled in he held out a wad of bills like a winning poker hand and laughed almost uncontrollably. The two bar girls jumped to his side and walked him to the bar. "You buy poor girls tea?" they asked.

"Tea, whisky, opium, anything you girls want as long as you slide your hands down the front of my pants." They faked shyness and took turns squeezing him between the crotch. "Oh, baby," he said, looking toward the ceiling and howling. "Maybe later." He pushed them back but they sandwiched him again massaging his neck and back.

"You the gunner?"

"My first time," said Pete, offering his hand.

"O-seventeen hundred," said Rose. "That's lift off." He pulled the whisky and water glass toward him. "It's nothing big, a short run and back. We have to have two gunners before we can fly."

"I don't even care," said Gypsy Lee. "If they waste me, they waste me. All I request is they bury me face down so everyone can kiss my ass."

"Give me the whole bottle," said Rose. "I can't wait for you to pour."

Rose was decent enough when sober but when drunk he was hard to take, obnoxious, demanding and crying for respect. He finished the bottle within the hour and ordered another. The bar girls, who had been quiet, sensed the weakened prey and stepped up their attack by rubbing his thighs and running their cheeks against him and leaving streaks of rouge on his skin. "Me very tight," said one, while the other said, "My mouth open wide and I no bite."

"I'm under a lot of stress," he said, grabbing one of the girls and walking between the beaded curtains to the back room.

"What kind of life is that?" said Gypsy Lee, adjusting his hat "and drinking and screwing. And on the base. Some officer must be getting a cut. Look at all the locals we have around here during the day: labourers, laundry girls, dishwashers, officer maids. The place is stinking with dinks."

"A soldier's life," said Pete. Within minutes Rose returned wearing nothing but his green boxer shorts.

"That's one she won't soon forget," he said, flipping up his arms and attempting, without success, to force muscles to rise from his fleshy arms. His pot belly seemed at odds to his boney hairless legs.

"You've forgotten something, Rose," said Gypsy Lee.

"Rose! Rose!" he screamed. "That's Mr. Rose,

soldier. Don't forget I'm an officer and you're just a non-com." His face swelled like an over-ripe potato.

"A warrant officer," said Gypsy Lee. He grabbed Pete's wrist, pointed to his watch, and shook his head with a wink enjoying the game. Pete didn't care. Rose would not remember anything later, anyway, and Gypsy Lee would probably deny everything. He would show up ready to fly with Rose and be just as friendly and charming as always, a perfect salesman.

"Let's get you dressed," said Gypsy Lee. Gypsy Lee ducked into the back room to get his uniform. The girls followed him and soon emerged looking disappointed. Gypsy Lee threw the clothes over the bar counter as Rose fell to his knees. He and Pete lifted him and he started to puke.

"My god, man," said Pete. "You're going to fly?"

"You bastards," said Rose, shoving them to the side and staggering toward the door. "I'm flying now."

They stood behind and watched him stagger outside walking zigzags across the road. A whistle blew and three M.P.s started toward him as he knocked over the wash table of a screaming woman.

"It's Rose," Gypsy Lee yelled to the police. "I'll leave his uniform on the bar." Pete looked at the door as if Rose might return. "Someday that bastard will be selling appliances at Sears or begging me for a job," said Gypsy Lee. "He'll be ready to fly. Don't worry. All the M.P.s know him."

Later, Pete thought of Minou as he sat on the Huey, his legs dangling over the side. They weren't leaving for three hours. Clifton walked up smoking a cigarette.

"I'm riding along," he said. It's not even an hour's flight." He leaned against the Huey's thin skin.

"What do you think of James and his woman?" Pete reached over for a drag on the cigarette. "He wants to take her home."

"Baggage," said Clifton. "She waits on James hand and foot but she's too smart for that to continue in the world. Too soon they all learn about independence and get bitchy and demanding and refuse to have sex except at her convenience and gain a hundred pounds and demand all the money and then has her whole family flown over to move in so they can all ride his ass. If he wants to stay with her he'll have to stay in Nam. She will never accept living on a farm in the south."

They talked away the afternoon, talked of home and women and Pete wondered if he had changed in any way, something he knew was impossible to know if they had all changed. He would only know that after going home and attempting to fit in.

"How's it going?" said Rose, as he walked to the Huey with Gypsy Lee. He patted Pete on the shoulder before doing his pre- flight check. He looked perfectly sober although Pete smelled the whisky on his breath. Gypsy Lee shrugged shoulders.

"I hope they fixed this crate," said Gypsy Lee.

"Sergeant Kelley said he is the best," said Pete, as he loaded a belt of ammo into the M-60.

"Crazy Kelley. They'll have to drag him home. He must be the only soldier in Nam that wants to stay here."

"Let's rock-and-roll," said Rose, climbing into the cockpit.

Pete scanned the field and saw two Vietnamese men just inside the perimeter wire and beside a watch tower. They talked to a little girl, a girl about four or five years old, and pointed her toward the chopper, directing her onto the field.

"There's a kid coming our way," said Pete. The whine from the engine twirled the blade but the engine refused to catch. Clifton sat on the floor, his feet hanging over the side an on the rail. "Don't let that little bitch get close," he said. "She has a school bag on her back.

"Come on," said Pete. "Take off." Heat shimmer rose from the ground along with a twirl of dust.

"I see her," said Rose, through his communication device. The blades whirled again and again refused catch.

"Waste her if she gets too close," said Clifton. "We can't take a chance of her blowing our asses to crap."

"You watching her?" said Rose.

"I can't shoot a kid."

"She's getting too close. Waste her," said Clifton. "She's probably packing explosives."

The little girl continued to trot toward the chopper. Pete could not yet make out her features. What if she had no explosives? What if she did? Was her life more important than theirs, or theirs more important than hers? Nothing ever went right in Nam, every decision a disaster, every decision wrong. Don't waste someone and get killed. Waste them and they are innocent. Take the left trail and get killed by a mine. Take the right trail and get ambushed by an NVA patrol. Don't move at all and catch a mortar round. Take a convoy to avoid an attack and get blown up with a road mine. Don't take a convoy and the trucks travel without incident while you su☐er an attack at camp. Every decision was wrong. Always wrong.

The chopper blades swirled again. The girl stopped a minute and picked up a rock from the tarmac. The Vietnamese seemed to be screaming at her and pushing their arms toward the field. Again she started walking. Pete pulled back the bolt and locked in the first round. She was close enough now to see her face, the face of a little girl, pretty and innocent with dirt rings around her lips and large eyes of hope.

"Dee dee Mau," Pete yelled, flapping his arms. She seemed to smile as she came closer and held out the rock. "Get this fucking thing going," he pleaded into his mouthpiece. Again the blades swirled then rolled to a stop.

"Don't let that cunt in," Rose insisted. "That's an order."

Gypsy Lee leaned across the chopper. "Come on, man, come on," he said. "Drop the fucking hammer on that little whore."

Clifton pushed Pete aside and grabbed the M-60 then breathed hard as he sighted along the barrel.

"Let me run out and grab her," said Pete. "She's just a little girl."

"She's too fucking close to be innocent."

"Come on, man, come on, you cocksucker," Gypsy Lee pleaded. "Rock her ass!"

Clifton placed the site on her chest. The blades of the chopper swirled. He fired a burst, knockingthe girlr over like a rolling football, the rocks flying into the air, as the engine finally caught and the chopper started to lift. The Huey continued rising as Pete watched the girl grow smaller and smaller on the tarmac and he prayed to god she would explode.

Chapter 15

Pete had been waiting for R and R, a chance to get away with James, find some peace and quiet, gather his thoughts, a time without Clifton. No luck. Clifton was there.

"I'm going across the street to the bar," said Clifton. "Get drunk and get a little ass."

They, and James, had been assigned to the Shamrock Hotel on Hong Kong. The arched entrance opened to an expanse of marble floor and Pete remembered breathing in the odors of cleanser and wax as he dragged his bag to the oak desk. Now, sitting on the stiff bed of the room, he toyed with the cotton bedspread. His bag slumped on a large cushy chair in the corner and he had draped his shirt over a smaller chair at the foot of the bed. A shamrock had been etched into the ashtray on the night table. Clifton had already changed into his jeans.

"You never used to be so crazy," said Pete. It was a bold statement, almost a confrontation.

"Well?" Clifton smelled under each armpit.

"I'm staying here for a while," said Pete. "I'll be over later."

"I could have bought all the ass in town by that time." Clifton winked. "War is good, damn good."

James lay on the bed and immediately fell asleep. The sun crawled behind the buildings. The yellow light, fat and dripping, was mirrored in a thousand windows throughout the city. Hong Kong seemed a land of buildings not of soil. The window was small and all Pete saw were buildings: buildings above, and buildings below; thin buildings of mottled gray; wide long buildings of brick, green under the eaves from heavy fogs; short buildings of glass and riveted girders. Bamboo scaffolding clung like webbing from buildings under repair and new ones going up. Dark creatures worked along the planks.

Pete rolled back to the bed. The setting sun yellowed the ceiling. The color grew deeper and widened down the wall. The sun set quickly like it did on ships or islands. The wall went colorless and Pete lay in the darkness and counted what he thought were seconds. How different they were from the seconds of home. Pete finally changed his clothes and moved onto the street. Clusters of solid light lit sidewalks of chipped concrete. Few vehicles drove the street, no bicycles, no rickshaws, just a motorcycle cop passing on his white Triumph. A black Mercedes and two yellow Austins followed. Colored neon lights worded large windows with Chinese and English letters. Pete moved across the street toward the bar Clifton had mentioned. A large Chinese in a bright shirt stopped him.

"G.I.," he said reaching out his stubby arm. You want woman?" He demonstrated by pumping a finger into his fist.

"No." Pete felt the condom nestled in a pocket with some change.

"Price good. Number one woman." The Chinese grinned broadly, his teeth yellow in the light.

"No." The lights cast the street in a dim kind of false daylight.

"Aaaah, but good one. Tight." His yellow teeth looked natural. "Got one woman. Tight one. You try; good price." He continued to flash his teeth and his pocked cheeks pushed his eyes tightly together.

"I'm on business." Pete looked toward the bar.

"Tight one. Must try." The Chinese was very insistent. "Clean. Good price." He grabbed Pete's shoulder as he pushed toward the bar. "I got boy too. Maybe you like a nice boy? Maybe even a duck or a goat? I got one nice duck, lay only small egg."

"I got no money," Pete said.

"Humph," the Chinese said, his grin now gone. He

reoccupied his corner by latching quickly onto another soldier.

The bar had a mystical quality to it, a certain unrealness of fog and gauze. Lights freckled the dark with hazy stars. Tables lined a wall opposite the well-stocked bar. Booths crouched deep in back under a smattering of drifting table candles. A girl in red silk danced with a tall skinny soldier on a small wooden dance floor. The rest of the floor was deeply padded and carpeted. The girls were shadows, shadows within shadows, small bits of fall, of changing leaves beautiful before pealing to the ground.

"Pete!" Clifton called from the dark. "Here. Here in the booth."

Pete walked toward the sound, past the dance floor. The dancing soldier, like a carried rug, groped over the girl's shoulders, his feet not moving, and she twisted him from side to side, a tiny pier holding a large dock. Pete stumbled through the dark, bouncing from table to table until Clifton grabbed his arm and pushed him into the booth.

"Thought you weren't coming," he said. He sat with two small women. One of them slid next to Pete. "This is the guy I been telling you about," Clifton said. "A real crazy bastard but one you can count on."

"You buy girl tea?" the girl asked Pete. She squeezed him between the legs.

"She's a regular sponge," said Clifton.

"Buy lonely girl tea?" she repeated. Pete nodded. She smiled. "What you drink?"

"Rum and Coke," he said. Before leaving to get the drinks she squeezed him again and placed her lips against his cheek.

"Ever seen so many beautiful whores?" said Clifton. "Ass everywhere." Another girl moved in next to him. He pushed them both forward. "Beauties aren't they?" One girl wore a tight blue silk dress, yellow flowers embroidered throughout. The other girl wore an identical dress in red, like the dancing woman. "Prime meat. Squeeze their tits and tell me which one I should screw first. Go ahead."

Both girls looked beautiful, flawless features covered in golden brown skin. Deep black hair flowed over their shoulders. Pete did not touch them, afraid he might fall in love with love rather than a woman.

"Go ahead," said Clifton. "I been here an hour and still can't decide." He scratched his temple. "Makes no difference. I'm going to fuck them both anyway." He was already drunk. "I'm going to fuck everyone in the place." He pulled the girls back. "Everyone but that bird dressed in yellow." Clifton pointed to a girl sitting alone at a small table. "Got V.D." The girl was small and looked like a clone of every other girl in the bar. "Only one here in yellow, too. I wanted to go through the entire rainbow before the night is over."

"Maybe she's not sick?" said Pete. The girls wore nothing low cut, all fabric went right to the neck. Slits rose lit up the sides of the dresses and the girls looked very proper and delightful.

"The other girls told me, some kind of rule I guess."

The girl returned with Pete's drink and moved in beside him. "Here." Pete threw a wad of bills on the table. "You keep hold of this money. It's stolen and I don't want any part of it."

Clifton fumbled with the bills, his eyes darting over each shoulder. The girls tipped toward the money like closing flowers.

"You crazy?" said Clifton. "You don't go throwing money around like that.

Pete leaned across the table. Clifton looked odd without his uniform. "The ass is on Biggilo." He stumbled over the sergeant's name. "Biggilo's buying all the ass you can screw." He nodded and sat back. The girl stroked his head.

"What do you mean?" Clifton asked. "Where did you get this?"

"Biggilo." Pete leaned forward again, tapped a finger to his lips and lowered his voice. "He's been saving this money in an ammo box under his tent floor. A friend of mine found it and gave it to me so we could have a good time. But I don't want nothing stolen. I knew it woulodn't bother you." He pulled Clifton by the arm and snared his head. "He should take better care of his shit." Pete flew back laughing. "Anyway, I took the money but he stole it, not me."

Clifton scratched at the table. "So, you're finally growing up," he said. "It's the first step leading to success. Be careful he doesn't find out."

"Careful, my ass." Pete slammed his hands to the

table. The girls jumped. "The bastard's got it coming." He almost spit on the table. "He's no fucking God." Pete quieted again trying to remember everything Clifton had told him. "Aren't we the first to be picked for patrols? Aren't we the first for convoys? Aren't we the first for every fucking thing around there? Bet your ass." His fist tightened around the glass. "You make a God out of him. Worship the bastard.

Not me. Not fucking me." Pete emptied the glass and sent the girl for another. "It's the money I don't want. Stealing isn't right. But I took it. I'm even starting to sound like you."

"Money's money," said Clifton, wadding the bills into his pocket.

Pete expected the drinks to be thin but they were filled with rum. The liquor felt good and bad at once and burned his stomach. Sweat sprang to his face. The girl licked his ear. "I rove you G.I.," she said. "No bull schick." She meant bullshit. They all meant bullshit. That's what love was - bullshit. Her soft hands rubbed between Pete's legs lifting them like two magnets. How could anyone fall in love with bullshit?

Clifton pushed his way between the girls and stood beside the table. "I'm injured," he said. He pointed to the wet lump in his pants. "I need medical assistance." He grabbed the girl in red. "I need help reducing this nasty swelling." The girl's black eyes reflected in the light. She was smaller than Pete thought.

The girl in blue pushed in beside Pete, her fingers running over his neck. He continued to sweat. I love you, no bullshit, he wanted to say, and say it with real feeling like bullshit had all the power of Christ Almighty. The first girl undid his shirt. Pete buttoned it. She undid it again. Pete smelled her soft neck, felt the warmth of her hands reading his chest like Braille. She rubbed inside his T-shirt. The girl in blue unzipped his pants. Pete leaned forward and gulped a quick drink. She fished for his prick. He wanted her hand there, wanted the touch but the lights were not dark enough in this dream, a dream where Pete sat naked in a classroom and no one, not even the math teacher flipping her curly blond hair and flaunting her big tits, noticed him shivering, his buttocks stuck to the hard chair.

"I think you dead, G.I.," she said. Pete jerked her hand off his limp prick, a flag with no wind. "Too long no woman." She replaced her hand. "You want me G.I.?" she said, with odorless breath as she squeezed his nuts. Pete emptied the glass. "Thirty dollar. Not much money for American G.I."

Pete yanked out her hand. "Later. Maybe later." He handed her the empty glass. She smiled and left for another drink. The other girl slid her hand in and Pete twisted it out and tried to zip his pants.

"Dance, G.I." she said. He buttoned his shirt. When he stood, the girl held out her hand and said, "Must have money for music."

They danced tightly to a slow song, feet dragging across the floor as she dry-fucked him. Through the silk of her dress, Pete felt her small tender frame. She smelled like an open field of flowers at sunset. In his ear, the girl sang off key. She scratched the back of his neck. He drew her closer. Pete thought of high school, American girls with their abundance of breasts, his '55 Hudson Hornet coupe and the midnight deadline to be home. But that was nother dream. Tonight's dream was a dance in small circles beside the swirling music. Pete got an erection. Pressing tightly against it, the girl blew on his chest.

When Clifton returned Pete was still dancing and slightly drunk. Clifton ordered a drink, slid into the booth and called to Pete. The liquor caused Pete to laugh and he kissed the girl on the forehead, pulled her tightly against his prick. After the dance, he stumbled to the table.

"Best ass I ever had," Clifton said kissing his girl hard. "Bite sized tits." He looked Pete in the eyes. "Get up there while the bed's still warm. War makes women vital and men feel alive. We like to breed when people are trying to kill us. It helps us know we will continue."

Pete weaved into the hotel room. Nothing in it was misplaced. Even the beds were made and James was gone. The wall steadied him and he started to sober. While the girl sat on the bed, he went into the bathroom and doused his face with water. He checked his wallet. The money was all there. The girl had not raised the price. He leaned against the door and lost all interest in sleeping with her. She scratched at the pockmarks on her face and her breasts were small dumplings and large feet hung from the ends of her thin legs. Lamplight worked against all relationships, changed perspectives. Beauty lived in the dark and he knew she was just one light switch away from beautiful. Pete felt nothing: no love, no hate, no emotion at all and somehow that seemed important. He sat on the bed opposite her and watched the floor, the thick dark carpet.

"Bath, G.I.," the girl said. She undid his shirt. His shoulders ached. She ran water into the tub. Outside, the lights of the city now sprinkled against the window. The girl helped him undress and she laid the clothes across the bed. Wearing just underwear Pete entered the bathroom. He felt the hot water, the bubbles snapping against his wrists. He slipped under the suds and let his arms float and the bubbles pop about his ears. He heard the door slam shut and he sat up, cocking his head. The room sounded unusually quiet. She must have changed her mind and left, he thought. He let the water flow back over him. No matter. He didn't want her, anyway. He had not felt so relaxed in months, no war, no Clifton.

He smacked the side of the tub, as if remembering something, jumped from the water and ran into the other room. The girl was certainly gone. His empty wallet lay open on the bed. He ran into the hall leaving a trail of wet footprints. An old lady with thick shoes glanced at him and smiled. He felt a draft and remembered he was naked. He jumped back into the room. The wallet resembled a small brown tent under the table light. He flipped on the radio and crawled back into the tub. The water felt even better this time, bubbles tingling his arms. The whole bathroom was white, clean, pure, inviting, a virgin inviting him to stay. Warm water held him tightly and he started to laugh at the situation, the missing money, the sex he didn't want and never had. He threw a bar of soap against the wall. Sticking his face in the water, he blew through his lips making little motor boat sounds. Money, after all, was the least valuable commodity in the world.

He returned to the bar and found Clifton with James at the same table. The dancing soldier had disappeared. Clifton appeared sober.

"I got screwed," he said.

"Atta boy," said Clifton. "You did it. Fucking-A." He slapped Pete's arm. "Didn't get the bitch in the yellow dress, the one with V.D.?"

"I been fucked."

"And I bet she was good. I knew it." Clifton stood. "A round of applause for my buddy." He clapped.

"Sit down. I been ripped off. The bitch took my money." '

"What?" Clifton pushed his way back between the girls.

"I took a bath and left the money in my pants. Shit!"

He hit the table with a fist. "What an ass hole."

"You ain't lying," said Clifton. "Can't let you out of my sight."

"Oldest trick in the book," said James. One of the girls rubbed his arm. Another one brought him a fresh drink. "Should of gone with you."

"Yes," said Clifton. "Stripped her down, spread her thighs and shoved it in for you." Moisture formed around the glass. Gloria played on the juke box. G-L-O-R-I-A. "How much she get?"

"Everything."

"You had nothing tucked away?" said James.

"Nothing. Four hundred big ones down the toilet." He tossed his head back and looked at the overhead light. "Four damn hundred." Another drunken soldier moved to the dance floor. The bar had grown crowded.

"I got enough of Biggilo's money to get us by," said Clifton. "Don't eat too fucking much and beat off if you're horny."

Clifton made another trip to the hotel. He returned later and found Pete almost passed out at the table. A young girl sat at his side rubbing his temples with her slender fingers. Clifton was just a dark haze. "You get your friend coffee," she said without looking up. James nodded. She moved his head to her shoulder. Her black hair shone in the dark. "Your friend very drunk. Must go to bed."

"That's what got him here."

"Coffee," she said.

The girl lifted Pete's head, pressed his temples gently and gave him a mild shake. Her nails worked over his collar-bone and she reached into his shirt and rubbed his chest. When Clifton returned with the coffee, she shot him a dirty look. She tipped back Pete's head and Clifton held his shoulders. The girl tried to pour coffee into his mouth. His shoulders quivered. The coffee slipped down, his mouth opened wider, he looked skyward, choked, then fell face forward onto the table and among the countless halt and lame in bars everywhere.

He awoke in his room with a cloudy head. His mind drifted beyond reach bobbing in a di□erent time, up one thought, down another and he fell back when he attempted to sit. A piece of time washed over him. Hopelessly he reached for it and tried to splash about in the countless seconds and minutes. Time, he thought, if I could just touch it, feel its shape. The dry rum tasted foul in his mouth.

Feeling, touching time was part of the enigma. Slicing, swatting or holding it was almost impossible. Time could not be infinitely divided because it was not a "thing" but a feeling. He splashed about in time trying to be saved. Waves of months, weeks and years washed over him. Bodies drifted past. Clifton. Sergeant Yama. Biggilo. Dead everywhere. He tried to put everything straight. Being and non-being were part of the same feeling, not two sides of the same coin but the coin itself. There was no side separate from here and the pain he felt and the rum he tasted. Yet, there was no here. Time and events could not be spent or saved. They simply floated about to be grasped at, but not reached, felt, or touched. Yet time remained buoyant and solid like an ocean floating upon itself layer upon layer able to float and to sink and to wrap itself within itself. He wondered if he had had this feeling before, this thought, or was he caught again. Who died, he thought? Someone. No one. He let time, before, present and after, soak in.

It was not time but a warm cloth that soaked his head. The cloth was removed and quiet footsteps entered the bathroom followed by running water. The footsteps returned along with the warm cloth. Smooth gentle fingers worked down his neck and onto his chest. Slowly he opened his eyes. A young Chinese girl kneeled over him. He could see his own reflection in her black eyes, deep and clear as if he had found a home there. Pete pulled her to his chest. "Yama," he said, remembering the sergeant, and cried quietly.

Clifton returned to the room later that morning. Pete sat alone reading a copy of In Hazard. "Where you been?" he asked quietly. "Breakfast, Pete boy. Have a doughnut." He threw a bag on the bed.

"Girl give you the book?" Clifton went to the bathroom and washed his face.

"You saw her?" He leaned over the edge of the bed to hear him better.

"I know everything about women. I helped her

carry you here."

"You know nothing."

"Women take to you. I know that much."

"She brought me breakfast before she left."

Clifton entered the room drying his face with a towel. "James fucked her," he said.

"What?" Pete put down the book.

"She wanted to stay with you and since all your damn money was gone, I let her." He finished drying his face and threw the towel on the table. "I got your watch. Didn't want her to steal it." He fell on his bed and pointed at the ceiling with a finger.

"What about the other?" Pete asked.

"What other?" Clifton piled his pillows and got comfortable. "Oh that." He started to light a cigarette and leaned over and offered Pete one. Pete shook his head. Clifton threw the pack on the nightstand. "James fucked her. She was that bitch in red. He said she was not a bad piece of ass." He drew heavily on the cigarette. "She paid for breakfast?"

"Not everyone's trying to cheat us." Somehow it did not matter who had slept with her. She had a job and she did it. The boy he had been at home would have been upset. Here, everybody fucked. It don't mean nothing.

"The shit they're not. She's a whore and you need to remember that. Sometimes, as musicians, you get confused."

Pete started pacing stopping only to look out the window. The city was covered in morning gold.

"She's a good woman," he said quietly.

Clifton jumped to the side of the bed and grabbed him by the shirt. The cigarette hung from his fingers. "Don't you fucking believe it." He pushed him to the bed and stuck his finger in his face. "You're here to get straight, not fucked up. Every bitch has a racket. She'll use that bush like some people use a credit card."

"She's nice, and decent," he protested, wanting to believe it. "You never used to be like this. We were kids once."

"Soldiers now, buddy - soldiers." Smoke rose around his face.

"You treated people differently," he said. "You act more and more like something evil, something bad."

"We all turn into something bad in the jungle. The longer people live the more bad they become. I only give people what they want. There's nothing bad about that."

"She's nice."

"She's seventeen and knows her shit. Cover your ass and your heart cause you're in for real trouble." Clifton turned away and mashed out the cigarette. "You want to be in love, want to be hurt, want to feel something just one more time. Days of emotions are over, just a distant memory you will eventually forget."

"She tried to help me." He grabbed Clifton by the arms and flipped him around. "She tried to help me."

"Don't be an asshole." Clifton spoke sternly. "Don't

fight me on this one. You can be a crazy, mean bastard, it's there in you, and I'm not looking for trouble. Just listen to me. Her name is Izanami and she came here to breed like all good Chinese girls. She wants something. All cunts want something." He lit another cigarette and handed it to Pete. "Look at buildings and walk around town. Leave the fucking to me and James. He likes it and doesn't take it seriously. You're the kind that always falls in love and then goes crazy."

The smoke rose from the cigarette. In the sunlight it mixed with particles of dust. He thought of what little time he had had with Izanami. She asked for nothing except to not report her sister for stealing his money. All the girls of Hong Kong were sisters. She needed the four hundred dollars for her family. Izanami would repair the damage. She promised to feed him and be his lover. Pete liked her. He knew that she liked him.

That evening, James and Pete went for a drink. The bar had already become familiar. Several girls, looking clean and lovely, danced to Purple Haze. Pete looked for Izanami. A sailor, already drunk, staggered around the floor dragging a girl with him. James and Pete sat at a booth. He had not seen Clifton since that morning. A tall Chinese woman with short hair sat beside them. She put her arm around James. "May I get you a drink?" she asked.

"Yes," said James. "You sound different."

Pete did not see Izanami, just the girl in the yellow

dress, the one with V.D. She sat alone. "Say something again."

"Heavens. Do you so enjoy the sound of proper English?"

"English. That's it," said James. "What gives? Aren't you Chinese?"

"One must remember that this is a British colony, of sorts. May I get you that drink now?" She walked to the bar.

"Quit looking," said James. "Your friend's a working girl. If you can't accept that, you can't accept anything."

"That doesn't bother me," said Pete. "Love and sex are not connected, not this time." He lied.

Two girls slid beside James. No one bothered Pete except to give him a free drink. As James got drunk, he excused himself and left with a girl. Pete returned to the room not knowing what he would find. James entered the room an hour later with two girls. Pete sat on the bed reading. "You need some cheering up," he said. "You're not going to piss away your R&R in this room."

"I'm going to take a bath."

"I can only have one of these at a time. Take one." James released the girls. "It's what you need and my Pap says to share with your friends if you have more than you need." He threw his arm around Pete. "Let's tie them down and beat them with our shorts." Pete smiled. "That's my Pete," he said. "Get some rope."

"You're a shit head. I'm taking a bath."

Pete locked himself in the bathroom and ran the water. In the tub he listened to a chorus of howling, wall banging, squeaking springs and screams from the other room. He stayed in the tub until he shriveled waiting for the noise to stop but the noise continued. Finally he dried, dressed and decided to sneak away. He opened the bathroom door slowly and stepped out.

"Thought I was screwing my head off," James laughed. You don't always have to fuck them to have a good time." He stood on the bed fully clothed, a girl on each side. He laughed again and jumped from the bed to grab him. Pete started laughing too. "That a boy," said James. He began to sing loudly. The girls joined in and they all locked arms and danced about the room in a wide circle twirling and twirling until they fell to the floor.

"Can we always keep it like this?" said Pete, his head resting on James' shoulder.

"Every good has to have a little bad," said James. "We can keep it like this until we can't stand it no more."

They all lay on the floor under the yellow glow of the overhead light and did not move or speak for a very long time.

As they had planned, Pete met Izanami after the bar closed and they walked the warm empty streets, sandy-colored buildings leaning in as if listening to a secret. He loved the feel of her, so tiny, so delicate, he could almost wrap his arms around her twice. He had never met anyone so precious. Fog rolled across their faces and they ran through the streets like lovers across empty fields, arm in arm, familiar in their shortness of time.

All of Hong Kong was open to them and Pete played an imaginary trumpet as Izanami danced and sang with a turquoise- colored voice. He swung her around and around, sweet salt air sticking to the night, finally placing her on a flat metal post like a jewel. She hugged him around the neck and smiled. He squeezed her tightly kissing the dew from her face. They stood quietly held by the fog, the empty street, the fruit colored lights, the buildings and the island. They needed no words. Each of them became the other, equally important and delicate.

All week long he filled the mornings and afternoons with Izanami losing himself in a dream where the characters rolled together and not one character could be plucked without a piece of the other clinging like morning mist. He forgot the war, forgot himself, forgot everything except time. He reached for it, tried to loop it around itself, tried to get it to run fast and slow at his bidding and tried to stop it from running from one place to another and tried to get time to run from here to here at his bidding. He wanted Izanami forever.

On his last night in Hong Kong, he held tightly to Izanami. They made love and ran through the streets and made love again as he tried to catch himself. He attempted to squeeze her into himself, suck her lips into his body, to hold and hold and hold and hold. He could not sleep, just watched her tiny head on the pillow, her face at peace. Twice he woke Izanami, held her, then let her sleep again. He thought he understood time but he understood nothing, only that, though the idea of love might linger, Izanami would be gone. He sat beside the bed, fully clothed and kissed her damp skin. Although he refused to watch it, the sun still rose.

"I'm not going," he mumbled to James when he entered the room. Izanami was dressed and sat beside him. "I'm not going back." She rubbed his back.

"You're going," said James. He stood by the door. "What are you going to do? You're no Chinese." He moved toward Pete. He held to Izanami like a kid with a new toy.

"Keep away. I'm not going." He jumped up holding Izanami in front of him like a small shield. "She'll take care of me. She said her friends will hide me and I will never have to go."

"Damn. No way, man." James look frustrated, pulled on his fingers. "Listen, you're out of balance and can't see straight. Follow me. Leave the girl. Your friends are in Nam, real friends. Any man who ducks his responsibility will die a coward. Cowards live forever and you don't want that guilt. Like all men you just need to fall in love again with the next woman you meet."

"No," Pete said, lunging forward and swinging at him. James stepped to the side and hugged him to the floor. "I won't go," he said. "They won't get me again." His voice quieted. "I'm happy and I won't go." As he lay there, he realized his refusal to leave was really an acceptance. In exchange for her love decency kindness, he had given her his last emotion. Nothing remained.

James handed him a twenty-dollar bill and hugged him. "Buy her breakfast. Say your good-byes and I'll see you on the bus."

That night they landed in Vietnam and the image of Izanami already started to mix with the growing clouds of his mind. He imagined her sitting alone at the bar in Hong Kong drinking unsweetened tea. She scraped a fingernail around the rough edge of the porcelain cup. Another woman slid across the table from her. She counted out two hundred dollars, Izanami's share of his stolen money. Izanami placed it into her dress and walked to the bar. She sat on a stool. Bob Dylan played on the juke box. Quietly she sang the words to herself. "...Take me on a trip upon your magic swirling ship..." She lit a cigarette and crossed her legs as they neatly kept time. Smoke framed her face and she looked into the street for passing soldiers. Life could be no other way for a soldier.

And besides, Clifton was with him.

Chapter 16

The flare hanging over the burnt sticks of the village revealed itself as something other than a star. The glare, the flutter, the core glowing white and brilliant and trailing off to the look of dirty glass made it something not to wish on, not to follow. Pete watched the light drift down trailing a faint cloud past his bunker opening. The flare cast hard shadows against the village where only lizards lived. Pete searched the sixteen rows of perimeter wire and beyond where the light dimmed into jungle. The flare, tied to a parachute and flickering out, was immediately replaced.

Pete leaned away from the opening. Nylon from his flak jacket irritated him, caused his back to sweat and run cold. The bunker was still damp from the last rain and smelled of dirt and old roots. Pete dropped his helmet to the clay, reached into a torn pocket for one of his last three unfiltered Camels, and placed one between his lips. He cupped the burning match close to the pack and read: "Earn your High School Diploma at Home." Throwing the matchbook to the ground, he inhaled deeply. The smoke twisted into the air, lit by the dying flare. In a corner, he heard a rat chewing. During the First World War they were called corpse rats. Here, they were just rats, huge ugly-toed creatures with wire tails and interlocking teeth.

Pete's hand shook as he drew the cigarette to his mouth. Where was Clifton? Pete wanted him back, wanted him close. Unless balling the washer woman, getting high, beating off in the can, Clifton was dependable.

Pete stepped to the rear of the bunker and stood in the shadow of the entrance. Another flare ignited casting light against a long row of bunkers. Sandbags, old, the color of red earth, tipped unevenly from the bunkers. The new plastic bags looked slick and gray in the light. Planks, runway stripping, sandbags, tarps and ponchos, covered the tops. A one-five-five fired two quick rounds. Light sparkled from the beer cans dangling on the barbed wire.

Pete finished his cigarette and returned to a seat of sandbags next to the front opening. Two rifle slits had been built into the bunker beside the main opening. The bunker smelled of mildew, sweat, semen, stale beer, dead rats, C-rations, brass, plastic, canvas, upturned earth, moldy air, and sweet burned gunpowder.

Pete heard footsteps outside. Clifton pushed his way into the bunker and unloaded an arm load of tin cans. "Party time," he said.

Pete remained motionless in the dark while Clifton rummaged through the cans. Slowly raising his arms, Pete pointed his Smith & Wesson 38 at Clifton's head. He had an idea about time and wanted to experiment. Time had something to do with the pistol, with Clifton, with war and with death. He was not sure of the connection, only sure that there was one.

Clifton fumbled for a flashlight. Pete aimed at the black shadow curling around the floor and placed the gun barrel directly at Clifton's head. Clifton finally scratched a match. The light outlined him in yellow. His hair was black and thick and the sweat on his neck had turned to a fine mud that discolored his collar. The match burned down lighting his thick red knuckles.

Pete placed his finger on the trigger. I'm going to blow your fucking brains right through a sandbag, he thought drawing back on the pistol's hammer. The seconds knocked together, swayed apart, as time teetered against his thoughts. The cylinder clicked into place. Clifton turned as the match dimmed out.

"Help me with this shit," Clifton said. "Where

is that fucking flashlight?" He reached under a cot. "Got you." When he clicked the switch nothing happened. He tightened the plastic end cap, rapped the flashlight against his palm until it flicked on. He shone the light against Pete who sat quietly smoking a cigarette.

"You're not homesick again?" said Clifton. "Look. I scrounged all kinds of crap for a Christmas Eve party." He cast the light over the cans and bags, then gathered up the pile and tossed each one onto a cot. There was a whole cooked chicken stuffed into a can, a blue can of Planter's nuts, cranberry sauce missing half a label, candied yams, colored marshmallows, and two aluminum tins of Jiffy Pop popcorn. A bottle of Sly Fox wine, a box of toothpicks, a paperback of Heart of Darkness, and a box of Trojan condoms completed a second pile.

Clifton sorted out the treasure placing the cans to one side and the bags to the other. "Smile," he said to Pete. Clifton knelt beside him and tugged on Pete's cheek and shook his face. "One little smile for Clif. Tomorrow is Christmas, for Christ's shake." He squeezed Pete's nose. Pete jerked away.

"That's the old Pete," Clifton said, sitting on the cot. "We got to make our own fun. A Cherry's coming out later and we need to break him in right."

"It's Biggilo," Pete said, not wanting to think about a new man. He hated Cherries, hated breaking them in.

"Big deal," Clifton said. "So the bastard sent us out

on Christmas Eve. What's one day from another over here? We'll survive like we always survive. Biggilo's dead meat anyway. Wait until we get him on a patrol, then see who returns." Clifton fumbled for his cigarettes. "Got a smoke?"

Pete shook his head.

Biggilo had been on their asses every since they landed; sent them on every patrol, on every convoy, on every listening post, on every dangerous and dirty detail he found. Pete had had enough. If anyone needed to find his place in time it was Biggilo.

Clifton tore open a box of C-rations and removed the slim carton of Kools. He lit one and handed the other one to Pete. "His time will come," Clifton said. He stuck the box between two sandbags. "Besides, tonight is Christmas Eve. Big John's got a whore in bunker eight and there's going to be ass for everyone." Like a fly, Clifton rubbed his hands together. "Light the stove, let's get things started."

Pete assembled the small sterno stove by clipping the four sides into place. He worked the stand into the clay. The cans of sterno were stored under the cot and Pete pried the lid off one with his bayonet, lit the grease and watched the quiet blue flame. Clifton cracked the edge of the chicken can to prevent it from exploding. Pete worked the key around the can of nuts and shared them with Clifton. Thick fat from the chicken started to liquefy and steam rose from the can. Pete stuck his finger into the fat seeping from around the lid. The fat tasted like tin and wet feathers.

Pete stepped outside. The night had thickened and pinched against stars and Pete found the air diﬃcult to breathe. With each breath he tried to catch time, organize the world in his mind. Lately no thoughts stayed with him. Pete understood something that could not be put into words, something about time, and about death, and about everything he knew.

He lit a Kool he had taken from the pack. Dark shadows moved across the road. Pete thought of Sergeant Yama and the days of confusion that now seemed so far away.

At first, with the death of Sergeant Yama, Pete felt confused about the world. Since then he had thought a lot about time and death. Pete realized that as each event happened, it no longer was. The fact of BEING stood as pylons marking the param-eters of NOT being. He leaned against the bunker watching the stars nailed to the night. Even they were a myth. He saw only the light cast off thousands of years ago. Many of the stars he could see did not exist. Pete thought of Sergeant Yama and remembered the convoy and the jeep carrying the sergeant. A mortar round had hit the jeep. The sergeant was there, then he was gone. Pete ran from his truck to hold the mangled sergeant. That is when he first thought about time.

Pete heard the faint patter of chopper blades mixed with the fine buzz of invisible gnats. He tried to hold his thoughts straight, line them up like telephone poles. There was no death in the world because there was no instant of death. By the time the news of death reached him, regardless of how immediate, how sudden, how instantaneous, whether he held the Sergeant or not, whether he tried to frantically knock life back in, dam it up or tie it off, the fact of death became irrelevant. Wasted energy. No point. What he knew of Sergeant Yama, was not Sergeant Yama. What happened, if it happened, happened before understanding, before time. The only reality that existed was the next instant even before it became the next instant. That was what Pete understood, was what kept him alive, shielded him from being homesick. Nothing had changed except his understanding.

Pete wanted to explain his idea to Clifton, let him know the secret. Yet he knew that Clifton would only laugh at his idea in a way that was not cruel. The blue light from the sterno stove sprinkled against Clifton's face as Pete entered the bunker. Clifton fumbled with the lid of the chicken can. Pete gouged a hole in the clay with his bayonet, dimpled his poncho into a bowl for the chicken. Another flare fizzled outside leaving a jagged cut in the night. A battery of 105's fired a salvo that shook the earth and brought comfort to Pete. Clifton worked the can over to the poncho and poured in the bird. Fat steamed under the wings.

Clifton pulled at a leg. The bone slid out. The meat peeled away. "Tender," he said jabbing the meat with a lint covered fork from his pocket. Pete joined in. The bird tasted better hot and was soft and creamy almost like a firm pudding. Clifton cracked the can of yams and placed them on the stove. Because of the cooking sequence, they had learned to eat one thing at a time. Clifton spooned out a large scoop of cranberry sauce.

Pete leaned forward and peered through the window. Something in the barbed wire moved. An animal was caught. Pete tried to identify the creature. Under the dying light of a flare it jumped shaking the wire. He knew the animal would free itself. Voices from outside caused Pete to tense. Clifton licked his fingers. Pete's stomach churned.

The cold sterno light halted the captain as he entered. He had thinned over the last few months and heavy crow's feet scratched around his eyes. He had been a captain for too long. Because he was not afraid to remove his shirt and string barbed wire, not afraid to make mistakes, not afraid to be afraid, the troops liked and respected him. The captain smiled. The Cherry stood stiffly beside him. The captain had aged. Gray streaked his dark hair and his lips were dried and cracked. Pete realized they had all grown together. Only the Cherry appeared young and fresh, his uniform still pressed.

Trying to ignore the new man, Pete thought of the convoy when Sergeant Yama died. Pete had held the body in his arms and cried, although there were no tears, and he was later sent to the hospital at Qui

Nhon. A doctor said Pete was homesick, that he would recover from the war. But Pete remained homesick until he sorted out death. One day, as he had coffee with Paul, an M-60 gunner, he tried to assemble his philosophy. Paul stood to stretch when an enemy sniper killed him. His face, half severed at the neck, blew apart like a dropped ripe tomato and he fell at Pete's feet. Pete kicked him away and finished his coffee. He understood that Paul, like Sergeant Yama, was caught in time and that nothing meant anything, and he was no longer homesick.

"Have some food," said Clifton.

The captain shook his head. "Duty, and all that shit," he replied pushing the Cherry forward. "This is Noons. Show him the ropes. No sense you being out here by yourself." The captain grabbed a handful of nuts and marshmallows before leaving.

Clifton stepped forward to shake the Cherry's hand. "Clifton's the name. That's Pete at the window." Pete looked away trying to spot the animal in the barbed wire. It resembled a rabbit. "We're having Christmas Eve dinner. The bird's about gone. Try something else, nuts or something." He steered Noons, who s ill had no night vision, to the cot. "Look around," aid Clifton. "It's the only home we've got."

Pete watched Noons take inventory, watched him frown at the stove's fire, the unguarded rifle slits and openings. Everything about Noons was Cherry: regulation polished combat boots, pressed uniform smelling of starch and Tide soap, untaped rifle sling, Old Spice, Brylcreme and Pepsodent. Even his stripes, Stateside yellow, glinted against the light.

"I just ate," said Noons. "Thanks anyway." Noons played with his rifle sling. Clifton crossed his legs on the clay, reached for more chicken, slobbered grease down his chin, and blew a wad of snot against the wall. Pete wondered whe

Noons would ask THE question.

"Been here long?" said Noons. He still fiddled with the sling. The

metal rattled.

"Came over on the boat, Pete and me. Been tight ever since." Clifton wiped the grease from his chin. "We go everywhere together, even screw the same women." Noons stiffened his head. "Pete in front, me in back. It's a buddy system that works."

Pete tried again to find the animal and waited for another flare to light the wire.

"Where you from?" Clifton said. He opened a can of crackers with his John Wayne. The lid cut his finger. The finger bled onto a cracker.

"Iowa," Noons said. "My dad's a trucker. Has a beautiful red International with a Cat engine."

"They proud of you?"

"They don't like this communist stuff."

"Wouldn't know." Clifton ate the bloody cracker. "Pete and me ain't never seen no communists."

"None?" Noons looked startled.

"Not a one."

"You mean you've never killed anyone?"

Pete jerked at the question, the one they all eventually asked. He tried to close his ears, tried to concentrate on the animal. A flare lit the wire. Pete wanted the animal to go free. It wrapped itself tightly around the sharp barbs.

"Killed lots of Gooks," said Clifton. "Look at this." Clifton eased a necklace of dried testicles over his head and handed it to Noons.

"Looks kind of odd," said Noons.

"You get one for killing Gooks," said Clifton. "No one gives a shit about killing commies." Noons fingered the necklace. "Try it on."

Noons placed the testicles over his head, pushed out his chest and attempted to see them in the dark. He had developed no night vision. The necklace fit loosely.

"They feel like wads of gum," said Noons.

Clifton worked the yams from the stove. They had burnt on the bottom. "I got that one for killing Gooks on a convoy," he said. He blew on his fingers. "Pete was there."

"Did you get one too?" Noons asked Pete. When Pete said nothing, Noons looked disappointed. He fingered the large beads again.

"Don't mind Pete," said Clifton. "Doc says he's homesick. He got one like the rest of us. Won't tell anyone, is all." He leaned over and slapped Pete on the back. Pete twisted away. "Pete started a lot of shit." Clifton sat back. "Now he's just homesick."

"What are these made of?" said Noons.

"Nuts." Clifton fished out a forkful of yams.

"I've never seen nuts like these." Noons compressed one.

"Only grow in Nam. Lots of them around." Clifton placed the yams into his mouth and quickly spit them out. "Damn that's hot." He blew on the next forkful.

"Can you eat them?" Noons scratched at his neck.

"Shit yes," said Clifton. "Tough though, especially when they're dried. Try and crack one open." He licked at the yams. "Go ahead, they'll make a man of you."

Noons placed one in his mouth.

"They feel spongy, like a dried prune," he said. "Where do you get them?"

"From the Gooks."

"They sell them, or what?" He bit again.

"Grow them like everyone else," said Clifton. "Got these at harvest time." He rubbed his tongue across the yams. Pete wanted to laugh but he thought laughing looked stupid on an old soldier. No true soldier ever laughed in the presence of a Cherry.

"Do they grow from trees, or in the ground?" Noons tried to crack a different one.

"Special place," said Clifton. "Got to cut them and let them dry before you get a necklace."

"Where can I get one?" said Noons.

"Find you a Gook and reach up between his legs."

"What's that?" Noons stopped chewing and cocked his head to one side.

"Gook nuts," said Clifton. "Haven't you been listening?" He drew his finger across the air like a knife. "You kill the little bastards and snip off their nuts."

Noons jumped to his feet ripping off the necklace and spitting.

"What kind of shit is this?" He gagged and smacked the wall.

"You don't have to kill them first, but we figure it's sort of a humanitarian thing." Clifton talked through a mouth full of yams. "Want some?" He held the fork to Noons.

"You're fucking crazy," Noons screamed. "I'm a corporal. You're asses are going on report." He continued to spit.

"Won't do no good," said Clifton. "No one gives a shit about rank. Try some of these nuts?" He handed the Planters peanuts can to Noons. Noons waved his arms at Clifton. "You're just flying off the handle. Sit. The captain told us to teach you some shit. You just learned something." Clifton grabbed his M-16. He placed the Jiffy Pop on the fire. "Give that a shake every few minutes. I'm inviting some of the guys over later for a party."

Quiet fell over the bunker when Clifton left. Outside a star shell swish-popped and floated aimlessly down. A momentary breeze jiggled the rock-filled cans tied to the rows of barbed wire. Pete lit another cigarette. Noons huffed about the bunker. The

Jiffy Pop started snapping and the aluminum foil swelled. Steam rushed from the top. Reluctantly, Noons shook the container. He placed the package on the clay.

Pete said nothing. Noons sat on the cot. The moon had grown round and large but cast little light. Pete counted the rows of wire and imagined crawling through each one trying to escape something, the war perhaps, or maybe even time. There was life beyond the wire, beyond the jungle. Pete saw the animal. It was dead.

Noons chewed a few kernels of popcorn. "Want some?" he asked Pete. Pete jerked on his dog tags and looked directly at Noons. "I done nothing to you," said Noons. "I've been friendly and everything and you have to pull that on me. I came here to kill Gooks same as everyone else."

Pete cringed. He hated Cherries using the slang. Noons had not earned the right to say Gooks, or Zips, or Slope-heads. That only came with time.

"I was first on the rifle range and can run a bayonet through a six- ply tire," said Noons. He shrugged, blew out the stove and rolled to the cot.

Murphy burst into the bunker. Packages of gum bulged from his pockets. "We got trouble," he said. He motioned slowly, his arms making horizontal circles. "Joe saw some shit with his star scope." From his pants he produced three cans of Tiger beer. "Sappers in the wire." He fumbled with the cans as he spiked the lids with his bayonet. "James sent them.

He got tied up." He handed one to Pete and one to Noons. Noons looked sick.

"There's a shitter out back, across the ditch and beside the tanks," said Pete. "Go!" Pete jerked his arm toward the exit. He knew Clifton stayed away because of Noons. Pete lit the stove and filled his canteen cup with water. He felt around for an open C-ration box and removed the coffee, tossing the cigarette box to the cot.

Noons returned quickly looking pale and breathless. Pete laid his M-16 in the bunker opening. Outside, nothing had changed. He checked his clips. They were taped end to end. He had stacked a small mound of clips behind a sandbag. Pete knew that Noons was holding back the panic. He would think there were not enough rounds, that they were too small, not capable of knocking a man down. Even Noons' marvelous feats with a bayonet and a six-ply tire would appear inadequate. The bayonet would not even fit an M-16. To Noons, everything would suddenly appear ridiculous.

Pete tapped the flashlight awake and moved the light around the bunker. Men had piled other clips into long open slits. Overhead, grenades dangled from strips of nylon parachute line. Bayonets protruded from between sandbags beside each rifle slit. Two unraveled condoms, one filled with cigarettes, the other with matches, dangled from a beam. A Colt .45 dangled from a belt below the slits and to the right. Five boxes of ammunition sat on the ground around the base of the sandbags. In the center of the bunker, a box of grenades was buried with only the top exposed. A 12 gauge shotgun, a Buddha, a crucifix, a Tao symbol, a star of David, a communist hammer and sickle, and a poster of a naked woman being screwed by a pig, were all jammed against the bags. Overhead, a horseshoe and a bra were nailed side by side. Pete let the light fall on each object and grinned. Nothing felt better than home.

The ground shook with the dull thud of artillery and the night burst alive with light and the jagged white bones of busted flares twisting to the ground. Too much light with too much contrast lit the wire. Pete could count every barb, every blade of grass. The area looked like a poor photograph, overdeveloped, contrasty. Noons jumped to a rifle slit and fumbled with his weapon. He drew back the bolt, tried to unlatch the safety.

"I can't see anything," said Noons. " Not even with the light. My hands are numb."

Pete watched Noons squint beside the slot. Because of the changing light, the ground and the wire appeared to shake slowly. Pete relaxed and stirred the coffee knowing the base camp was too large for any full scale attack. Charlie might pitch in a few rockets, fling in a mortar round or two, maybe some small arms fire, nothing more. This was no Dien Bien Phu, no beautiful French defeat.

Weapons crackled from the bunker line. Artillery

fired another salvo. A tank, rattling the bunker, moved quickly on the road clattering evenly, smoothly. Pete glanced out the large opening and saw lights high in the sky. Noons shoved his weapon through the slit.

"Still blind?" said Pete.

"I can't see anything on the ground."

"You will," said Pete, holding back a smile. "This is the farthest you'll ever get from home."

The lights drew lower and flickered out replaced with the sound of airplane engines. Colored flares ignited across the wire. A solid stream of red and yellow tracers ripped from the sky, painting the earth. Bullets arched down from Puff, a gunship flying in a wide circle. The hosing continued, tracers eating across the landscape. Blue-green rounds from the enemy spun from the ground into the sky and fanned out. The bunker line opened up with red-yellow tracers. Lines of blue-green answered from beyond the wire. The horizon flashed with bursts of artillery fire. Everything appeared to be splattered with puffs of electric paint, streaks of neon, and smears of dusty-colored star shells.

Murphy fired from the opening. Noons did the same, every round a tracer, a stupid Cherry mistake because they made a straight line back to the shooter. Pete watched the yellow streaks cut past the wire into the brush. He poured two cups of coffee and handed one to Noons. Noons knocked it away and started to cuss.

"Just trying to be friendly," said Pete. "It's tough when you're out this far. Some men never find their way back."

Pete placed the cup in the rifle slit, felt the tension of Noons' finger clutching the trigger. Murphy occasionally quit firing and drank Tiger beer. Pete brewed more coffee and ate a marshmallow.

"Goddamnit," Noons cried out.

Pete shined the flashlight on Noons. His weapon had jammed. Noons jerked it back through the slit, banged it against the wall. Murphy turned for another drink of beer and changed clips. Several enemy rounds chipped at the bunker. Noons ducked below the slit. He slugged the bolt, twisted, hammered, sliced his hand on the steel. Blood squirted down the weapon.

"Jammed shell in the extractor," said Pete, calmly like an instructor. "Use your bayonet."

Pete pointed with the flashlight. Noons grabbed the bayonet and rammed the blade into the M-16 attempting to work out the shell. More rounds chipped the bunker. Murphy drank again. Light from a shell-burst caught Noons slamming the bolt of his weapon forward. Pete spotlighted Noons again. Noons fumbled with a full clip, panicked, pounded the clip in and shook the gun wildly. Blue tracers hit the bunker as Noons' weapon discharged knocking Murphy back into the darkness, shot through the throat. Noons stopped, looked at his weapon in disbelief.

Pete threw down his coffee, ripped apart a fresh medical dressing, and jumped to Murphy's side. His pulse was gone. Pete did not bother to turn him and instead, blew out the sterno stove. Noons had not moved. Pete turned Noons around and shoved his weapon through the rifle slit. He placed Noons' hand around the grip, his finger around the trigger. Already the action had started to slow. Pete sat at the opening, took careful aim and fired 1 ke a clock every few seconds. He never flinched. He never missed. A beer can flipped around the wire with every shot. Noons continued to fire, even after the action had ceased.

Pete stepped outside to piss. He returned to find Noons still at the slit, holding the weapon, the barrel glowing red in the middle, his hands knocking against the metal. Pete grabbed Noons by the shoulder, let him drop to his knees. Pete relit the stove to heat more coffee. Clifton entered the bunker.

"Give you a hard-on?" Clifton asked Noons. Murphy's body was barely visible in the sterno light.

"Got the flashlight?" said Clifton, when he saw Murphy. Clifton slapped it awake. Murphy lay face down in the Jiffy-Pop, the back of his head split open like a wet red and gray flower. The bullet had apparently hit his spine and bounced through his skull. Packs of gum and empty shells surrounded him. Clifton rolled him over. Popcorn stuck to his face. Clifton shone the light in his eyes. "A clean kill," he said. "Opened his throat and climbed out his skull.

That ruins the whole damn party." He kicked Murphy hard in the side. "I'll bag him and tell the others." He dragged Murphy to the exit. Pete helped thread him through the opening.

Noons started to puke. Pete shoved his head out of the opening. When Noons finished, he lay across the sandbags and cried. Pete poured him a cup of scotch from Clifton's canteen and felt in the dark for the necklace. Lifting Noons by the shoulders, Pete placed the necklace around his neck. He handed him the drink. Noons still shook. The bunker was empty. A star shell fizzled in the distance. Pete placed his arm around Noons.

"It's OK," said Pete. "You're just a little homesick."

Chapter 17

The artillery had done its work. Little remained of the village - an occasional smoking hooch, some bodies twisted into grotesque art sculptures, smoldering cooking fires and overturned water buckets. Only two rounds had fallen short, killing a soldier named Whitmore from a farm in Nebraska. His father would receive the condolence letter knowing the contents even before he folded back the envelope flap as if turning down new sheets on the bed. His wife would stand away from the light, her hands, flowered with pie dough, holding her cheeks, her breath unwillingly pumping in and out. Although feeling staggered and dizzy, his chest suddenly emptying through his tightened throat as if a great knock-out blow had slammed into his stomach, he would stand stoically, silently – an attempt to drown all emotions or, at the least, toss them into the dark – catching the toes of escaping energy in an effort to drag back enough power to turn to her, raise an enfolding arm as she staggered to his chest, unable to speak or to think, her alluvial emotions flowing over them both, yet unable to penetrate his defense. She would place the Purple heart (maybe a bronze star might have been thrown in as an extra salute to heroism by a cynical clerk) in a frame with the triangular folded flag on the mantelpiece. Occasionally she might retrieve the letter from its special place in the drawer and believe he had given his life – no marriage, or kids, or grandkids, or growing old together and all the love and disappointment an average life entails - for his country. Died heroically in combat while defending America's freedoms.

On the field the men found little of him remaining, a few smoking bits of bloodless flesh, (the blood having completely vaporized) that fit easily into a beer can. Surprisingly, his boots remained intact and empty. A short-timer tied the laces together knowing they would fetch a blowjob in any village with several more in the bank for future visits.

Pete led the men to the village edge and flopped down against a tree stump, his M-16 across his lap, boonie hat tossed to the side allowing the sweat to squeeze from his forehead without restriction. James squatted, Vietnamese style, as Fibo placed one leg on a log, resting the butt of the M-60 machinegun on the ground. Sonny, the only soldier with pressed fatigues and shinned boots, blew dust from his weapon. Other soldiers gathered around followed by sergeant Henderson, thin, bewildered, an average saxophone player whose sunken cheeks gave him the appearance of constantly sucking a lollypop. The men liked, but did not trust him, knowing that he often made poor decisions and realizing that rank never equaled leadership.

"OK men," he said. "We're not finished. Move out and sweep the village."

No one moved. He had been in country too long to expect a positive outcome so he lit a cigarette and moved ahead alone keeping, out of embarrassment, any farther comments or commands to himself. He passed a crying baby, just old enough to sit, bare arms raised at the elbows and, quivering with shock and confusion, a fluffy brown and white mottled puppy sniffng at its side.

Pete breathed deeply letting the cigarette smoke fill his chest. So this was home, he thought, the only home he knew, a watery smoking landscape smelling of cordite, napalm, and burning flesh, an unbelievable home too soon comfortable and natural. How quickly we all adapt, he thought. Scarce food? Eat less. No shelter? Curl up in the rain. No money? Who needs it? Pete had learned that money was the most overrated commodity there is. People could adapt to anything: cold, heat, suffering, sickness, slavery, conquest, poverty, peace or war. People could adapt to any situation and often thrive. The soldiers were rapidly adapting to aggression and sufering. Is it wrong or am I wrong, Pete thought. Is it possible that the natural state of mankind is war and madness, and kindness and peace are askew? War felt so comfortable, so honest. No bullshit existed here, honesty yes, but no bullshit. Men counted and depended on one another. They had a purpose here, one they would probably never have in the states. Yet everything real seemed unreal, like no place in the world held such an honest yet illusive existence. The thoughts refused to square in his head. How could the most real place in the world, a place that felt genuine and authentic, reveal itself behind mist? Pete watched the baby and the puppy.

James stood and said, "Christ! I've never seen such a bunch of cruel bastards. What the hell have we become?" He walked to the baby, looked down and shook his head as if in disgust. He reached down and tenderly picked up the puppy, rubbing it against his cheek. "When are these stinking pricks going to realize a dog is more than a tasty snack?" James returned to his original spot and opened a can of stew for the puppy. When it finished eating he placed it inside his fatigue shirt. Its head protruded from between the buttons and quickly fell asleep.

An old lady ran from the bushes and grabbed the baby. As she started to run back a soldier from the

25th shot her three times in the back. She fell forward on top of the baby and her hands. Her legs splayed to the sides. Pete watched her legs quiver momentarily, her heels slapping the clay. He thought the bullets had probably gone clean through killing the baby. If not it would probably smother soon enough. In any case, no noise crept from under her body. Pete hoped the puppy would survive. A good dog was a comfort at camp, something warm to hug and to pet, to curl beside a man as he slept. A dog became a protector asking nothing except a little food and water, not unlike the other soldiers.

Pete looked at his hands, held them in front of him. They held a glow about them, a hazy image. Everything had a hazy image, an aura like the light reflected from a movie. Everything was visible on the screen as real but without depth. It could be seen and touched but not penetrated. Some mystery lay behind the images, but what? No one spoke. Only occasional gunfire, like heavy drops of rain against a metal roof, sounded.

"I need a piece of ass," Clifton said, as he stood. "Nothing works up my blood like more blood." He stroked his fist between his legs and pumped his hips. "What do you say we all get one?"

"There ain't no shitting ass around here," said Noons. "The last piece is lying in that fucking pile."

"Don't you believe it," said Clifton. "Where there are soldiers of the grand fucking American army there is ass for sale. War is all buying and selling and people will do whatever it takes to make a buck."

"Don't underestimate him," said James, stroking the head of the puppy. "If anyone can sniff out a piece of tail it's him."

Noons popped the clip from his M-16, loaded and topped it off at 19 rounds from a pile he had in his pocket. It might have been a myth but no one filled it with 20 because it caused a jam. "You go find one and let us know," he said.

Clifton tipped his hat and bowed low before moving cautiously into the village. Fibo, wearing a green T-shirt, retrieved a deck of cards and several of them gathered for a quick game, no money, just a chance to relax. Clifton returned later hiking up his pants and saying, "Yahoo! I got a piece you won't believe. She's in the next hooch over, legs spread and waiting to take on all comers."

"You're crazy," said Noons. "You're always making shit up."

"Right. Why don't you come over here and smell my cock?"

"There's really a woman back there?"

"Like I said..."

"I don't have a condom," said Fibo. "Besides, I'm winning."

"Oh, little faggot boy has an excuse," said Clifton. He glanced at Sonny who smiled back. "You stupid fuck, you're not winning anything. Everyone is loosing. What is a condom, anyway? A wrapper that goes around your prick. What do you think your skin does? The same damn thing."

"She's probably a hundred years old," said Noons.

Clifton slapped him on the back of the head. "Old, my ass. She's as sweet as a daisy and she's everything a man wants in a woman. Sure, she won't give you a blowjob but she's willing for anything else. Twist and fold her anyway you like. She won't protest one bit. Who's in?"

They all stood. "OK," said Fibo. "Lead the way. I always feel like breeding after killing."

"That's more like it," said Clifton. "Are we men, or what?" He led them to another bamboo hooch, one almost complere. "She's stark naked and lying on the table. It's dark in there so just walk straight ahead and go at it. Show her what you're made of, Fibo, although she can take anything you've got. In fact, I've got a five that says you can't make her scream, in horror or delight. You can't get a sound out of her."

Fibo placed the M-60 on the clay and covered it with the belt of rounds. Giving two thumbs up he said, "Wish me luck, boys. I'm going in."

Clifton passed out several victory cigarettes as they listed to Fibo making "yahoo" sounds and saying things like "take that, baby" and, "do you want it all the way?" Finally a cry emerged, a small screech followed by a moaning wail, the sound of a man. Fibo stumbled from the hooch, pants still down, his hands covered in blood. He fell to the ground and started to puke.

"You stinking bastard," he said. "You motherfucking stinking cock-sucking bastard." He looked pale and shaken.

"What is it?" said James. He placed his arms around the puppy for protection as the others lifted their weapons.

Fibo rolled to his back, his wet prick sliding between his legs, and placed a bloody arm across his forehead. With the other hand he tried to pull up his pants. "You sick fuck," he said to Clifton. "I felt my way in and found the table. She was there, just like you said. I ran my hands up her legs and pulled her to the edge and stood at the end of the table giving it to here. No complaints, just like you said. I pulled up her knees to really get it in." He moaned slightly. "You sick fucking bastard. I finished, I finished all right, then lay forward for a kiss, a chance to hold her head and give her a kiss to show my appreciation. God damn you, God damn you!"

"She was great, wasn't she," said Clifton. "You couldn't ask for more in a woman, just like I said."

"You bastard!" Fibo said, rising to his knees and pointing his bloody fingers at him. "Something wasn't right. I leaned in and felt around." He dropped his head, raised it and shouted, "She had no fucking head!" Everyone looked at Fibo, then at Clifton.

"I said she wouldn't give you a blow job? She had everything you wanted and you took it well enough."

Fibo rolled back to the ground. "Sick bastard, sick, sick bastard," he said.

"What are you complaining about? You didn't even

have to pay her." Clifton looked to the others as if he had been falsely accused. "Are you some kind of Icky-Bob Crane? Some kind of wimp afraid of the headless horseman, or, in this case, headless horse-woman? Get on and ride, that's what I say. Bes ides, when someone says 'man, that was a dead piece of ass' you can smile and say 'buddy, you don't know what a dead piece of ass is."

James started first, a little growl that grew into a chuckling cough followed by loud hiccupping guf-faws then bone rattling laughter. Everyone followed, the laughter squeezing out tears, some of them rolling to the ground. As they started to quiet, Noons raised his hand as if to ask a teacher a ques-tion. "Can I be next?" he said. The laughter exploded again, more raucously this time and with more tears. Fibo, pants around his ankles, laughed loudest and fired his M-60 into the air with one hand while at-tempting to catch the hot casings with his mouth. Even Pete laughed, although he felt the others laughed far too loudly and for much too long.

Chapter 18

Sergeant Biggilo finally led his first patrol, finally left the base camp, finally decided to show the men he was good as any of them, even better. Pete had changed dramatically after R&R, a dark change like a shadow gradually creeping across the lawn. He became even more quiet and withdrawn and he stayed isolated for long periods of time. The war had pushed all sound and emotion into one small box someplace within his head that he could not reach. The box had quickly snapped shut, pinching his emotions into a pain so terrible that their very scream was inaudible, high and wrenching and he refused to acknowledge them, refused to claim he had any at all. He was aware of nothing except the ever- present tick-tock of time within his chest.

The world no longerrotated smoothly to the east catching early morning rays of sun. The world bounced on its side like a cube.

Maybe Biggilo had something to prove. One day before he took out his own patrol, he stopped a returning patrol. The men carried the superior look soldiers get when they have been too long in the jungle, an indifferent and indignant look that refuses authority. Sergeant Biggilo still had the look of a REMF (rear echelon mother- fucker). He ventured to compensate by standing taller than the rest of them and by chewing out asses. Lately it had been his favorite sport and he often met patrols at the inside gate. He cut Pete from the group.

Everyone else, covered with red mud and tired, stood in loose formation. Biggilo, like a steam train starting up, yelled about Pete's appearance as if starched uniforms and shined boots were prerequisites for killing. Pete knelt on his haunches, Vietnamese style, and drew a heart in the clay. He scrawled an arrow through the heart and wrote Izanami's name, childish he knew but necessary.

"Stand up, you bastard, stand up when I'm talking to you," Biggilo said.

When Pete refused to move, Biggilo grabbed him by the shoulder, jumped on the drawn heart and slapped him in the head. Clifton knocked Biggilo to the ground and drew the bolt on his M-16.

"You're dead meat," he said and pointed the weapon at Biggilo's head. Biggilo tensed, ground his teeth together. "Shoot the son-of- a-bitch," someone said. Clifton grinned and stepped back.

Biggilo, realizing he was safe, screwed his lips tightly together until the pressure burst them apart and he screamed a spit-full of obscenities followed by "Your ass is getting an article-15."

"Ooooooooooooooohhh, hot shit," said Clifton, squeezing his prick and knocking his knees together in mock fear. Everyone burst out laughing. There was no comparison between facing death almost daily and a paper write-up saying you have been a bad boy.

Clifton lowered the weapon and pulled Pete to his feet and carried him to the new company club. Biggilo jumped up, his starched uniform covered with mud. He stood there powerless and resentful, his mouth moving but only silence emerging. Because Pete no longer cared, because Clifton no longer cared, because none of them cared, the sergeant hated them all. Mostly he hated Pete. Clifton laughed about it at the club while Pete sat outside buckled back on his haunches and drinking a beer.

"Way to go," said James. "We don't have to take any shit from that guy, or any guy."

Fibo said, "I thought you were going to waste him."

Pete did not care, not anymore. If Clifton killed Biggilo, that was his problem. Maybe killing was the thing that made people most human.

Biggilo assembled the men at 1600 hours the following day. Pete was at the top of the assignment roster. They were all tired from yesterday's patrol. Biggilo looked tough in his freshly pressed uniform, like a general on a fox-hunt. He inspected everyone, taking close looks at the rifles. He carried too much gear. Extra ammo pouches hung from his harness. No one had ever seen him sight in his weapon. The sling was not taped, to prevent it from rattling, and he carried only one canteen of water, not enough for him to last the morning at this altitude and in this heat, not without practice. Biggilo sat in the front of the deuce-and-a-half

Pete thought of his mind as a star-shell that would not descend, a dirty glowing light burning quickly before flickering out. He sat quiet and fully aware of himself.

"You're stir crazy," said Clifton. The truck bounced their thin faces. "You need to get a new girl, see the sights." They passed a field where two water buffalo were screwing in the dim morning.

"Don't let it build into something dangerous."

Pete started to say something, then turned away. Everyone was looking at him. Clifton kept blinking in and out of the rising sun. Pete watched dust falling to the road behind the truck. "I don't like it," he said. "Yards and yards of nothing."

"The road?" He heard Clifton plain enough.

"All of us," said Pete. Dust puddled on his clothes. "I want a big hand of air to catch me whenever I fall." The truck hit a rut and Clifton dropped a clip.

He bent to pick it up.

"There's nothing real in that," he said.

Everyone kept looking at Pete, James, all the rest.

"What is it?" Pete said.

"You're mumbling's getting on our nerves," James replied. The deuce-and-a-half drove several miles from the base camp, turned down a thin rutted red road and passed an open field and a stand of brush and bamboo before stopping beside a Montagnard graveyard. A fence surrounded the graveyard. On poles small houses sheltered souls. The fence was tied together with strips of bamboo. An American helmet hung from a post. Scattered above the houses, carved wooden helicopters appeared to be flying to protect the dead.

Biggilo attempted to form the men, put them in order. They knew where they belonged. In the bush, every man was equal. As point man, Pete scouted the map for reference points before moving down a Montagnard trail that circled back toward camp. The brush became thick and darkened the trail. The patrol tunneled through until the trail opened on a small treeless field. A stream split the field and on the far side rose a gentle ridge. Trees and brush ringed the field on three sides, perfect for an ambush.

Pete knelt beside the trail behind the tall grass and motioned the others forward. James dropped to his knee ten feet to the side. Everyone else flowed into the opening while Pete and James watched the clearing. Two men filled their canteens at the creek and scrambled back up the ridge. Pete thought the grass moved on the hill and he readied his weapon. Biggilo stood like a Civil War general beside the water while the other men filled up. The short walk had emptied their canteens.   James and Pete filled up last dropping iodine tablets into the canteens before replacing the tops. Biggilo eyed the water, a green scummy a□ air that slowly slapped against the red bank. He dipped a finger into the slimy film and flicked away a large black bug. Moss covered the fallen tree that acted as the bridge. Two men crouched on the ridge. Pete moved ahead to regain the point. Biggilo shook his canteen and moved on without filling it.   Any man afraid of water was afraid of war. He deserved killing, thought Pete.

The patrol crossed a stand of bamboo a mile from the base camp. Pete thought of how far he had walked since landing in Vietnam: hundreds and hundreds of miles yet he had never traveled more than a few miles from the camp, a few miles from safety. The last of the light, trickling through the trees, fell across them. Another day had died. Pete stopped and looked into the leaves constantly aware of small green snakes tumbling from the limbs, snakes whose bite could kill him before he snapped them o□. Every clump of brush remained a sanctuary for vermin.

They moved to a position on a ridge next to a unit from the 25th. The ridge overlooked a clearing and a trail. Biggilo strutted about the position giving orders that everyone ignored. His chin dipped close to his chest, like a boxer, and his arms, inflexible, crowded his sides. His hands choked the ammo belt where two fingers knocked against the buckle in rhythm with his ticking shoulders. He was a man who had seen many war movies.

Pete remained close to Clifton, nestling into the tall grass beside a small knoll. He rolled out his poncho, to deflect the moisture, and positioned his gear at one end. Clifton dropped his poncho to the ground and surveyed the area. The rest of the unit had dug in to their left. James and Fibo were already placing Claymores beside the trail, pushing their metal stakes into the dirt and unraveling the ignition wire and stretching the wire to his position. Biggilo motioned them to hurry. The sun had already set. Clifton dropped his gear beside Pete. "Use my poncho for a blanket," he said. "I'll take the first watch."

The poncho had a liner that felt warm when Pete rolled it over him. The night air stuck to his skin leaving him gummy. Already gnats had buzzed into the poncho and zipped about his ears crawling through the sweat on his face. Of all things in the war he hated them most. He tried to swat them unsuccessfully before falling asleep. Clifton woke him from a hard sleep and, when he tried to sit, he felt dizzy and disoriented. The grass twirled under him. It was midnight.

"Give me a couple hours," said Clifton, "and you

can have your bed back."

Pete gulped a big drink of water, more than usual. The taste of iodine lingered in his mouth, a taste he had grown to enjoy. An intense heat caused him to sweat and kept him groggy. The entire jungle was a fever, a flaming mania of black passion. Pete splashed his face with water. Patrols were no place for nightmares. The moon cast the land in an eerie green glow as if the world were being seen through a star-scope of flickering shadows. Pete almost expected wolves to howl and shapes from the other men appeared like dark gargoyles featureless in the dark. Trees rose like towers; the clearing became a moor of bubbling fog.

Pete stomped his feet and pissed. God, he could not keep awake. His prick felt hot and stiff and he thought of jacking off but it was too much effort, and the night, above the valley, was too clear for any secrecy. He peered through the sight of his M-16. The moon would be completely full in a few days and the night even more devious, more sinful and beautiful.

Nights made Pete feel alive and important. He started to nod and jerked awake. The sleep would not leave. The M-16 felt good and comfortable and secure in his hands as he placed the muzzle into his mouth. That was too easy and he replaced the weapon on the grass and grabbed his .38. The gun felt warm from the night air. He lowered it into his belt and thought of going to see Sergeant Biggilo.

His water would be gone and Pete wanted to take him a fresh canteen knowing Biggilo would be too full of himself to take any. He thought of leaving the canteen beside his gear like an unknown lover leaves a valentine. Clifton was going to kill him so it was important to treat Biggilo with some kindness.

Pete started through the brush with the canteen. He tried to stay awake and he dropped to his knees and placed his lips against the gun's barrel. He could warn Biggilo, a quick note perhaps, maybe scare him by attaching the note to a bloody bayonet. Meaty arms of the jungle closed around him. Trees eclipsed the moon and heavy leaves handled Pete softly. His footsteps became air and he could not tell if he stood upright, floated upside down or drifted sideways. They blanketed him with hot breath and he lay in her arms sleeping somewhere between heaven and earth. A cloud drifted close and led him naked, out of himself, out of the jungle, to a holy place where he knelt to worship the Gods of war, the Gods of understanding. All was war, all killing, all love and grace.

A gnat buzzed him awake. He lay beside the empty poncho, the canteen on the grass. Clifton was gone. A dream, he thought. He had a wonderful dream and Clifton let him sleep all night. It was 4 a.m. Clifton would return soon. He won't mind if I take a nap, Pete thought. He's out there somewhere. Pete crawled under the poncho. The liner was still warm and smelled of Clifton.

The morning sun rose colorless and large and rapidly started to dry the wet grass. Air smelled green crisp and new and birds clipped by overhead chipping the sky awake. Across the clearing elephant grass bumped against the jungle and the stream. The thin mist rising skyward, looked yellow and muddy. Men were already moving and steam drifted from cooking C-rations filling the air with the smell of canned eggs. Clifton worked his way up from the clearing. He looked tired and out of breath.

"Biggilo's gone," he said. He looked in a wide circle. "We can't find him anywhere."

"Gone?" Pete asked. He had started a fire and he nibbled the edges on a sticky orange roll.

"No one can find him." He pinched o□ a chunk of the roll. Except for the dough sticking to his fingers, the roll broke apart in his hand. "We found blood on his poncho. Nothing else."

"Maybe Charlie got him," said Pete. "They take a man just for fun."

"No fucking slope-head did this. Someone here got him." He pushed down the roll and licked his fingers. Pete opened a can of peaches and cut some cinnamon roll from the can. Peaches were always good. "Noons called the base for Captain Druxman. He'll be here soon." Clifton knelt on one knee and drank some coffee. He did not look well. "We're supposed to look for the bastard. Fat chance." He looked around again as if he had lost something. "He's in a hundred pieces by now. Nothing but meat."

Pete finished eating and joined the search, working alone, quietly, methodically. By the third day, Biggilo still had not been found. Pete started watching Clifton. Clifton appeared uneasy, anxious and rambled on and on about leaving this place, leaving the sergeant. Heavy moods crowded him and he took a swing at James knocking his turkey roll across the grass. On the fourth day, Pete decided to follow Clifton.

Clifton carried a piece of burnt toast, an ammo box and his M-16. Pete felt fresh and good from a bath in the stream and he followed Clifton from a distance. The morning had turned warm but the jungle, into which Clifton disappeared, was cool. Clifton followed a small trail that smelled faintly of sweet ugly decay. Moss clung to the sides of trees in heavy blankets. Twice Clifton turned to look back. Pete crouched in the side brush. Clifton worked his way down a ravine where the grass had been previously pushed flat and lay like an arrow in one direction. The area appeared familiar, like all jungle appeared familiar.

Ahead, the trees arched high like a temple, the dome shot with small holes where the light above was seen but refused to enter. Every few feet Pete stopped to listen. The light from a small clearing glimmered ahead and the faint smell of something old, rotten, continued to fill the air. Pete proceeded to the edge of the clearing and nestled into the grass. Vietnam was Eden, he thought. He never wanted to be tossed out, would refuse to eat the apple, would stay forever in the quiet and peace. All he had to do was to stay good, stay decent and moral. Foul air blew from a distance. He sat back and drank from the canteen. The taste of iodine had become natural, a cleanser, a purifier, a gourmet defense against sickness. This was a holy place, a holy place where he could rest.

Below, Clifton removed his clothes and bathed in the small creek in the clearing. The odor of decay grew stronger as wind bent the grass. The temple smelled of death. Pete heard Music. Clifton sang a line from *Saint James Infirmary Blues*. The notes tumbled, badly spaced and out of tune. Clifton bent over the bank and opened the ammo box. He grabbed a bar of soap.

Shit, Pete thought. A bath. He came here for a fucking bath. He felt ashamed, ashamed he had suspected Clifton, here in this familiar place of holy cleanliness. Clifton was his buddy, had watched over him throughout the war. Pete sighed and slid a shaft of grass into his mouth. A large green bug crawled over his boot and he flicked it off, crushing it with his heel.

Clifton flopped against the creek bank. He quit singing and dried himself with a small towel. The sun climbed halfway up the trees. The world, except for Clifton, became motionless. His clothes were piled on the ground and he reached into the ammo box.

Pete decided to enter the clearing. Another breeze blew the odor of death his way. He wanted to apologize to Clifton, to tell him he was sorry for his disbelief. Clifton extracted a roll of nylon parachute cord and his Gerber knife from the box. The odor of death became so strong that Pete could smell it on his own hands. Clifton took three steps forward, stopped and looked toward the trees hugging the clearing. Shadows covered them. He drew in a deep breath.

There, on a tree, tied around the forearms and nailed through the wrists with two bayonets, hung Sergeant Biggilo. Pete ducked, smelled the death on his legs. Biggilo hung naked. Clifton gasped another breath and ran his finger across the blade of the knife. Biggilo had swollen like an enormous purple grape. Flies ate at his empty eye sockets and maggots wriggled from his bloated lips and fell to the grass. A large dripping hole gaped from between his thighs.

Clifton placed his towel on a bush, drew in a final deep breath and dashed for Biggilo. He scampered up the tree behind the sergeant and threw the rope in a noose around his neck. He jumped to the ground, tightened the rope, and tied the rope to a limb. Biggilo's head twisted to one side as if he had missed a question. Clifton stuck the knife between his teeth and, using an adjoining tree, struggled up beside Biggilo. With a sawing motion, he severed one of Biggilo's arms at the elbow.

The forearm and wrist remained bayoneted to the tree. Biggilo rocked forward against the rope and the tree. Clifton worked his way up the other side cutting at that elbow. The dried tendons snapped one at a time. Clifton jabbed at the joint. The arm came away and the sergeant swung from the rope, ticked like a clock back and forth, back and forth, his neck slowly stretching out and pinching up his head like a fat black ball.

Clifton sprang to the ground and ran to the nylon cord. He wrapped the cord around his wrist and quickly cut the tied end from the tree in an attempt to lower the swinging sergeant. Biggilo's neck squeezed tighter and, like parting lips, began to tear apart below the chin. Clifton had diffculty holding him. Biggilo split apart at the neck, his head flipping over the jungle like a tiddlywinks chip. Clifton stumbled, snapping back on the rope as it cracked in the air. With handless arms, Biggilo caught Clifton around the chest and threw him to the ground. Clifton struggled free, covered in maggots, and ran for the creek where he spun into a shallow dive. He rose slowly, his face plastered with mud.

It might have been then that Pete became the war. He only remembered the feelings he carried and the image of Biggilo bursting forth in a wild celebration of death. The world smelled of decay, an odor that clawed at his nostrils, and he loved it. He returned to the unit where he became a tight ball watching for long moments toward the black woods.

Chapter - 19

That afternoon Captain Druxman gathered the men from the patrol where they stood or sat in a half circle around him. He paced as usual. "No sight of the sergeant?" he asked. Shoulders shrugged. He asked again, directing the question toward Pete. "I understand you didn't like him." Pete said nothing just picked mud from between the cleats in his boots. The Captain bounced on his heels before drifting around the half circle. He spoke to each man individually asking, not just about Biggilo, but about something personal in their lives, if they had written home, if they were feeling OK "Sure you haven't seen anything," he asked Clifton.

"Nothing," said Clifton. "We've seen this thing before. Some guy goes for a crap and never returns.

He didn't know anything about being a soldier, not a real soldier." Clifton chewed a wad of gum. "We going back to camp?"

The captain shook his head. "Got a call an hour ago." He flipped his thumb over his shoulder. "Expecting some trouble off that way. We're done here and we'll be departing in twenty." He handed Pete the map. "The coordinates are clearly marked. It's an old French position." He squeezed Pete's shoulder like a man concerned, a priest maybe. "You want to talk about anything, come to me." And then, real close and quiet. "It won't go any farther."

"Full of ghosts," said Clifton, helping Pete up.

"Piss off," said Pete.

"French positions are always full of ghosts, legionnaires marching through the night, armless, legless, headless."

Pete jerked away. Clifton, killing the sergeant, had finally crossed the line. Pete was finished with him.

The column moved out with Pete on point. Sunlight splintered through the trees and onto their faces. Every time they hit a patch of clear trail, red dust filled their noses. Face dust turned to mud and sweat covered bodies. After crossing streams they stopped to dig clay from between boot cleats otherwise the boots became too heavy and exhausted them too quickly. The column hit a short stretch of road, easy walking, but they quickly moved back into the bush. Not that it made any difference. Charlie put mines in the roads. When soldiers refused to walk down them, he put them beside the roads so they were everywhere. The men felt better walking beside the road, anyway. Pete led them over a bare hill to be followed by more hills. The walking no longer made any difference, one hill was as good as the next. Always they traveled in the same place. Pete's thoughts overlapped like double exposed film. Sometimes they seemed soft and dry like cotton, other times hard and wet like misty morning glass. He did not know what a mind is, where the ideas came from. This large conglomeration of contradictions encompassed everything in his life and either totaled what he was, or meant nothing at all.

Late afternoon sunlight broke through cracks of bamboo and dribbled onto the giant stalks. When the column stopped, silence covered the jungle, except for the rustle from Pete cutting through the brush. He liked the idea that his hands bled from the elephant grass, that he had the guts to chop through it. Ahead, the grass, twisting one way then another, bent across a clearing. Pete knifed the machete into the ground and unfolded the map. The M-16 pulled at his shoulder. He eyed the map and the clearing, squatted, placed the weapon across his lap, gathered in the sun, the clearing, the elephant grass, the uneven slope of the hill where it nuzzled the jungle. He gathered in the images, shrank them down and placed them on the map, a paper world he controlled. This was the perfect place for killing.

The Captain moved through the brush and knelt

beside Pete. Pete remained still and felt warm, ubiquitous and eternal. He ran things in the bush, he was the boss, the leader, the lead soloist. He had become THE MAN, THE EVERYTHING. Here was a chance to redeem himself, for once stand atop his own mountain.

The captain surveyed the map. Pete reached for his canteen, the water warm and still tasting of plastic, iodine, medicine, sickness, a healing power rushing through his stomach. Captain Druxman had grown sad in this country. Each death had added years on him. The men were boys to him, his boys. No concerned officer lasted long in a war zone. With heavy eyes, like those of a dying dog, he stared from between dry eyelids. Dirty creases in several places crossed the map at his feet. Pete handed him the canteen. The Captain looked toward the sky and folded his hands between his knees. Drooping his head he fingered the dirty creases and rolled his hands across the contour lines as if to feel the hills and valleys. When his finger touched a jagged blue line he pulled his hand back as if the water had splashed over him. He looked at Pete. "It's there," he said. The captain drank some and spit out the rest of the water as if trying to wash away his authority.

"It's a good spot for killing," said Pete.

"Maybe not," said Druxman. He moved back into the brush. "There," he said, and motioned the patrol forward, pointing across the clearing. They moved ahead, the forward men peeling to the sides like a snake shedding its skin. Clifton looked at Pete with cold, watermelon-seed eyes. The patrol crossed the small creek that Pete had not seen, but knew was there.

Foliage had overgrown the old French position. A few impressions in the ground remained, a partially collapsed bunker and several rows of rusted concertina wire. It must have been an artillery position since empty 75mm shell casings were scattered about the ground and covered with grass. The men dug in among the old position.

Pete found a spot alone, one above the rest of the unit that overlooked the clearing they had crossed. He smoothed the poncho over the grass, placed his gear at one end and himself at the other.

It looked like Clifton had teamed with James. Pete could see them not far from the last row of wire. They had the M-60 machine gun and had macheted an opening in the grass for a better field of fire. Clifton opened the bi-pod and checked the barrel. He snuggled in behind the piece and rocked from side to side. James practiced changing the barrels. They could cover the entire clearing.

Should the enemy come from behind, Clifton could have spun all the way around. He thought he saw Pete on the hill and he sighted the weapon on his chest. Pete stared back, not moving. Clifton's face was a blur, but it was him. No one else wanted to kill Pete. Clifton worked his way back around and James locked in the first of a long row of cartridges.

The sun, like a naked lover, slumped below the horizon leaving a translucent gown of red-orange drifting slowly behind. Mist edged from the ground and blended with the last light of day as the sky went from day-light to day-night. The mist became evening, the air wet with dark, the kind of night that lifted dead Frenchmen from the soil.

A fire smoked and rolled in Pete's eyes. For a moment, reflected in his canteen cup, he resembled a bewildered and revengeful Quasimodo, bent and twisted by hatred and love, and confused by them both. His fingers turned pale as he strangled the cup. Like a whore takes on lovers he took in the night, unafraid, uncaring, wanting the payment of another day. Nothing more, just another day, a day without Clifton. Pete wanted to be rather than not be in this little piece of time and he wanted it alone, as one man.

The Captain emerged from the brush. The rest of the band huddled together like birds in a nest. "Everything OK?" he asked. Pete had watched day go into night realizing there was never a breaking point between the two. One simply became the other, just like life became death, like Sergeant Yama. Dew had become an internal part of him and he felt the night stick to his flesh.

"Well?" said the Captain, irritation in his voice.

"Fine," Pete replied.

"Good boy." The captain smiled and squeezed him on the shoulder before slipping back into the brush.

Pete covered himself with the poncho and lit a smoke where the flame could not be seen. He imagined himself in Hong Kong leading Izanami to the room. She was smaller than ever, too small and too young to be a whore. But she was. If Pete needed to understand anything, he needed to understand that. We are not what we are, but what we are not. With one finger he touched her smallness and watched the overhead light of the hotel room stroke her skin in yellow-tan layers. Everything unimaginable, incomprehensible had been melted down into a thin layer of lust and poured over Izanami. She was everything good, everything important. Yet she was still a whore. Pete loved the thought of her. She made war an insignificant twit fizzling itself out in a tantrum.

A gnat buzzed in his ear causing him to jump. The hairy hands of night held to his chest. Dozing o□ in the night was a dangerous thing. Gnats swirled and zipped, invisible and impossible in the dark. In the distance someone threw a C-ration can. Quiet voices scratched over the radio. Pete pissed and fell back asleep.

He woke with a jerk, sweat pouring from his forehead as if he were about to be sick. The brightness of the night caught him by surprise and he rolled to one side and felt the grass, damp and thick and foreign in its fatness. For a moment he thought it was too late, that the dream of death that caught him was a reality and he was no longer Pete but a part of the grass or something under the grass that had gone through the skins of thousands of maggots. Never again would he be something that thought or felt or was. Time had him by the throat. Pete stroked the ground like a woman, in the quiet time after love, strokes the chest of her lover. He was alive, damn it, alive.

Pete rolled to his back and shot his hands toward the sky. The world quivered, about to break apart and his hands shook violently. It was not like him to fall asleep, to lose track of time. After all, he had been awake since landing in Nam. It was not like him to shake. The easy time in Hong Kong had ruined him. Clifton was right. He rubbed his chest feeling the warmth, making sure he was not a cold slab of meat, overgrown with weeds and resting at the bottom of a forgotten ravine. The shaking continued. It was not fear. Fear only happened once. This was something different. The full moon caused him to squint and he jumped up, grabbed the M- 16, screamed loudly and fired seven lucky shots into the air.

James and Clifton dropped to their weapon, must have removed the safety, and waited for the onrush of enemy. Nothing. Pete knew they both breathed heavily with anticipation. Everything was quiet, everything except the indifferent sound of evening scraping against the moon and mist. Like his own weapon, condensation covered the machine- gun barrel. Clifton's chest pressed against the ground. Pete watched him through the grass as he looked down the machine-gun barrel. The front, exposed by the moon, expressed a perfect picture of calmness, steam rising from the stream, a short meadow of deep green, and further on a forest of bamboo that became increasingly heavy and darker until nothing could be seen or known.

"What the hell's going on," said James. He chewed a piece of hard tack. "That wasn't no '47. Sounded like a '16."

Clifton looked up the hill. "Came from there." Captain Druxman moved behind them. He and Noons walked toward Pete's position. Noons carried the radio and must have been sleeping because he stumbled as he walked, trying to balance on his night legs.

Pete rolled into tight ball. He rubbed the barrel of the M-16 with a handkerchief. A half full clip tipped against his boot. "A mistake," said Pete, without looking up. "The moon blinded me and I saw death approach." Back in the world Pete might have been considered crazy and locked up in a V.A. hospital. Not here.   Not now in the middle of an N.V.A. Infested jungle. Noons, rubbing his eyes, and the Captain returned to their position. The world never looked more clear.

It's better now, Pete thought. Everyone knows we're here. He was not frightened although the moon had crept up and fingered him for execution. The harder Pete hid the brighter the moon became, relentless, ever present. The beams burned through his closed eyes. He had to silence the light and the quiet.

Stars freckled the night. Pete did not feel like talking to the Captain, or to anyone else. It was too late for them both and conversation fit like a kid's coat, tight and rough. Words had no meaning. If the world was merely a metaphor pointing to emotions, what good was it now that Pete had no emotions, no feelings? The barbed wire glowed under the moonlight. Pete thought of Hong Kong and of Izanami. He could still feel her passion. But something had changed. Pete snapped his head to one side. The thought that she might also be a dream startled him. Perhaps she came from some mist in his mind one lonely night on perimeter guard. Perhaps she was nothing more than a sandbag catching juice from his pumped prick. What did it matter? "Don't mean nothing," Pete mumbled. She drowned out the rumble of battle, the sounds of pain and suffering, the noise of passing from one person to another person, from boyhood to manhood, from manhood to warrior. It did not matter if the intensity of her love making was feigned. It was real enough to him. She, above all other people, must exist.

The battle for Camp Holloway, the air force base, started with a ring of flares miles in the distance. Quick yellow artillery flashed through the trees. The camp rested beside Pleiku and was too far away for anyone to hear the battle. The enemy force that hit the band's patrol was small and may have only been sent, or distracted from their path of engagement, to investigate the noise Pete had caused.

Clifton heard them first, when one stumbled into the stream. He nudged James. Shadows crossed the field. From the hill, Pete opened a can of C-rations and picked at the jam and crackers. There was no hurry. Death always waited. He locked a full clip into place and went back to the crackers. The jam spread like a thick wax.

Clifton squeezed the trigger on the M-60 and James snapped a hand flare against the ground. The flare shot high overhead and fizzled to life. The M-60 spit red tracers into the brightening night as the N.V.A., crossing the clearing, went from ghostly images to crouching, vicious creatures whose brush-covered backs burst alive with light from the flare. Twigs waved from their helmets and they dropped quickly from sight as the onslaught of bullets nipped the grass like a rabid goat. Clifton fired short bursts of seven to ten rounds each while James jerked on his asbestos gloves holding the extra barrel in case the barrel went from red to yellow to white.

A grid of blue and red tracers etched the clearing below as Charlie fired back. The battle would not be long. Already the sky started to lighten toward the east. Charlie was a vampire who hid from the sun. All artillery was in action. The real battle was against camp Holloway with a diversionary strike against Dragon Mountain. Hueys and shit-hooks could be heard overhead on their way to Holloway. The steady chop of rotors shook the ground as they passed.

Pete eased down the hill, working through the tall grass and brush. Towards the bottom of the hill, Clifton still sparked the machine gun. There was not enough ammunition to continue a long engagement or to heat up the barrel. Yet during a lull in the action, James elected to replace it. He snapped back the catch lever and, as his asbestos glove smoked, twisted the barrel off and placed the rod at his side. An occasional shot zipped from the clearing and was answered with one from the band. In the darkness James tried to replace the cold barrel. Clifton lay impatiently. Two N.V.A. sprang from the grass and rushed forward, their AK 47s clacking loudly as they moved. Clifton fumbled for his 16. The sun almost topped the horizon and the N.V.A. were clearly seen, both young men hardly larger than their weapons. One of them lost his pith helmet and crouched for a better shot.

James tried frantically to jam in the barrel. He looked up. Fibo came running to help. A hot blue tracer zinged James and tore out the back of Fibo's skull like a broken pumpkin.

Clifton spun to his knees and tried to fire. The safety was on. The stopped N.V.A. ran to join his comrade who had gotten caught in the wire. An M-79 round exploded beside them knocking one of them down. The other one fired at Clifton winging him in the arm. Clifton pinched off the safety as another enemy round snapped into his bolt, disabling the weapon and knocking it to the ground.

Clifton jumped for Fibo's M-16 and landed with his elbow in the back of his head. The enemy fired again as his comrade staggered to his feet and worked his way over the rusted wire.

Noons, no longer a cherry, took careful aim from the dug-out and fired. One N.V.A. crumpled to the ground. Noons fired again and missed. Clifton jumped up. Blood and chunks of Fibo's brain dripped from his arm. He fired, the little Mattel weapon rapidly ejecting shells. The enemy knocked back into the wire. Clifton twisted around and pointed the weapon at a movement he sensed. Pete stood there quietly smoking a cigarette. Let Clifton do all the killings. Pete wasn't going to get involved. He passed Clifton and inserted the barrel into the M-60. Clifton dropped behind the gun looking intensely through the brush for any movement, anything that might seem alive.

All signs of the enemy were gone, driven back by the morning light. Pete heard the Captain make a radio check back in the dug-out. Noons, who looked hardly shaken by the battle and rejuvenated from the sun, sat on a fallen tree drinking a cup of coffee. Empty clips had piled on the dirt. Pete was also low on rounds having cut several bamboo trees almost in half. Clifton and he never spoke.

Clifton rolled to his back. "Fucking-A night," he said. Fibo lay cold and empty against Pete. Clifton flipped the finger to Noons who quickly returned it. "Harvest time," Noons called from the hill.

Clifton, stiff from the fighting, bent over Fibo with some difficulty and kicked him hard in the chest, his usual test for death. Pete grabbed for Clifton's leg but missed as Clifton stepped aside and shook his finger at him. The Captain emerged from the dug- out and joined Noons for the coﬀee. James walked up the hill.

One N.V.A. was caught and tangled in the wire. The other one, although badly scratched and bleeding, had made it through. A fly gathered around his lips and the lips twitched. He tried to roll to his side and started breathing deeply. Blood bubbled from his chest. Clifton leaned Fibo's weapon against the wire where it rocked slowly. The N.V.A. staggered to his hands and knees. From behind, Clifton kicked him hard in the nuts. He fell forward tumbling to one side and grabbing himself. He puked a wad of black creamy blood.

"Got a live one," said Clifton, stepping forward and drawing out his Gerber knife. "A live one," he yelled to the men on the hill. He pointed the knife at the soldier. Clifton pushed the N.V.A. flat to his back and crouched down on the small bleeding chest. He held the man's forehead and waved the blade across his eyes before turning the edge toward the soldier. The soldier closed his eyes, trying to pry Clifton's hand off.

Pete grabbed the M-16 and looked toward the Captain expecting some kind of help, some word or command to stop the killing. Everyone in the band hooted and whistled. Had they forgotten life so quickly? The Captain stood on the log, hardly able to balance himself, and raised the canteen cup as in a toast.

Clifton flipped the knife twice in his hand. His arm was bleeding as he tried to force the head to look upright, to look at him. The soldier pinched his eyes tighter, no longer able to keep his head twisted. Clifton crawled his fingers over the soldier's forehead until they reached the left eyelid.

Pete cried to the Captain, "No! Don't make me do this." He held his arms straight to the sides. "No more."

The Captain, having steadied himself on the log, never moved. Even Noons stood to watch.

"Pete, you're the best one for it," said Noons. "You've taught us all something about surviving."

"Help me stop," cried Pete. "No more killing." He heard them cheer, chant his name. The captain looked at them all, his face confused and concerned.

"What's with that crazy bastard?" he said. "Either kill him or get back up here," he sad to Pete.

Clifton pried up the eyelid. The soldier was choking on his own blood. His one eye screamed in terror. Clifton placed the edge of the blade on the eyeball and drew the steel slowly to the right. The eye peeled apart like a fat, slit grape.

"No!" Pete cried at Clifton. "It stops here."

The ground spit a wide arch of dust when Pete fired

into it. Clifton plunged the knife quickly into the soldier's throat. Blood spit into his face and he laughed into it, laughed like the blood was a part of him. He did not bother to wipe the blood off. Clifton's eyes were as cold as river rocks. Sweat, or something wet, dripped down Pete's shoulder.

"I'll fucking do what I will," said Clifton.

Pete threw the weapon to his shoulder, taking aim on Clifton.

"He's already dead," called the Captain. "Quit screwing around down there by yourself and get back up here. You're making me nervous."

"You've done a good job," yelled James.

Pete swung around, firing toward his voice. The Captain, Noons, James and the rest of the band ducked. Pete turned back around. In that instant, Clifton had already cut away the soldier's pants and had the knife at his nuts.

"No!" Pete repeated, his voice like a quick jab.

"Shit man." Clifton straightened and looked from the corner of his eye for his M-16.

"It stops now." Spit dribbled from Pete's lips and his face burned. He wanted something more than this.

"Quit acting crazy," said James from the hill. "Come on, Pete. Leave that dead Zip alone and come up here. Stop yelling crazy stu□ . Come on up for some coffee before the Captain turns you over to the shrinks."

"What the hell's he doing?" said the captain.

"Every now and then he gets all kind of worked up. You don't know him well but he's a good guy inside."

"He knows his killing," said Noons. "He taught me a thing or two when most guys wouldn't. Look at him go down there."

"O.K." Clifton tried to calm Pete with his hands. "This fucker killed Fibo, I killed the fucker." He stiffened. "The nuts are mine. He asked for it."

"No more killing," Pete screamed. "Everything here is finished."

Pete put his weight on one foot, then the other. No one from the

hill rose above the brush and no one spoke.

"Don't get crazy." Clifton moved to his feet and edged toward the weapon, slowly, almost imperceptibly. "The killing goes on because we go on, because men go on. It always has and it always will."

"You've killed your own, one of us. Now it's over." Pete tightened his fists around the weapon. He felt the plastic, the metal, the oil and the burnt powder. There was never a time when his head felt so clear, never.

Clifton appeared startled and confused. "What the fuck you spitting about?"

"The sergeant - in the clearing," Pete said. "I saw everything."

"I'm not buying it over that bastard." Clifton started shaking his fist with the knife toward Pete. "Remember the night, the morning. This is no fucking dream.

Remember the Sergeant."

"The sergeant's dead." Pete wanted Izanami and his Hudson and rolling down a forest road from Mount Rainier. Where the hell is the music? he thought. "I looked for you. You were missing."

The Captain peered above the grass and motioned for Noons to crawl back and retrieve the radio. Noons, reluctantly, moved backwards until he tripped, scraping his arm badly.

"I found the sergeant," said Clifton, lowering his voice and almost pleading. "You grabbed all your hate and ate it. I couldn't find you that night. I looked everywhere. The sergeant was missing so I knew something was up." Clifton's pants caught on the wire and a rusted barb cut into his leg. "You ate yourself and got raw. Taste the blood on your lips. Even the bones shine through."

Pete closed his eyes and started to relax. Then he yelled again, "It's got to stop. No more killing."

"Everything you know is a lie," said Clifton. "You're sick and you killed the sergeant, like you said you would." Pete did not want to listen. "I found you covered with blood, saw the look of a fresh kill in your eyes. Remember, bastard, because I'm not buying it for you. No one is killing me because of you. Biggilo hated us and you wasted him."

"You were in the field." Pete's eyes watered. Was that night overhead or a giant hand blocking out the sun?

"I found him hanging on a tree," Clifton continued,

"just where you nailed him, and I waited. You came toward evening." Clifton tried to eye the M-16 but the weapon had fallen to the ground, knocked loose by the shaking wire stuck to his pants. "You carried a torn pocket bible and worshiped him like a black, twisted Christ. Remember the smell? Death. You found death coiled in your mind when you prayed." Clifton said the words slowly and distinctly. "I cut him down the next morning. You killed him and I covered your ass like I've always covered your ass."

"No," said Pete, his voice an echo. "I followed you. You wasted the sergeant." He started to lean, step closer to Clifton and placed his left hand to his head.

"We, are the killer," said Clifton said. "WE!" His face contorted. "I taught. You learned." Clifton turned the knife in his hand. "Biggilo goes to you. Take his nuts."

"He's all right, captain, really he is," said James. "We've been buddies for a long time. He just goes crazy sometimes. It don't mean nothing. He been in the bush too long, that's all. He'll come out of it. I'll show you." The Captain reached for him but missed as he started walking down the hill. "Pete, come on man. You're all worked up."

Sweat ran from Pete's forehead . He reached toward the air as if it were solid, something he could grab and cover himself with.

"Noons just made some coffee up on the hill," said James, his grin wide and inviting. "You know what my pap says about this kind of thing...?

"No more killing," said Pete, dropping to his knees. "And goodness shall reign." He grabbed the rifle and fired. James stumbled back, his smile turning to confusion. Pete fired again and again and again....

That evening, back in base camp, Pete walked to the morgue escorted by two MP's. In the distance, the new band replacements rehearsed Stars and Stripes Forever. A tank chased its own dust down the road. From the N.C.O. Club tumbled the sounds of laughter and drinking.

"Why are we taking him here?' said one of the MP's.

"The doctor said to give him one look at the guy he zapped, then return him."

Pete entered the morgue wearing no shirt and his dog tags jangled against his chest. A rifle hung from the shoulder of the guard closest to him. Pete felt for the Gerber knife that was no longer there. He imagined Clifton stretched out on the table. Pete circled him, checking the toe tag that listed his name. It read K.I.A. Pete felt Izanami in the hospital ward and he smiled. He made love to her until past midnight, until the sound of guns, cackling from the bunker line, signaled another attack. The guard had fallen asleep.

Pete knocked him over and tried to rush to the fighting, now eager to go. Blue-green tracers buzzed the air and flares spotted the night like bright paint thrown on black canvas. Pete waved to everyone, pushed along by the surge of gunpowder. Overhead a lone gunship locked into a circle and rainbowed the night with streaks of red. He had never seen anything so beautiful. He thought of Clifton, lying against the last wire bent solid as stone, one finger plugging the hole in his forehead and, even in death, wincing like some frightened confused Dutch boy trying hopelessly to hold back time.

Unprotected, his own man, Pete knelt before the perimeter wire, rolled back on his ankles and, laughing and pretending to fire madly at the moon, tried desperately to separate himself from the guards dragging him away.

Chapter 20

So, if any of you doctors were listening, it's just like
I said. There was no story here about men at war, just
a story about war itself, the war within all of us and
a man who knew himself too well, a man who was
war. You never would have guessed. Why? Because
all the people in the hot–shot colleges and universi-
ties don't know a damn thing about war. You start
them but you never go. There are no mirrors in the
books cluttering up this office, no people bursting
with emotion. Words – that's all you have here are
words, crooked bits of ink clinging to dead trees.
If you want to know about war, you have to touch
soldiers, share a cigarette, a swig of Jim Beam. You
can't ask them about war, you have to feel the war in
them and find it in a place words don't go.

Half a person cannot live. Pete could not accept the evil inside all of us so he kept it outside, refused to confront it inside. We must accept war, the evil in all of us, and constantly do battle with it knowing we will eventually fail because evil is the temptation of fascination and resides in a world of porn, whiskey, fast cars, religion, easy women, greed, and arrogance, while good lives in literature, poetry, music, religion, nature, respect, and kindness. Evil will always win, will eventually break through the lines of defense but good can constantly fight a holding action, a slow retreat, and when evil breaks through, attempt to fill the gaps with decency and continue to fight.

How did suicide enter into all of it? Because I'm someone who cares. There is something you need to know about soldiers. If your buddy's got his guts blown out and he begs you to put him away, you put him away. That's making the ultimate sacrifice, not him, but you. He's gone, dust, air. You must go on. Now I must live with my decision, something you doctors forgot to do years ago. Maybe our whole country's got the same problem: unable to shoulder any kind of responsibility. Everything that happens here is someone else's fault. No one takes the rap for anything. Well, that stopped with me. If I run a red light, it's my fault; if I beat my wife, it's my fault; if I let the government constantly wage illegal wars, that's my fault too.

I gave Pete the wire to hang himself, the extension cord wire off the buffing machine. There was nothing even implied about his request. One day he said, "I'm checking out." He was reading a copy of The Old Man and the Sea. I thought he wanted to escape, have me leave one of the doors open, or bring him a key. He wanted out all right. He didn't care if the big fish ate the little fish or if sharks ate the world's biggest fish or if business men eat working men. He finally understood – you don't need a fish to make a decision. All you need is the extension cord wire off the buffing machine and an exposed hot water pipe above the toilet.

Pete realized what we are, what we all are whether we're in the bush looking for Zips, or in law school waiting to stuff our pockets from the troubles of others. He could not live with that mirror. An hour later, when I saw him sleeping from the pipe, peaceful as anyone on a Sunday picnic, I didn't even bother to cut him down. I sat against the wall and thought of everything he had told me; and I swear to God, he looked contented. I did what none of you bastards would do. I took him from his nightmare, busted his mirror, let his picture on the wall never grow old.

He's out of his war now. And I'm out of a job. So what? It wasn't much of a job anyway.

7231938R00174

Printed in Great Britain
by Amazon.co.uk, Ltd.,
Marston Gate.